DARK DREAM'S
TEMPTATION

THE CHILDREN OF THE GODS BOOK 26

I. T. LUCAS

Also by I. T. Lucas

THE CHILDREN OF THE GODS ORIGINS

1: GODDESS'S CHOICE

2: GODDESS'S HOPE

THE CHILDREN OF THE GODS

DARK STRANGER

1: DARK STRANGER THE DREAM

2: DARK STRANGER REVEALED

3: DARK STRANGER IMMORTAL

DARK ENEMY

4: DARK ENEMY TAKEN

5: DARK ENEMY CAPTIVE

6: DARK ENEMY REDEEMED

KRI & MICHAEL'S STORY

6.5: MY DARK AMAZON

DARK WARRIOR

7: DARK WARRIOR MINE

8: DARK WARRIOR'S PROMISE

9: DARK WARRIOR'S DESTINY

10: DARK WARRIOR'S LEGACY

DARK GUARDIAN

11: DARK GUARDIAN FOUND

12: DARK GUARDIAN CRAVED

13: DARK GUARDIAN'S MATE

DARK ANGEL

14: DARK ANGEL'S OBSESSION

15: DARK ANGEL'S SEDUCTION

16: DARK ANGEL'S SURRENDER

DARK OPERATIVE

17: DARK OPERATIVE: A SHADOW OF DEATH

18: DARK OPERATIVE: A GLIMMER OF HOPE

19: DARK OPERATIVE: THE DAWN OF LOVE

DARK SURVIVOR

20: DARK SURVIVOR AWAKENED

21: DARK SURVIVOR ECHOES OF LOVE

22: DARK SURVIVOR REUNITED

DARK WIDOW

23: DARK WIDOW'S SECRET

24: DARK WIDOW'S CURSE

25: DARK WIDOW'S BLESSING

DARK DREAM

26: DARK DREAM'S TEMPTATION

27: DARK DREAM'S UNRAVELING

28: DARK DREAM'S TRAP

DARK PRINCE

29: DARK PRINCE'S ENIGMA

30: DARK PRINCE'S DILEMMA

31: DARK PRINCE'S AGENDA

DARK QUEEN

32: DARK QUEEN'S QUEST

33: DARK QUEEN'S KNIGHT

34: DARK QUEEN'S ARMY

DARK SPY

35: DARK SPY CONSCRIPTED

36: DARK SPY'S MISSION

37: DARK SPY'S RESOLUTION

DARK OVERLORD

38: DARK OVERLORD NEW HORIZON

39: DARK OVERLORD'S WIFE

40: DARK OVERLORD'S CLAN

DARK CHOICES

41: DARK CHOICES THE QUANDARY

42: DARK CHOICES PARADIGM SHIFT

PERFECT MATCH
PERFECT MATCH 1: VAMPIRE'S CONSORT
PERFECT MATCH 2: KING'S CHOSEN
PERFECT MATCH 3: CAPTAIN'S CONQUEST

SETS

THE CHILDREN OF THE GODS BOOKS 1-3: DARK STRANGER TRILOGY—INCLUDES A BONUS SHORT STORY: **THE FATES TAKE A VACATION**

THE CHILDREN OF THE GODS: BOOKS 1-6—INCLUDES CHARACTER LISTS

THE CHILDREN OF THE GODS: BOOKS 6.5-10—INCLUDES CHARACTER LISTS

TRY THE CHILDREN OF THE GODS SERIES ON
AUDIBLE
2 FREE audiobooks with your new Audible subscription!

NOTE FROM THE AUTHOR:
Dark Dream's Temptation is a work of fiction!
Names, characters, places and incidents are products of the author's
imagination or are used fictitiously and are not to be construed as real. Any
similarity to actual persons, organizations and/or events is purely coincidental.

PRELUDE

"Ella? Are you even listening?"

Despite how fascinated she was by Julian's story, Ella was drifting off. With the hum of the private jet's engines lulling her to sleep, she was fighting a losing battle with her eyelids. They simply refused to stay up no matter how hard she tried to stay awake and hear more about the mythological gods, their immortal offspring, the immortals' split into two warring factions, and their millennia-long fight over humanity's future.

It was a riveting tale, especially since it pertained to her and finally explained her telepathic ability. According to Julian, she was a descendant of the gods and a carrier of their godly genes.

At any other time, Ella would've hung on Julian's every word. But not today, not after what she'd been through.

"I'm sorry, Julian, but I can't keep my eyes open."

"I understand." He looked disappointed. "It's too much information for you to absorb, especially so soon after all of that excitement. You need to rest."

A wave of guilt washed over Ella.

She owed her freedom to Julian. The least she could do was

keep her eyes open and listen to him as he revealed his most guarded secrets to her.

Without his help, Ella would've still belonged to the Russian mafia boss who'd bought her, his wife for the rest of her freaking life and a mother at eighteen.

She'd been spared the first part; however, a pregnancy was still a possibility.

Her period was a week late. She could be carrying Gorchenco's child.

But then, stress had caused delays before, and Ella prayed it was the culprit this time as well.

She had to believe that Fate had arranged the chance meeting between Julian and her mother for a reason. After that, and then all the trouble that went into rescuing Ella, it didn't make sense that Fate would abandon her now.

What also didn't make sense was that one conversation with a woman he'd met at a psychic convention had such a profound effect on Julian, prompting him to mobilize his entire clan to help Vivian rescue her daughter.

He must've done one hell of a sales job convincing them to take on a powerful Russian mafia boss. Especially since Gorchenco was known as paranoid about security and never stayed in one place for more than a couple of days. Planning a rescue around that had been difficult and costly in the extreme.

She owed Julian her life.

If she'd stayed with the Russian, Ella would have died. Either literally or figuratively. Her soul would've shriveled and withered away.

"It's not that I don't find your story interesting. It's fascinating, and I don't want to miss any detail. But I'm just so damn tired." She smiled apologetically. "If I had known that the part of a damsel in distress getting rescued was such an exhausting job, I would've never signed up for that movie."

Julian's expression softened. "You're crashing from the adrenaline high. It's perfectly normal. Getting away from an exploding gas tanker will do that to a person."

"Yeah, I guess." Even though she'd known that the explosion had been staged and perfectly timed, it had still been a terrifying experience.

But it was more than that.

The rescue had been a *Mission Impossible* style operation, and its complexity and perfection of execution had been awe-inspiring, but that was just the last straw, the explosive climax that had come on the heels of a traumatic month.

She wasn't a doctor like Julian, but Ella could figure it out on her own.

Ever since her ordeal had begun, her stress levels had been sky-high, and her body had gotten used to operating on that super-charged fuel. Now that the reasons for her flight-or-fight response were gone, she was deflating like an overblown balloon.

God, she could imagine staying in bed for two weeks straight with her mom coddling her like a little girl.

Yeah, that sounded like a plan.

Despite it all having been her own fault, Ella deserved a little tender loving care after what she'd been through.

Her only crime had been stupidity, and the price she'd paid was too high for that. Nevertheless, it could have been even worse.

If only she hadn't been so gullible.

She should never have fallen for Romeo and gone with him to New York. Except, in her worst nightmares, Ella could not have imagined something like that happening to her. Suburban girls from good homes just didn't get lured into a trap by pretend boyfriends and sold into sexual slavery.

"The seats recline all the way." Julian got up and opened an overhead compartment. "You can take a nap until we land."

He pulled out a folded blanket and a pillow, then waited for her to turn the seat into a flat surface. When she was ready, he handed her the pillow and put the blanket over her. "We should be landing in about two hours."

"Thank you. You're an angel."

"You're welcome."

Gazing at her for a long moment, Julian looked like he wanted to tuck the blanket around her or kiss her, but he did neither.

Instead, he raked his fingers through his hair. "I'll wake you up when we start the descent."

What a sweet guy.

Her guardian angel.

Gorgeous, kind, and a doctor, Julian was too good to be true, but she was too tired to speculate as to his motives. Whatever they were, they couldn't be worse than Romeo's. Most likely, Julian was precisely who he seemed to be.

Except, Ella was never again going to trust anyone implicitly.

Curling up on her side, she tucked the pillow under her cheek and closed her eyes. As Yamanu started humming another tune, a small smile curled her lips. Was he singing for her?

It was nice of him. But she didn't need a lullaby. In no time, Ella was dreaming.

She was in a cemetery?

That was odd. What was she doing there?

Who'd died?

"You did." A man appeared next to her, his face hidden behind a huge bouquet of red roses.

Turning to look at the tombstone that they were both standing in front of, she read the inscription on the granite slab. Most of it was written in the Cyrillic script which she couldn't decipher, but the name of the deceased was written in English.

Ella Gorchenco.

Cool, her subconscious had provided burial for her sham of a marriage.

But who was the guy with the roses?

As if moving in slow motion, he took a step forward, bent to put the bouquet down, and then straightened and turned to her.

The moment she saw his face, Ella sucked in a breath and prepared to scream.

He lifted both hands. "I come in peace. Please don't scream murder."

"What are you doing in my dreams, Logan, or rather nightmares?"

He shrugged. "I'm a figment of your subconscious."

"Right. And my subconscious also conjured the kiss you forced on me the other night?"

Smirking, he leaned forward and got in her face. "But that didn't really happen, did it? The lunch meeting with your former fiancé was the only time we've actually met in person, and we've done nothing but talk. The rest was created by your mind." He waggled his brows. "Maybe you fancy me? Could I be the mysterious and dangerous stranger that you want to explore your dark side with?"

Hmm. There was something to that.

She was both attracted and repulsed by Logan, and it wasn't even about his good looks, although he was one of the most striking men she'd ever met. The other being Julian. But where

Julian seemed to be pure light and goodness, Logan was the opposite.

One was her Jedi Knight, and the other the Sith Lord.

The question was, who was she?

The way she was feeling now, Julian's light was almost too bright for her. He belonged to a universe she was no longer a member of. Maybe in time she would feel worthy of someone like him, but not yet.

Logan's pull, on the other hand, was as undeniable as it was disturbing. Something about his darkness resonated with her.

Like recognizing like.

Ella would've never tolerated the presence of the real Logan. He was too scary and too intense. But in her dreams, he posed no threat to her.

After all, if he did something she wasn't happy with, she could always wake up.

Pushing his hands into his pockets, Logan started walking. "By the way, congratulations on your escape. You must have really powerful friends."

Ella followed him, compelled to keep the conversation going. "It seems that I do. Although I've never met any of them before. They are my mother's friends. Not mine."

Logan slowed down, waiting for her to catch up to him. "Gorchenco is probably heartbroken."

"Yeah, I know. And I hate feeling guilty for making him go through the grief. But it's his fault. He should never have bought me."

"He saved you from a much worse fate. Anyone else would've raped you on day one."

Ugh, that was blunt. Dream Logan was just as rough around the edges as the real one.

"That's true. But if not for Gorchenco, Stefano would have never hunted me down. After seeing my picture in a magazine and realizing that I looked exactly like the Russian's long-lost love, Stefano seized the opportunity to make some quick money. He knew Dimitri would pay any price to get her back from beyond the grave, even knowing he was buying only a lookalike."

For some reason, Logan seemed fascinated by her story as if he was hearing it for the first time. The real Logan had probably never heard it, but since he was a figment of her imagination, he should not have looked so surprised.

Except the mind was a strange thing, creating realistic scenarios where she could pretend that she was having a conversation with the real Logan.

In a way, it was liberating.

She could tell him her darkest thoughts and let her subconscious react to them. There was no need to pretend that she was a nice girl with nothing but goodness inside of her. Maybe if she gave that dark energy an outlet, she could get rid of it.

"Gorchenco seemed enamored with you, Ella, not with the ghost of his long-lost love."

She shrugged. "What is it to you? You wanted to buy me from him."

Logan laughed. "I did. I still want you."

Ella stopped and turned to him. "Why? Is it the pretty face?" She waved her hand in front of her.

"That too, but it's not the main reason. I've had plenty of girls who were even prettier than you. But you're special. One of a kind."

Ella rolled her eyes. "Did you also lose a girlfriend who looked exactly like me?"

"No, Ella. You're one of a kind not because of what you look like but because of what you can do." He pointed to her head. "You and your mother are probably the only two in the world with such powerful telepathic ability, and that's what makes you both so special."

Ella was a much more powerful telepath than her mother. Except, she wasn't going to point it out because it wasn't important. Besides, she didn't like to boast.

JULIAN

*A*fter the limo with Ella and her family had left, Julian dropped his duffle bag in Turner's trunk and joined Arwel in the back seat. With Yamanu sitting shotgun, it wasn't as if he had much choice, but it was fine. His conversation with Turner could wait for later, and Arwel was good company.

Tagging along with Ella's rescue team had produced two unexpected side benefits. Julian had made friends with several of the Guardians, and he'd even made some progress with Turner.

His mother's mate was a good man with an exceptional mind, but he wasn't easy to befriend and was as warm as a calculator. This mission had brought them closer. Not close enough to start calling the guy by his given name, that was a privilege only Bridget was allowed.

But still, it was progress, and Julian wasn't going to let it fizzle away. "I'm glad you left your car here, Turner. It would've been awkward riding with Ella in the limo and intruding on the family reunion."

Turner glanced at him through the rearview mirror. "How did it go with her? I had my noise-canceling earphones on throughout the flight, but she didn't seem overly distraught to me."

Julian raked his fingers through his hair. "I think Ella was in a state of overload. In the beginning, she asked some questions, but the longer I droned on, the more her eyes glazed over, and finally she just flat out told me that she was too tired and couldn't keep her eyes open."

One thing Julian was sure of. Ella had shown absolutely no interest in him. Hopefully, it was just a side effect of what she'd been through, and not something deeper and more permanent.

He hadn't encountered a problem like that in a while. In fact, the only times he'd been rejected were when the ladies were already in committed relationships, and even then, their refusal was usually accompanied by wistful looks.

It wasn't vanity, it was just the way things were.

Being a single, handsome young doctor put him at the very top of the food chain as far as desirability went.

But maybe he'd overestimated his appeal.

Julian was kind, which he'd been told showed on his face, he was cordial, which was so ingrained in him that he couldn't be any other way, and he wasn't pushy, which just wasn't in his nature. In short, Julian was as far from a bad boy as a guy could get.

He'd never even cheated on a test.

Was Ella one of those girls who preferred jerks?

Why some women liked to be treated poorly was an inexplicable phenomenon, but during his extended stay among humans, Julian had seen it happen time and again. It wasn't just an urban legend.

"I'm sorry," Arwel said.

"What for?"

"That Ella didn't fall in love with you at first sight. I know that it was what you'd been hoping for."

Damn. Was everyone going to give him pitying looks from now on?

Julian shrugged. "That rarely happens in real life, and when it does, it's usually an infatuation or just lust. I much prefer for us to get to know each other first, and then fall in love with the person inside and not the superficial shell."

Except, he'd fallen for even less than that. Ella's damn picture had been enough to turn him into a man obsessed.

Arwel patted his shoulder. "You are right. I wish you luck." The guy didn't even try to mask the sad look in his eyes.

"Give her time." Yamanu turned his head back. "Ella has been to hell and back. You can't expect your pretty face to magically melt all that crap away. Right now, she's probably wary of men."

It would've been easier if she were. But Ella hadn't been wary of him, or Turner, or even Yamanu with his impressive height and creepy eyes. Arwel, with his ever-suffering expression, was not the type anyone felt wary of, so he didn't count.

Ella had been at ease with all of them, even friendly, and it hadn't been only a show of confidence. Her scent had been free of fear.

Being placed in the friend zone by an attractive young woman was a first for Julian, but that was precisely where Ella had put him. She'd followed him to his hotel room, borrowed his clothes, including his underwear, and had even joked about the stink that she had thought he'd left in the bathroom.

She was treating him like a brother, or a close cousin.

If he weren't an immortal with extra sharp senses, Julian might have entertained the hope that Ella was putting on an act while secretly thinking he was hot. Regrettably, though, he hadn't sniffed even a whiff of arousal from her.

But then, that was too much to expect from a girl just rescued from what had been basically sexual slavery.

Fates only knew what Gorchenco had done to her.

Perhaps she'd told her mother some of it, but it wasn't as if Julian could've asked Vivian for details. Besides, Ella probably hadn't told her mother the worst parts.

From the little he'd managed to glean of her personality, Ella believed herself to be strong and didn't like to burden anyone with her troubles.

Both were admirable qualities, but Julian had a feeling that they would be detrimental to her recovery. No one could force Ella to get psychological help if she refused it. But without it, her mental wounds would either fester or heal all wrong.

He couldn't let that happen.

Worst case scenario, he would thrall the nasty memories away, provided she agreed, of course. Julian wasn't a psychologist, but if he were in her shoes, he would never tolerate his choices being taken away from him again, no matter how good the intentions.

"I hope no one is planning a welcome home party for Ella," Arwel said. "She's not going to like it."

Turner lifted his eyes to the rearview mirror. "I know Bridget is going to be there to give her a checkup."

That was news to Julian. "Why? I already did that, and she's fine. There wasn't even a scratch on her."

Turner shook his head. "Ella might want to talk to a female doctor."

"Oh." He should've realized that.

"Kian and Syssi are going to be there too, and I'm guessing Amanda as well. But don't worry. Your mother is going to take charge of the situation and kick them out after the obligatory introductions, and welcome words are done. Bridget takes shit from no one, and that includes Kian."

Turner was right. Bridget was an assertive lady, and not just in her capacity as a doctor. His mother would take care of Ella.

"Do you think I should be there?"

"No," Arwel and Turner said simultaneously.

"You'll just look desperate," Turner said.

Arwel waved a dismissive hand. "It's not about that. Ella needs space to breathe and time to recuperate. You need to be patient, Julian. When she's ready, she'll come to you."

ELLA

*S*quashed in the back seat of the limousine between her mother and her brother, Ella ran her hand over the fabric of her jeans. They were stretchy, comfortable, and probably had cost no more than thirty bucks. They felt wonderful.

Even though there were panties in the paper bag her mother had brought, Ella was still wearing Julian's boxer briefs. They were roomy. That's why. And the panties her mother bought were too skimpy.

The first chance she got, Ella was going to buy a pack of boy shorts that were just as comfy as Julian's.

"Tell me more about the village, Mom," she said, mainly to stop her mother's sniffling. "Where is it?"

They'd had their cry, but enough was enough.

"Somewhere in the Los Angeles area. We are not supposed to know exactly where it is. The limo's windows will turn opaque when we get near it, and the car will switch to autonomous driving."

"It's so cool," Parker said. "Not even Magnus knows where

the village is. So, if the bad guys catch anyone, they can't torture the information out of us."

Ella grimaced. "The things you consider cool are weird. Is it really that dangerous to be an immortal?"

"To us, it is," Magnus said. "We need to hide from humans and from our enemies alike. Though for different reasons."

On the plane, Julian had given her an abbreviated history lesson, so she knew about the Devout Order of Mortdh, or Doomers as they were called for short. She also remembered the love story that had started the conflict between the two groups of immortals, but many of the other details were fuzzy, probably because she hadn't let him finish the story and had fallen asleep.

"It's like a real village," her mother said. "In the center of it, there is a nice park with ponds and walkways, and the buildings around it house the offices and the clinic and the like. The residences are not too close together, and there is lots of greenery between them. It's like living in a park. And it's so quiet, nothing but birds chirping and crickets."

"There are no kids," Parker said, looking grim. "Just two babies. All the rest are grownups."

That was weird. "Where are all the kids? In boarding schools?"

Magnus shook his head. "I wish. The price of immortality is a very low fertility rate."

"I see." Ella's gut clenched.

She needed to get that pregnancy test as soon as possible.

Mom, is there any way we can stop at a pharmacy on the way? It was a good thing she didn't need to wait to be alone with her mother to ask.

Why? What do you need? I have tampons if it's that time of the month.

I wish. I need to get a pregnancy test.

7

Her mother turned to her with a pair of worried eyes. *Are you late?*

One week.

Shit.

Yeah, you could say so. I hope it's only stress. It happened before. Remember the SATs? I was supposed to get my period then but didn't because I was so stressed out before the tests.

Her mother let out a breath. *I hope you're right. But in any case. I'm sure Bridget has some in the clinic.*

Who is Bridget?

Julian's mother. She's a doctor too.

"Mom, are you and Ella talking to each other in your heads? Because if you are, it's rude."

"I'm sorry." Ella wrapped her arm around Parker's shoulders. "It was girl talk." She leaned to whisper in his ear, "I'm sure you didn't want to hear us talking about tampons."

Making a face, Parker shuddered. "No, gross. But next time wait until we get home instead of that weird staring into each other's eyes that you do. It looks creepy. I don't know how come I didn't notice it before."

Because they'd been more circumspect about it and hadn't done it often. Parker had been too young to be told about their telepathic connection. He would've blabbered about it to his friends and endangered their family.

But a lot had changed during the time Ella had been gone. Her little brother had been turned immortal, and her mother had found love with her immortal bodyguard.

Freaking unbelievable.

Now with Magnus in the house, they would have to limit their telepathic communication even more. Keeping it a secret was no longer an issue, but Parker was right, and it was rude to do it in front of other people.

Peeking from under her lashes, Ella glanced at the

Guardian. No wonder her mother had fallen for him. Magnus was a handsome man, but it was more than that. He had that aura about him of someone a woman could depend on.

Then again, Ella was a lousy judge of character, so maybe she was wrong.

The Russian had been dependable too, but it came with a price no sane woman would be willing to pay. Besides, he'd bought her and coerced her into having sex with him. That was not dependable, it was despicable. She should hate him, despise him, and not feel sorry for him. He deserved the suffering he was most likely feeling right now.

Ella closed her eyes.

If only there was a way to forget the last month, erase it from her memory as if it had never happened.

She remembered Julian mentioning something about the immortals' thralling ability. It was like hypnosis that they could use on humans, but some were immune to it. Russians in particular, which was one of the reasons her rescue had been so complicated. The Guardians, as the clan's fighters were called, couldn't just assume that they could thrall Gorchenco and his people. They had to use more mundane methods to get her out.

Was that also the reason Parker had volunteered to transition first, or was she confusing the stories?

Ella tightened her arm around her brother's slim shoulders. "So, you're an immortal now, eh?"

"Not yet. But I'm going to be. Doctor Bridget says that my body can heal faster and better already, but it's not at full power yet. I need to grow my fangs and venom glands first, and she says it can take six months or more."

"Was it difficult?"

"The fight?"

Ella frowned. Julian had said that Parker had been brave to

volunteer to go first so she and her mother wouldn't have to rush into it. But when she'd asked him what was involved in a Dormant's activation, Julian had started telling her the entire history from the beginning of civilization, and then she'd fallen asleep.

"What do you mean by a fight?" she asked. "Julian didn't explain how it works."

Squaring his shoulders, Parker lifted his chin. "I had to fight an immortal male. But they didn't have anyone my age, so I had to fight Jackson who is nineteen and really strong. But I head-butted him, and he almost fell on his ass, but because he's immortal and has great reflexes, he didn't, and he came after me. I was a little scared, but it was okay. The bite didn't hurt so bad. And after that, when the venom hit, I was so loopy that I saw stars." He chuckled. "I didn't just see them, I flew by them. It was like a hallucinogenic trip."

Ella waved a dismissive hand. "Like you would know how that feels." But then the rest of what he'd said registered. "Hold on one sec. Why did that Jackson guy bite you? Is that some warped part of a coming of age ceremony?"

"It is, but the bite is what induces the transition. The venom is what activates the dormant genes."

Now Julian's comment about Parker's bravery made sense. It must have been really scary.

"But why did you have to fight him first? Couldn't he just bite you and be done with it? Or is that the ceremonial part?"

"In order for the fangs to elongate and the venom glands to produce venom, immortal males need to turn aggressive," Magnus said. "That's what the fight is for."

"It's why I head-butted Jackson. He didn't see it coming." Parker sounded smug. "And that is also why Magnus couldn't induce me. He likes me too much."

KIAN

"Do you think Gorchenco will buy it?" Kian asked after Turner was done with his update.

"I wouldn't if it were me, and given his security measures, it seems that we think alike. So no, I don't think he is going to buy it. But proving it isn't true is another thing altogether. He won't find anything no matter how much he digs."

Kian wished he could share Turner's confidence. But then he had no reason to doubt him either. In matters of this kind, he should rely on the guy's expertise and not on his gut.

Except, his gut refused to calm down.

"I don't want Ella leaving the village until we can ascertain it's safe. It will take a long time before Gorchenco concedes defeat and stops looking for her."

"Couldn't agree more." Turner reached into his pocket and pulled out a diamond ring that made the one Kian had gotten Syssi look small and modest.

"This is a donation from Ella. Or rather Gorchenco." He put it on Kian's desk.

"What do you want me to do with it?"

Turner shrugged. "Ella suggested that we use it to cover the cost of her rescue and finance others."

Kian lifted the ring and turned on his desk lamp. "I'm no great expert, but this looks flawless to me. It's worth a fortune, but who are we going to sell it to? It's probably one of a kind and easily traceable."

"I can think of a few potential buyers. My friend Arturo might be interested. Not necessarily to keep it for himself or give to his wife, but to sell it to some rich sheik or one of the new Asian billionaires. Those are the kinds of people we don't have access to, but he does."

"Would he keep the source confidential?"

"Of course. He wouldn't have been in business for so long if he didn't. The rules of conduct are even stricter for the black-market traders than they are for the legit ones."

Kian chuckled. "I bet. Legitimate business people don't kill each other for bending the rules."

"Sometimes they do."

Handing the ring back to Turner, Kian leaned back in his chair and crossed his arms over his chest. "How are you going to get it to him? It's not like you can mail it or entrust someone to deliver it."

Turner put it back in his pocket. "First I need to check if he's interested. Then I'll figure out the logistics."

"Just make sure to tell him not to offer it to any Russians. Imagine Gorchenco buying back his own ring."

"I don't see how that's a problem. Anyone could've taken the ring off Ella and sold it on the black market. If he wants to buy it back for sentimental reasons, so be it."

Kian shook his head. "I'll feel better knowing it's not getting back to him."

"As you wish. But I'm sure you can put the proceeds to good use, and it might be difficult to move."

"No doubt about it. But let's see how it goes first. If it doesn't sell, I'll reconsider."

Since they'd started the new operation, Kian had found himself making business decisions based on costs more than anything else.

Which meant that promising technologies didn't get funding when they required too much capital to get going, and that wasn't good. But as hard as he tried, and as many hours as he worked, Kian couldn't increase profits fast enough to cover the ever-increasing costs of their humanitarian initiative.

"Julian and I had an interesting conversation," Turner said. "Apparently, Vanessa is running out of space in the sanctuary. The idea of a halfway house came up."

Kian shook his head. "Unless we can find a donor to finance it, I'm afraid it will have to wait. We will need to buy a place and hire people to run it. I'm doing my best to keep all the balls up in the air, but I'm not a magician."

"The proceeds from the sale of this ring will cover several buildings. And as for hiring people, you may get away with only two paid staffers, and the rest could be done by volunteers."

"And where do you suggest that I get those?"

Turner waved his hand in an arc. "You have an entire clan of people who are getting paid every month just for breathing. You can demand that in exchange for getting their share of the clan's profits, they volunteer a few days a month at the halfway house."

The idea had merit, but it wasn't going to be an easy sell. Perhaps Bridget could pull off the same kind of miracle convincing the civilians to volunteer as she'd done convincing the Guardians to come back from retirement.

"If I do that, I risk alienating my clan members. There is a limit to what people are willing to do for a cause, no matter how worthy."

Turner nodded. "It's just an idea. What you do with it is your decision."

"Right. Let's run it by Bridget and see what she thinks. Of the three of us, she is probably the only one with a good grasp on what our people are willing or not willing to give up. I never expected her to be so successful with luring back the retired Guardians. She pulled a fucking miracle."

The satisfied grin on Turner's face was a rare sight. "Bridget is the best. You made a good choice putting her in charge of this operation."

"Indeed."

ELLA

"Someone pinch me," Ella said when they walked out of the entry pavilion. "This is unreal."

As the glass doors slid open onto the picturesque grounds of the village, a gentle breeze brought with it the smell of freshly-cut grass. To see all that lush greenery was as surreal as what it had taken to get up there.

Parker hadn't been kidding about the clan's use of futuristic technology. He'd warned Ella about the limousine's windows getting opaque, but he hadn't said anything about driving into the belly of a mountain and then taking an elevator ride up to the surface.

It was like a scene from a sci-fi movie.

Men in Black came to mind. Was she going to open a locker door and discover an entire civilization living there too?

"It's beautiful, isn't it?" Vivian wrapped her arm around Ella's waist. "Just listen to how quiet it is. From up here, you can't even hear the cars driving down on the road below. That's what I call true serenity."

"Or *The Twilight Zone*." Ella looked around.

The village was beautiful, but it seemed deserted. Other

than the chirping of birds, it was devoid of human or animal sounds.

Even Gorchenco's Russian estate hadn't been this quiet. There had been gardeners with their air blowers and grass mowers, people talking and arguing, dogs barking, horses neighing, and even the occasional sheep bleating. Being isolated and far away from the city didn't mean it was devoid of life.

She turned to Magnus. "Where is everyone?"

"The café is closed at this time, so there is no reason for anyone to be out and about. I just hope they are not in our house preparing a welcome party for you." His grimace didn't bode well.

On the way, Magnus had said that the welcome wagon would only include Julian's mother, the big boss and his wife, and maybe the boss's sister. Four new people she would have to smile and chitchat with were too many already. All Ella wanted was to take a shower in her own private bathroom, crawl into her own bed, and go to sleep without fear of anyone joining her.

Except, even that was too much to hope for because she might be stuck with the specter of Logan following her around in her dreams.

"I thought that only a few people were going to come."

Magnus rubbed the back of his neck. "That was what I've been told. But as you are about to discover, our clan is full of busybodies. They mean well, but it gets annoying at times."

"Don't worry about it," Parker said. "They are all very nice."

"I'm sure they are, and I'm grateful for everything the clan has done for my family and me, but I would've appreciated a softer landing."

Whatever, she would survive. She'd smile, and shake hands, and thank everyone for their help. It was the least she could do.

Eventually, everyone would go home, and she could get that shower she was yearning for.

"This is our house." Her mother pointed. "I don't see a crowd, so that's a good sign."

The door opened, and a short redhead stepped out, smiling and waving. "Welcome to the village, Ella."

"That's Bridget, Julian's mom," Parker said.

She looked like his sister, but Julian had warned Ella that everyone looked about the same age, although they weren't. For some reason, she found it easy to make a mental switch and not assign an age to any of the immortals based on how they looked. What bothered her, though, was that it seemed that the village was like a commune, and people walked into each other's homes even when the owner wasn't there.

"Is it always like this here?"

Her mother frowned. "What do you mean?"

"People going into other people's houses whether they are invited or not?"

Vivian paled and leaned to whisper in her ear. "Didn't Julian tell you about their exceptional hearing? Your comment was very rude."

He had, but she'd forgotten about it. "I didn't mean for it to sound like that. I'm just curious how things work here."

Bridget walked down the steps and offered Ella her hand. "Normally, no. We don't go into each other's houses uninvited. But your mother allowed us to wait for you here." She clapped Ella on the back. "Don't worry, for now it's only me. Kian, Syssi, and Amanda are coming a little later, but none of us is going to stay long. I know you must be tired after all of that excitement and can't wait to get in bed."

Feeling like a jerk, Ella nodded. "Thank you for organizing my rescue. Julian told me that you were in charge of the entire operation."

"I'm the one who coordinates everything. But the actual missions are Turner's department. He plans them, although normally he doesn't join the teams on the ground."

"Come on, Ella." Parker waved her in from the door. "I want you to see my room."

"I'll take Scarlet for a short walk." Magnus patted the dog's head. "She was too shy to do her business with Ella around."

Scarlet adored Parker, but she seemed suspicious of the newcomer joining her family. Or maybe she just didn't like Ella for some reason.

Whatever, the dog liking her was the least of her concerns. Ella had an entire village of immortals to befriend.

Not yet, though. Maybe after two or three weeks of hibernation.

"That's a gorgeous house," she said as she entered. "Did it come like that? No offense, but I know it's not your work."

It was evident that the decor had been done by a professional. Everything was high-quality and perfectly coordinated, but it wasn't ostentatious or over the top like Gorchenco's homes. It felt cozy and homey and nothing like the estates Ella had been living in lately.

Thank God for that.

She wanted no reminders.

No more fancy houses, no more limousine rides, and no more private jets with bedrooms and a staff of servants on hand.

"Thank you for the non-compliment," Vivian said. "But you're right. All the homes in the village are furnished and decorated by the clan's interior designer, and they come ready and supplied with everything. And I mean *everything*. There was even food in the fridge."

"Excuse me," Bridget said when her phone rang. "I'll take this outside."

As Bridget stepped out into the backyard, Vivian beckoned Ella to follow her to the kitchen. "Just look at this cookware. It's almost a shame to use it. I would hate for these beautiful pots and pans to get scorch marks."

"So why cook if we can get takeout?" Parker asked.

Vivian ruffled his hair. "Your brother has developed a taste for restaurant food. He treats what I make like punishment."

"No, I don't. I just like eating tasty food."

Ella rolled her eyes. "I love you, but you're such a dweeb."

As the door opened and Magnus entered with Scarlet, the dog rushed in and headed straight for Ella, then stopped a couple of feet away from her and sat back on her haunches.

It seemed that Scarlet had changed her mind and was ready to be friends.

"She wants you to pat her," Parker said.

Scarlet tilted her head as if saying, "What are you waiting for? I'm ready to be friends with you."

Crouching in front of her, Ella reached with her hand, letting Scarlet sniff it first. She knew the ice had been broken when the dog licked her hand and started wagging her tail.

"You're such a good girl." Ella patted her solid head. "How old is she?"

"A little over five months. But she's big for her age." Magnus sounded like a proud father.

As Bridget opened the living room's sliding glass doors, Scarlet bounded outside, and a moment later returned with a rubber ball between her teeth.

"That thing doesn't belong in the house, and you know it!" Vivian pointed to the backyard.

Tail tucked between her legs, Scarlet trotted out.

It was such a homey scene that it was almost surreal.

Ella felt as if she'd crossed into an alternate reality. Even though she was in a secret village whose occupants were immortals, everything seemed so normal here, so familiar.

After having everything taken away from her, she had her mother and brother back, and even a dog, and a future stepfather who seemed like an awesome guy.

So why the hell did she feel like an intruder in someone else's life?

"Do you want to meet Merlin?" Parker asked. "He's our only neighbor, and he's the coolest guy ever. He's teaching me magic tricks."

Ella pushed up to her feet. "Maybe some other time."

"Come see your room," Vivian threaded her arm through hers, and then glanced at Bridget. "Do you want to see what I've done with it?"

Ella didn't need to communicate with her mother telepathically to know what this was about, and apparently neither did Bridget.

"Sure. Lead the way." The doctor waved her hand.

The room was much bigger than the one she had in her old house, and it was better furnished and decorated, but Ella missed her old room and the innocence she'd left behind there.

Bridget closed the door and motioned for Ella to sit on the bed. "Julian said that you weren't injured during the rescue. Is there anything else you'd like me to check on?"

Ella nodded. "I need a pregnancy test," she whispered. "I'm late."

"You're not pregnant."

That was as unexpected as it was welcome. Except, Julian hadn't said anything about immortals' ability to sense early pregnancies. Then again, he had no reason to. The subject hadn't come up.

"How could you know that?"

Bridget tapped her nose. "Immortal sense of smell. The

hormonal changes start right away, and I've trained myself to detect them in humans. But if you want to make sure, I can give you a kit. But since I need to take blood samples anyway, we might as well test for that too."

"Why?"

Bridget cast a quick glance at Vivian, who shook her head, saying no to Bridget's implied question.

Ella wondered what that was all about.

"Every newcomer to our village gets thorough blood work done as well as other tests."

That sounded ominous. "What tests?"

Bridget waved a dismissive hand. "Nothing to get all worked up about. Mostly it's bloodwork and measurements. Naturally, I'll also check your lungs and your heart, just to make sure everything is running like it should."

"So, it's like a physical?"

"Precisely."

"So why didn't you say so from the start? You had me scared for a moment."

"My apologies." Bridget cast her a pitying look.

Here it goes.

Up until now, no one had looked at her like that. Ella had been wondering when that would come, and she'd just gotten her answer.

As long as she acted as if she was fine, people treated her like everyone else, but the moment she showed fear, it was a reminder of what she'd been through and a catalyst for the sad faces.

The take-home lesson was clear. Fake it till you make it, or in her case, show no fear and hold your chin up.

5

VIVIAN

*B*ridget's confident assertion that Ella wasn't pregnant had done a lot to improve the girl's mood. Still, it was obvious that Ella didn't consider the doctor's nose a reliable test.

Except, Ella didn't know Bridget as well as Vivian did. Not that she and the doctor were close, but Vivian was convinced that Bridget would've never made a claim she wasn't absolutely sure of.

Bottom line, a huge weight had been lifted off her chest, and if Bridget weren't such an intimidating woman, Vivian would've hugged her and kissed her on both cheeks to express her gratitude.

There was so much to be thankful for, and the doctor had been instrumental in bringing most of it about.

Ella was back, and she seemed in better emotional shape than Vivian had expected. Not only that, her daughter and Magnus had hit it off from the first moment. There hadn't been any awkwardness between them, and they seemed to genuinely like each other.

But if everything was going so well, why was Vivian's gut

still churning?

Perhaps because she was predisposed not to believe in happy endings, and when things seemed too good to be true, it was because they probably were.

Or, maybe she just didn't know how to be any other way.

Her life up till now had been one disaster after another, and her natural state was to expect the next one in line.

"I can swing by tomorrow and take the blood tests and measurements," Bridget said as she opened the door.

In the living room, Magnus and Parker were setting up the table for the late dinner Vivian had planned to have with her family. Hopefully, there was enough food to share with their guests.

"Kian and Syssi are on their way, and so is Amanda," Magnus said. "It's good that Callie prepared a welcome feast big enough to feed a unit of Guardians."

"Who is Callie?" Ella asked.

"She's the fiancée of one of the Guardians and an amateur chef." Vivian cast an apologetic glance at Bridget. "I wanted to prepare the dinner myself, but she wouldn't hear of it. She said that an occasion like this called for a celebration feast."

"And thank goodness for that," Parker said. "Callie is an awesome cook."

A loud knock preceded Amanda, who didn't wait for anyone to open the door for her. "Hello, Ella." Entering with her usual dramatic flair, she sauntered in with a smile and wide open arms. "Come give your Auntie Amanda a hug."

Ella cast Vivian a sidelong glance and mouthed, "Auntie?"

"It's a figure of speech, darling." She pulled Ella into a crushing hug. "Aren't you a beauty." She pushed her away but kept her close with a hand on her shoulder. "Let me get a good look at you." She gave Ella a thorough appraisal. "You rock the sweet girl-next-door look. Just so you know, though, if you're sick of that and desire a makeover, I'm the one to turn to."

"Thank you. In fact, I would love one. What do you think I should do to change my appearance as much as possible?"

Vivian didn't like where this was going, but Amanda seemed to side with her daughter. "We can change your hair color." She reached behind Ella, pulled the rubber band off her ponytail, and fluffed her shoulder-length hair out. "What do you think about going short? Like me."

"No," Vivian said.

"Sure," was Ella's enthusiastic response. "That's different for sure. I also like your hair color. Do you think black will look good on me?"

"No way." Vivian put her hands on her hips. "Your hair is beautiful. Why would you want to change it?"

Ella pinned her with a pair of hard eyes. "Because I want to change everything about me."

That was new. Vivian had seen Ella upset, angry, and even furious, but her eyes had always remained soft.

As she imagined what had put that hard expression on her baby's angelic face, a lump formed in her throat.

Amanda wrapped an arm around her shoulders. "Relax. We are not going to do anything today." She leaned closer and whispered in her ear, "There are all kinds of methods to exorcize demons. Some of them involve dancing naked in the woods, and some involve a pair of scissors and a box of hair dye."

"Someone is at the door," Parker said.

Vivian hadn't heard anything, but a moment later there was a knock. Undoubtedly, Parker's hearing was improving by the day.

That must be the big boss and his wife, she sent to Ella. *Kian and Syssi.*

As Magnus opened the door for the couple, Ella sucked in a breath.

"Wow, you look so much like Julian," she exclaimed.

Kian smiled. "Hello, Ella, and you look a lot like your mother."

She and Ella exchanged looks.

"I don't see it," Ella said.

Behave, Vivian sent.

Do I need to agree to everything he says?

No, but try to be polite.

I am.

"Mom," Parker said. "You're doing that thing again."

An awkward silence followed, which Syssi broke by walking up to Ella and pulling her into a quick hug. "Welcome to the clan. We are overjoyed to have you here, free at last."

"Thank you. I'm forever grateful to you and everyone who took part in getting me out. I don't know how I'll ever be able to repay you."

"You already did," Kian said.

Vivian arched a brow. What was he talking about? Was it a figure of speech? Maybe he'd meant that the joy of rescuing Ella was worth the huge effort and all the resources that had gone into it?

Somehow that didn't fit what she knew about Kian. The guy was too pragmatic to say something nice like that.

"That ring you gave Turner will finance a halfway house for the girls that are ready to graduate from the sanctuary and transition into semi-independence."

"What ring?" Parker asked.

Ella shifted from foot to foot. "The engagement ring from the Russian. I thought it was the least I could do to repay the clan for what it has done for us."

That was news to Vivian. "You didn't tell me that he gave you a ring."

"Yeah, well. It wasn't important." She shrugged. "I wasn't going to keep it anyway."

Vivian knew her daughter well enough to tell when she was being evasive. But this wasn't the time for a frank conversation. It was up to Ella to decide when she was ready to share more of what had happened to her.

Until then, Vivian would have to wait patiently.

6

ELLA

"The guy in booth four is looking at you," Maddie whispered in Ella's ear as she passed by her on the way to the kitchen. "He's cute. Do you want to take his order?"

Casting a quick glance in the guy's direction, Ella wondered if she was experiencing a *Groundhog Day* phenomenon and reliving that pivotal day.

Except, in the movie, it had happened right away and not a month later. Which meant that she was probably dreaming.

Since the guy's face and most of his body were hidden behind the diner's tall menu, all she could see were his hands holding it up. They were long-fingered and olive-toned.

If that was Romeo, and it most likely was him, she was going to empty the carafe of hot coffee on his head. After all, this was a dream, so she wouldn't get fired for it, or arrested for assaulting a customer.

It would be so satisfying.

She wondered what had happened to him and Stefano in real life. But to find that out, she would have to ask questions and bring up things she preferred to forget. Thankfully, no one had volunteered any information, and other than her mother, no one had tried to coax it out of her either.

Not yet, anyway.

The full coffee carafe heavy in her hand and an evil smirk on her lips, Ella strode toward booth four and its olive-skinned occupant.

He sensed her approach and lowered the menu. "Hello, Ella."

"Logan." The smirk dissipated and was replaced by a frown. "What are you doing in my dream again?"

He looked around as if surprised. "This is a dream? It feels so real." He smiled up at her. "You have a very vivid imagination."

"Not really." Ella sat down across from him. "I used to work in this diner, and I remember every little detail about it. The only thing different is you. What are you doing here?"

He shrugged. "How should I know? I'm a figment of your imagination. You brought me here."

Yeah, she probably did. But why?

Was it a warning that Logan wasn't who he seemed to be, the same as Romeo? Was that why she was replaying the scene, just with a different actor?

But then Ella had no illusions as to who and what Logan was. The guy bought weapons from Gorchenco, so he was probably some sort of a mercenary or a warlord. He was dangerous and reeked of evil. Well, not literally, but figuratively.

"I don't know why I would do that. But since you are created by my subconscious, you must have an idea why we are meeting here of all places. It's not like I miss this diner."

He looked around. "Yeah, I see what you mean. It's quite drab. Where would you like to go? Is there a place you miss?"

"The beach."

Pushing up to his feet, Logan offered her a hand up. "Then let's go."

Even though she didn't like the real Logan and feared him, she took it. The moment his hand closed around hers, they were both transported to the boardwalk.

Dreams were fun that way.

"That's so cool." She pulled her hand out of his clasp. "One moment we were at the diner, and the next we are on the beach."

He smirked. "That's one of the many reasons I love dreaming. Unfortunately, I can't spend all my days sleeping."

"Yeah. You are too busy buying weapons from the Russian mafia. What do you do with them?"

"I supply my army. Technology keeps improving, and if we want to stay on top of things, we need the latest weapons."

She arched a brow. "You have an army? Are you a mercenary?"

"Not the way I see it. It depends on how you define a mercenary."

Ella thought it was self-explanatory. Mercenaries were soldiers for hire. They fought for whomever paid them.

"What's your definition?"

"A mercenary fights for money. But although I do that too, it's only to finance my people's cause. Fighters for a cause are either rebels, defenders, or conquerors. Not mercenaries."

"Which one are you? Rebel, defender, or conqueror?"

"Conqueror, of course."

Rolling her eyes, she waved a hand. "Why am I not surprised? And who or what do you intend to conquer?"

"The world."

"Naturally." She shook her head.

In books and movies, all evil masterminds wanted to rule the world. No wonder her imagination came up with that answer.

He smiled, looking actually friendly and not terrifying. "What about you? Is there anything you want to conquer?"

"My fears, mainly. And my disgust with myself."

The second part of her answer surprised her. She hadn't felt disgusted with herself when awake, not consciously anyway.

Logan seemed surprised too. "Why would you feel like that?"

"I should've resisted the Russian. I should have been braver and at least put up a fight, but I was too scared, too weak."

"To resist him would have been stupid, and you're too smart for that. You did precisely what you needed to do to survive and to eventually escape." Logan stopped walking and turned to her. "The truth is that you impress the hell out of me. Gorchenco is a smart and cautious guy, and yet you managed to fool him, lulling him into a false sense of security. Quite an achievement for an eighteen-year-old girl from the suburbs."

Well, that made her feel a little better. "Thank you. I thought so too, logically." She put a hand over her heart. "But in here, I feel icky, and nothing I do makes it better."

He tilted his head. "And what is it that you do? You've just gotten free this morning, and you expect to feel better right away?"

"Yeah, you're right. I need to give it time. It's just that I'm afraid the taint is going to stay."

Reaching for her cheek, he cupped it gently and smiled down at her. "Sweet, innocent Ella. There is nothing more boring than squeaky clean. The taint you're imagining makes you stronger and more interesting. It also makes you less fearful, not more. Once you've experienced the dark side and dealt with it, you know that you can survive it."

"Spoken like a real Sith Lord." Ella laughed and then continued in a deepened voice. "Welcome to the dark side, my young apprentice."

7

JULIAN

*I*t was a quiet morning in the clinic, and Julian had nothing to do. In moments like this, he found it difficult to resist his obsession. Not that he'd put much effort into it.

His addiction was harmless.

Pulling out his phone, he gazed at his screensaver.

How ironic was it that he was seeing as much of Ella now as he had prior to her rescue ten days ago? Which amounted to staring at her picture longingly and trying to convince himself that all she needed was time.

Like a lovesick human teenager, he'd altered his evening running route so he could pass by her house and get a glimpse of her through the windows before the nighttime shutters came down. He'd managed to steal a few, which had only made his torment worse.

It seemed that Ella never left the house.

In case he was mistaken, Julian had asked Magnus, who'd confirmed that she was spending her days in her room, reading, or surfing the net, or just vegging in front of the television.

Had she given up on life?

Not that ten days was a long time, not even by human standards, but Julian had hoped for some interaction with Ella.

Nothing major, just a hello-how-are-you sort of thing. Heck, he would've been happy to watch her from afar.

But knowing she was so near and yet unapproachable was pure torture.

The pitying glances he was getting from everyone didn't help make him feel any better.

His life officially sucked.

Except, feeling sorry for himself because of such minor things made him feel even worse. Ella had been to hell and back, and here he was, acting as if it was all about him.

Instead of moping around, he should get busy and actually do something, like sinking his teeth into the halfway house project.

With Merlin taking over the clinic, Julian had been relegated to the role of an intern, and the truth was that even with the miscellaneous tasks Merlin was assigning to him, he didn't have much to do.

It was ten o'clock on Monday morning, and other than rearranging the medicine cabinet and checking expiration dates, Julian hadn't done one useful thing.

Staring at Ella's picture didn't count.

"Do you need me for anything today?" he asked Merlin.

As he waved Julian away, the guy didn't even lift his head from whatever he was reading. "You can take the rest of the day off. Tomorrow too. I'll have a load of things for you to do Wednesday, so don't make plans for that day."

Julian arched a brow. "Are we brewing potions again?"

On more than one occasion, he'd had the passing thought that Merlin might be nuts, believing that he was indeed a wizard who could wield magic.

Or the guy could be a genius who was really creating new natural remedies.

Merlin was trying to come up with natural ways to enhance immortals' fertility, males and females alike, but to Julian, it seemed like the guy was delving in witchcraft. Especially since he was poring over a bunch of archaic pseudo-medical books that he'd brought with him from Scotland and then brewing stinky potions from Gertrude's herbs.

He'd overheard Merlin and the nurse having long-winded discussions about the different plants she was growing in her garden and their medicinal use.

It was possible that Gertrude was just as crazy as Merlin, but if she was as sane as she appeared and was supplying ingredients for Merlin's creations, then maybe the two were onto something.

"No potions, my dear boy. I'm compiling a list of research papers that I want you to read and summarize for me. If we tackle them together, we can cover twice as much material in the same time."

"No problem. I'm all yours on Wednesday."

As he left the clinic, Julian headed to his mother's office.

Her door was open, and he walked right in. "Do you have a moment?"

She put her tablet down and smiled at him. "For you, always. What's on your mind?"

A lot, but he wasn't going to bother his mother with his unrequited love.

"I want to talk to you about the halfway house project. I would like to get it going."

She sighed. "I gave Turner's mandatory volunteering idea a lot of thought, and I believe that it's not the right approach. It will create resentment toward the entire project. With the right presentation, I'm sure I can get people to volunteer their time without conditioning their share in the clan profits on it."

"You won't get many."

Smirking, she crossed her arms over her chest. "That's what Kian said about bringing back the retired Guardians. I think I've proved that my methods work."

"They worked once. It doesn't mean they would work again. You've played your ace. Every clan member has seen your presentation. What else can you show them?"

Leaning forward, Bridget smiled. "I can show them progress. I can prepare one hell of a presentation showing them success stories, and then tell them how many more of those we could be having with their help."

That was good. His mother was a natural at manipulating people's emotions and getting them to do what she wanted.

"You missed your calling, Mom. You should've gone into politics or fundraising."

"Nah, I just know our people and what works on them."

He nodded. "Assuming that you're right and that you can rope them into volunteering, we still need an actual house."

Uncrossing her arms, she put her hands on the table. "That's Kian's department. You should talk to him."

"I'll do it right now." He got up.

"Good luck."

"Thanks."

Pausing in front of Kian's door, Julian took a deep breath before knocking and braced for a refusal.

"Come in." The boss sounded impatient.

"Do you have a moment?"

"No. But take a seat anyway. What can I help you with?"

"Did Turner talk to you about the halfway house?"

"He did." Kian put down his pen and leaned back in his chair. "Right now we don't have the funds to purchase a property. I've recently made several investments in new promising startups, which I believe will begin bringing in nice profits in a year or two. But at the moment we are at the red line. I'm not willing to dip below it."

"What about Ella's ring? Turner said that it could finance several projects."

Kian nodded. "But he hasn't sold it yet, and I'm not sure when he'll find a buyer. So, until that happens, you'll need to find some other solution."

Julian arched a brow. "Me?"

"Yes, you. It seems to me that you're passionate about this project. Make it your baby. I certainly don't have the time for it, and neither does Bridget."

Taken aback, Julian swallowed. He was a doctor, not a businessman. What did he know about raising money and purchasing properties?

"I'm not sure I'm qualified."

"You're a smart man. You'll figure it out." Kian picked his pen up, indicating that Julian's time was up.

"Thank you for the vote of confidence. I'll see what I can do."

Lifting his head, Kian cast him an amused glance. "I'm sure you'll come up with something."

I'm not sure at all.

Maybe Turner could be of help. The guy's mental gears worked at triple the average speed, if not more.

Outside of Kian's office, Julian leaned against the wall and pulled out his phone. He shot Turner a quick text. *Any idea when the ring will be sold? We need that halfway house and Kian wants me to come up with the financing.*

He didn't have to wait long for the response.

Kian is overthinking this. All you need is a down payment on a property. The rest can be financed. I can provide the down payment from my personal funds, and once the ring is sold, the clan can pay me back and pay off the mortgage.

Julian read the text twice. Could it be as simple as that?

He fired off another text. *How come Kian didn't think of that?*

Habit. He's not accustomed to the use of financing for purchasing clan properties.

That still left the remodeling and furnishing and other necessities, but that wasn't where the big money went.

Pocketing his phone, Julian smiled. This was doable. But first, he needed to find a suitable property. How did one go about that?

Kian should know. With the number of properties he was purchasing, he must have people who found them for him. Turning on his heel, Julian headed back to the boss's office.

8

ELLA

*T*here were several advantages to having a private bathroom, Ella thought as she submerged herself in the tub's warm water. Aside from the obvious one of not having to share it with Parker so she could soak for as long as she wished, it was also a good place to hide from her well-meaning family and their expectant looks.

"Would you like to join me at the café?" Her mother.

"I can take you to the gym and show you around." Magnus.

"Do you want to take Scarlet for a walk?" Parker.

"Would you like to go to a cooking class with me?" Her mother.

And other variations on the same theme of trying to get her out of the house, or at least to interact more with her family.

With a sigh, Ella scooped two handfuls of frothy bubbles and combined them into a small mountain over her chest. Another scoop went on top, looking like a castle on top of a cliff.

If she were a princess, and her home were a castle, she wouldn't need the wicked witch to lock her up in the tower. She would choose to live there and allow no visitors. Sitting on the windowsill, she would gaze at her people living their lives down below. And when she got bored with that, she could read a book and live between its pages.

"Ella!" Parker knocked on the door.

Annoying kid.

Apparently, having his own bathroom didn't mean he was going to stop bothering her during her relaxing soak. "What do you want?"

"Do you know where the pain meds that Dr. Bridget left for me are?"

Ella pushed up to a sitting position, her mountain together with the castle on top sliding down into the water. "I put them on top of the fridge. Why? Are your fangs finally coming out?"

"I think so. I have the worst toothache ever."

Poor kid.

"I'll be out in a minute."

"I can get the meds myself."

"I know you can." In the month she'd been gone, her little brother must've grown an inch. "I just want to take a look at your gums." She got out of the tub and grabbed a towel.

"I'll be in the kitchen."

"Take two pills," she called after him before heading into her closet.

Bridget had warned them that once the fangs started coming out, the pain was going to be intense.

She'd also confirmed that Ella wasn't pregnant.

It had been such a huge relief to know that for sure. Now she could really forget about the Russian. Except, it was easier said than done. Every time someone mentioned his name, bile rose in Ella's throat.

Which was a weird reaction.

Was she suffering from a post-traumatic stress disorder?

While it had been happening, she'd dealt with it and hadn't

thought it was horrible, so why such a strong reaction now when it was over?

Normally, Ella would've talked about whatever bothered her with her mom, but Vivian was already worried sick about her and didn't need more fuel thrown on top of that.

Logan would have been a better choice as someone to figure things out with. Somehow, he'd managed to lift her spirits when no one else could, maybe because he'd said that she had impressed the hell out of him.

He didn't think of her as a victim.

Logan thought of her as a fighter, a survivor, and that gave her strength, while pity made her weak.

But Logan wasn't real, and she was basically talking to herself.

Then again, self-talk was a powerful tool for shaping one's opinion about oneself, so she shouldn't feel guilty about hoping to see him in her dreams again.

Talking to her subconscious while sleeping seemed to have a therapeutic effect on her, and it didn't matter who her weird brain had chosen for the role. Although selecting Logan, of all people, must say something about her and who her psyche gravitated toward.

Except, Ella hadn't dreamt about Logan since her first night in the village, and it seemed that her subconscious had entered the same sloth mode that her conscious self had.

The therapist her mother kept harping on about could probably shed light on what was going on in her head, but Ella wasn't going to see her. Her current issues would resolve with time, the same way her grief over her father's death had.

No therapist could talk the pain away, and Ella wasn't willing to take antidepressants either.

It was like putting a bandage over a bullet wound but leaving the bullet in. From the outside, everything would seem just peachy, which would make everyone happy, but the insides would fester, eventually killing the patient.

Ella chuckled. That analogy would no longer work when she was an immortal, but there was plenty of time before she attempted that.

Instinctively, she felt she had to get better first.

With a sigh, Ella pushed her feet into a pair of flip-flops and opened the bedroom's door.

The mental break she'd taken from life had to end, even though ten days were not nearly enough for the brain reboot she needed.

It was back to putting on a smile and acting as if everything was fine.

She was a pro at that. Pretending had become second nature to her, so much so that she'd even believed in the lies she'd told herself.

She'd done it twice already—once after her father's death, and the second time with the Russian.

She could do it again.

The first two times had been necessary for her survival. This time she was going to do it for the sake of her family.

And who knew?

Maybe pretending to be okay would actually help her feel that way?

9

VIVIAN

*T*he sun was setting, and it was getting cold, but Vivian dreaded going home. The evening walks with Magnus were a much-needed respite from the dark mood permeating their house, and as guilty as it made her feel to think like that, she wasn't ready to get back yet.

"You seem chilly." Magnus shrugged his jacket off and draped it over her shoulders.

The warmth that was trapped inside enveloped her like a cozy blanket, and when she pushed her arms into the sleeves, Vivian let out a contented sigh.

"What gave me away? The goosebumps on my arms, or the chattering teeth?"

"The goosebumps. I would've never allowed you to get so cold that your teeth chattered." He rubbed his hands over her arms.

Stretching on her tiptoes, she kissed his cheek. "My knight in a fancy suit."

"I think it's time to go back."

"Yeah, we should. It's going to be dark soon."

As they neared their house and Magnus unhooked the leash

from Scarlet's collar, she loped toward the front door. The dog seemed equally excited about going out for walks as she was about coming back.

"Mom!" Parker opened the door. "My fangs are finally coming out." He fended off Scarlet, who lifted up on her hind legs and was trying to climb up his thighs. "Come take a look!"

From behind him, Ella grinned.

It was the first genuine smile Vivian had seen on her daughter's face since the day she'd been rescued.

Ella put her hand on Parker's shoulder. "The very tips are out, and they are pointy. So cute. He looks like a baby vampire."

"Let me see." Vivian hooked a finger under Parker's chin and lifted his head up to the setting sun. "Yep. I can see them."

"This calls for a celebration," Magnus said. "How about we go to a restaurant tonight?"

Vivian shook her head. "I already cooked dinner."

Ella looked relieved. Apparently, the grin didn't mean she was ready to go out yet.

Parker, on the other hand, was disappointed. "We can eat yours tomorrow."

Vivian wrapped her arms around him and kissed his soft cheek. "You don't have the teeth to eat a steak with, so what's the point? That's the only thing you order when we go out."

His old canines had fallen out on Friday, and it would be a long time before his fangs were long enough to bite into a steak again. "But even if you did, it would've hurt too much. Your gums are swollen. Did you take the pain meds Bridget gave you?"

"Yes."

"Good. I think you should stick to the mashed potatoes tonight."

"Blah. I don't like them. Why didn't you make fries?"

She patted his back. "You'll thank me once you start eating."

"I'll set the table." Ella flip-flopped to the kitchen.

Was it her imagination, or did Ella look a little more upbeat?

Perhaps she was caught up in the excitement over Parker's fangs finally coming out.

Vivian shook her head.

Her sweet baby boy was growing fangs. Reality was indeed stranger than fiction.

When the table was set, Vivian opened the warming drawer and pulled out the meatloaf and mashed potatoes she'd made before going out on a walk with Magnus.

"It's Monday," Parker said.

Ella lifted a brow. "So?"

"Mondays and Wednesdays are supposed to be steak days." He sounded so despondent that it was almost funny.

"Says who?"

"We made a deal. Each of us got to choose what we eat two days of the week, and Sundays we eat out. I guess now that you're back we need to redo the schedule. But Mondays are still steak days." He cast Vivian an accusing look. "Meatloaf is for Fridays."

"I know, sweetie. But as I explained before, you can't eat meat without canines, and your gums will hurt even when chewing something softer. I made these easy to chew dishes especially for you."

With a long-suffering sigh, Parker put a small chunk of meatloaf on his fork. "The fangs are worth it." He closed his eyes and pushed the chunk into his mouth.

"I can make you an awesome ravioli with mushrooms dish," Ella said. "It will melt in your mouth."

"I don't like mushrooms."

"Since when are you so picky?"

Vivian put her fork down and wiped her mouth with a

napkin. "When we stayed at the other location, Magnus spoiled him with restaurant food takeout. Now he doesn't want to eat anything home cooked."

"I'm still good with steaks and anything else barbecued."

Ella eyed him with an evil smirk. "Oh, yeah? I can barbecue some zucchini and eggplant for you. Comes out delicious."

The banter between her kids that had used to annoy Vivian was now the best table conversation she could hope for.

It was familiar and reassuring.

"I almost forgot," Magnus said. "Roni asks what name do you want to put on your fake papers?" He reached behind him to the suit jacket he'd hung over the back of the chair. "I have a list of possible names." He pulled out a folded piece of paper and handed it to Ella.

"Can't I just make up my own?" She took the note and opened it.

"Good fake documents use the names of real people who've passed away, and in your case, it is doubly important to have the best possible. Gorchenco might be still looking for you."

Ignoring his comment about the Russian, Ella asked, "So Magnus is not your real name?"

"It is. The MacBain isn't."

"What is it then?"

"I don't have one. It's just Magnus."

"And what's Mom's fake name?"

"Victoria MacBain."

Ella glanced at the note and frowned. "I don't see MacBain on the list." She seemed disappointed.

"It's better for you and your mom not to share the same fake last name."

"Yeah, makes sense." Ella looked at the note for a long time. "I like Kelly Rubinstein, age twenty-one." She smirked. "It opens all kinds of possibilities."

As long as it got her out of the house, Vivian didn't mind Ella going to a bar and getting herself a drink or two. Anything was better than rotting away in her room for days on end.

"Indeed," Magnus said. "I'll tell Roni. Now, all we need is to get your picture."

Since the drinking age in Scotland was sixteen when accompanied by an adult and eighteen to order their own, Magnus probably hadn't suspected Ella's motive for choosing the name of a twenty-one-year-old.

"Can he wait with it for a few days? Amanda offered to give me a makeover, and I would like to take her up on that. I want the picture to look nothing like I look now."

Magnus took the note and put it back in his suit jacket's pocket. "There's no rush. For now, we can take you wherever you need to go, but if you want to get a car and drive yourself places, you'll need a driver's license."

Ella waved a dismissive hand. "I'm not in a hurry. Even with the wig and glasses, I'm still scared to leave the safety of the village."

"Even when you're with us?" Magnus asked.

"Even with you. I know he's still looking for me."

Leaning back in his chair, Magnus nodded. "Right now, Gorchenco is back in Russia, and rumors are that he's mourning the death of his young wife. But that doesn't mean that his people are not looking for you."

Vivian's eyes widened. Did Magnus say wife?

"But don't worry," he said. "We've covered our tracks well and the staging was impeccable. His people will snoop around and double-check every piece of information, and eventually, they will have to give up and accept that you are really dead."

Closing her eyes, Ella put a hand over her heart and slumped in her chair. "That would be the best news ever. I'm afraid he'll never stop looking for me."

"Because you are his wife?" Vivian bit out.

It rankled that Ella hadn't shared that information with her. Had Gorchenco forced her to marry him?

"No, not because I'm his damn wife, or was. But because he knows he'll never find another lookalike of his lost love." Ella opened her eyes and leveled them at Vivian. "Can we please never talk about this again? I'm about to barf out the meatloaf, and it's not going to be pretty."

MAGNUS

"Why didn't you tell me he married her?" Vivian asked when Ella excused herself and went back to her room.

"I thought you knew." Magnus rose to his feet and started collecting the dishes.

She handed him her plate. "If I did, I would've told you."

"It's not a big deal. Ella is dead to the world. That marriage is null and void. I don't know why you're so upset about it." He carried the plates to the sink.

Following him, Vivian sighed. "I don't like to put Ella and dead in the same sentence. And I'm upset that she didn't tell me about marrying Gorchenco. The only reason she wouldn't was that my daughter didn't think I could handle it."

"Don't take it too hard. It was her way of protecting her family, and it probably made her feel like she had at least some control over what was happening to her. She couldn't refuse Gorchenco, but she could choose whether to tell you or not."

His explanation seemed to mollify Vivian. Leaning against the counter, she crossed her arms over her chest. "I need to find a way to get her out of the house. Sitting in her room all day and cooking in her own juices is not doing her any good. She needs to meet people."

Magnus put the last plate in the dishwasher and closed it. "The obvious solution is to invite people over here. But you said she didn't want you to do that."

"She said she didn't want pity visits and threatened to go to her room if I invited girls I thought could become her friends. Like Tessa and Wonder. They are not much older than Ella. Sylvia too, even though she's in her mid-twenties. She's mated to Roni who's not even twenty yet."

Magnus chuckled. "Technically, Wonder is ancient." He'd told Vivian Wonder's story, but she must've forgotten.

Vivian waved a dismissive hand. "She didn't actually live for all those years, so they don't count."

As Parker walked into the kitchen and reached for his pain meds, Vivian put a hand on his shoulder. "When was the last time you took them? Bridget said no more than two every four hours."

He grimaced. "Are three and a half hours okay? My gums are killing me."

She nodded. "Maybe we should get you some topical numbing."

"Like for babies?"

"Yeah." She ruffled his hair. "You're my baby, and you're always going to be even when you're six feet tall and have a beard on that beautiful face."

He pretended to grimace, but it was more of a crooked smile. Despite protests to the contrary, the boy loved being babied by his mother.

Magnus handed him a glass of water. "Here you go, buddy. If you want, we can go over to Merlin's and ask him for that stinky stuff he makes to numb pain. If you don't mind the smell and taste of it, the paste is effective."

"I'm willing to give it a try. Do you want to go now?"

"Let me check with Merlin."

Magnus fired off a quick text to which Merlin replied with a thumbs up.

"Grab a jacket, Parker. It's getting cold outside."

The kid rolled his eyes. "It's less than a hundred feet to Merlin's house, and I can't catch a cold anymore."

"As you wish. Don't complain to me when you're shivering." Magnus turned to Vivian. "I'm going to leave Scarlet with you. Merlin has too much breakable stuff for her to get into."

The guy's house was a mess. Stacks of books were tucked into every corner, and the lab equipment was strewn over every surface. Not to mention the smell. For some reason, all of Merlin's creations stank.

Vivian kissed his cheek. "Don't take long. I'm making coffee."

When they got there, Merlin's door was open, which Magnus took to mean they were invited to just walk in.

"Wow, it stinks in here." He pinched his nose closed.

Parker looked up at him with a raised brow. "It's not so bad. I like the smell of cooking potions."

"You're a weird kid. This is okay, but your mother's meat-loaf is not?"

"Smell and taste are not the same. It's like the cologne you put on. It smells good, but you wouldn't drink it, right?"

"You have a point."

"Hello, neighbors." Merlin walked into his living room, wearing purple pajamas with little white stars and moons printed on them, a long, gray house robe, and a pair of fluffy orange slippers. "I have just the thing for you, my young friend." He pulled a tube out of his robe's pocket. "Smear it all over your gums whenever they bother you."

Magnus eyed the thing suspiciously. "What's in it?"

"Just some medicinal herbs. Organically grown without the use of harmful pesticides. It's perfectly safe."

Taking a quick sniff, Magnus crinkled his nose. As a boy, he hadn't given much thought to what was in the paste. As long as it helped with the pain, he'd been willing to smear cockroach juice on his gums. But as an adult, he now knew of several herbs that although safe were not something a kid should ingest. "You sure about it?"

Merlin waved a dismissive hand. "Positive." Removing a stack of newspapers from the couch, he put them on the coffee table. "Now come sit with me and tell me how Ella is doing."

The couch, which had been brand new just a few short weeks ago, was covered in stains and burn marks.

"I would love to stay and chat, but Vivian is expecting me back home for coffee." Feeling uncomfortable about leaving right after getting what he'd come for, Magnus added, "You're more than welcome to come and join us."

Merlin grinned. "I would love to. It gets a bit lonely here in the evenings." He walked toward the door, and then glanced at them over his shoulder. "Are you coming?"

"Don't you want to change first?" Parker asked.

"No. I'm very comfortable." Merlin tightened the belt around his waist. "This will do."

Magnus shrugged. As long as the guy wasn't naked, he could wear whatever he wanted. "Let's go."

"Is Ella still staying in the house all day?" Merlin asked as they stepped out the door.

"I'm afraid so."

"It's so sad." Merlin shook his head. "Maybe I can prepare a potion for her. Something to lift her mood."

"Ella will never take anything like that," Parker said. "What we need to do is invite Julian for dinner at our house."

"Ella doesn't want anyone visiting her."

"He won't. Julian will come because you and Mom want to thank him for organizing the rescue. And then he can stay and play computer games with me."

"I don't know if he plays."

"Come on. Julian is a young dude. Of course, he plays. He can come every evening to keep me company." Parker rolled his eyes and made air quotes. "If he hangs around the house enough, Ella will get used to having him there, and maybe they'll start talking, and then maybe he'll ask her out on a date."

"The kid is a genius." Merlin patted Parker's back.

Parker shrugged. "I just know my sister. Ella is stubborn, and she wants to do things her way, but she is a nice person. She will not be rude to Julian and go hide in her room when he comes. And when she gets to know him better, she'll see that he is a really cool guy."

It sounded like a good plan, but Ella might see right through it.

Then again, it didn't matter whether she did or not. The excuse for Julian's invitation was valid, and so was him staying after dinner, especially if he and Parker seemed to hit it off, which they already had.

11

SYSSI

"Welcome to my humble abode." Merlin made an exaggerated bow, waving Syssi and Kian inside.

As usual, he was dressed in a ridiculously colorful outfit. Red skinny pants that made his slim legs look even scrawnier, and a blue sweater with little white stars that was at least three sizes too big for him. Somehow, though, it all worked for Merlin. It was his signature look.

"I still don't understand why we couldn't meet at the clinic," Kian grumbled.

Syssi smiled and gave Merlin a quick hug. "Thank you for inviting us."

It was hard to believe that the house had been brand new when Merlin moved in. Aside from the clutter, which was just staggering, the place looked like it hadn't been cleaned even once. No wonder Merlin didn't want roommates. No one would've tolerated living like that.

"Please, take a seat. I cleaned up the couch." Merlin winked. "Nothing is going to jump at you from between the cushions."

Kian wasn't amused. His lips pressed tightly together, he sat on the sofa and glared at the doctor. "This is not a social call, Merlin. I don't have time for that."

"Right."

Merlin removed a stack of books from a dining room chair, dusted it with his hand, and brought it over to face the couch. Crossing one long leg over the other, he smoothed his hand over his nearly white beard.

Syssi wondered how he could work with that thing on his face. It looked clean, but it was long and messy and, in general, beards weren't sanitary, which should have been a concern for a doctor. And since it seemed that Merlin was brewing potions in his house, that beard was also dangerous.

It could catch fire.

"You're probably wondering why I invited both of you here."

"Indeed." Kian crossed his arms over his chest.

Syssi was waiting for an explanation as well. Kian's presence wasn't really necessary, and she could've come alone.

He had promised to be there for her throughout the fertility treatments, except, knowing her husband, in addition to wanting to be supportive he wanted to make sure that she wasn't submitting herself to anything dangerous.

Kian had admitted as much, saying that she was desperate for a baby and not thinking clearly, and that Merlin was loony.

"As you can see," Merlin waved his hand around the room, "I've been doing a lot of research. My approach to the problem of immortals' infertility is somewhat unorthodox." He chuckled. "Or maybe I should rephrase that since my sources are ancient. But anyway, I believe in holistic medicine. Which means taking into consideration both the physical and mental states of my patients."

Kian groaned. "I don't have the patience for this New Age crap."

"Oh, but it's not New Age. If anything, it's old age." Merlin scratched his head. "Since you've interrupted my well-prepared speech, I have to start at the beginning."

The low growl vibrating in Kian's throat would've scared anyone except for Merlin, who either pretended not to hear or was too distracted to notice.

"As I was saying, my approach is holistic." He made an air circle with his hand. "That's why both of you should start treatment at the same time. Our low fertility is not only a female issue, immortal males are not fruitful either."

Kian shrugged. "Fine with me. What do I need to do?"

Merlin smirked. "First of all, you need to relax. You're a stress ball, and in turn, you're stressing out your lovely mate. Excess stress hormones create an environment that is far from optimal for conception."

Syssi's heart sank. If in order for her to get pregnant Kian needed to relax, they would never have a child.

"And how do you suggest that I do that?" Kian asked. "Do you have a relaxing potion?" he scoffed.

"Indeed, I do, but because you need a clear head for what you do, you can't take it. I'm talking about daily meditation sessions and romantic vacations."

"I don't have the time or the patience for those either."

"Type A personalities are the most difficult to deal with." Merlin sighed. "Very well. I can put you on a bio-feedback program. You can teach yourself how to calm down."

"How long does it take?"

"At least an hour a day. You may still wish to consider meditation, which in my experience is more effective."

Kian shook his head. "I tried it once. It's a catch-22. Meditation is supposed to be conducive to relaxation, but in order to meditate, I need to calm down first. I don't see how it can work."

"Bio-feedback it is, then," Merlin said and pushed to his feet. "The other part of the treatment is the natural fertility enhancers I've prepared."

He walked over to the dining table and lifted two small decanters. One had a blue ribbon tied around its neck and the other pink.

"So you don't get confused." He handed the pink one to Syssi and the other one to Kian. "Drink one ounce twice a day. When these are finished, come to me for more."

Lifting the decanter, Kian pulled out the stopper. "Phew, this stinks." He turned his face away from the fumes. "And you expect us to drink it?"

Bracing for hers to smell just as bad, Syssi unplugged the pink-bowed decanter. The smell was different but just as repulsive.

"It's a good idea to have a piece of chocolate at the ready," Merlin suggested.

Braving another sniff, Kian asked, "What's in it?"

Merlin waved a hand. "A little bit of this, and a little bit of that, with a touch of magic." He winked at Syssi. "I want to start with this and see if it works before we attempt the human-made commercial medicines."

"Are there any side effects?" Kian asked.

"Enhanced libido is one." Merlin smirked. "I know that you don't need any enhancers in that department, but it was unavoidable. I'm afraid that throughout the treatment the two of you will be frolicking like bunnies."

Syssi felt her face turn red.

"You're embarrassing my wife." Kian wrapped a protective arm around her shoulders.

Merlin dipped his head. "My apologies. I meant no disrespect, but as a doctor, I have to be direct." He cast Syssi an apologetic glance. "In this line of treatment, I expect many more embarrassing moments. You should prepare yourself for it."

She had. But if the potion worked, there would be no need for the more invasive methods she'd read about.

Syssi crossed her fingers.

Lifting the decanter to the light, Kian gave it a little shake, stirring the sediment. "Do you have other test subjects, or are Syssi and I the only ones?" He glared at Merlin. "I want others to try it, so my intense personality won't be blamed for your potions' failure."

"Naturally," Merlin said. "Right now, other than the two of you I have Hildegard and Gertrude on board. Bridget wants to try it too, but she needs to sweet-talk her mate into it first."

Kian chuckled. "Good luck with that. You'll have to offer him the same advice you offered to me. Turner is not exactly a chill kind of guy either."

Crossing his arms over his chest, Merlin nodded. "I have a feeling Magnus and Vivian would want to join the program too. But first, Vivian needs to transition."

"It's going to be easier for her to conceive as a human," Syssi pointed out.

"Yes, this is true. But then she will have to wait for the transition until after her baby is born, and she's not getting any younger."

Syssi nodded. "I still remember how difficult it was for Nathalie and Andrew. He was going insane because he couldn't bite her. Bridget was afraid that it would trigger Nathalie's transition, which might have endangered the baby."

"I don't think she would've gone into transition while pregnant." Merlin smoothed his hand over his beard. "But I would hesitate to test that hypothesis."

12

JULIAN

*I*n the bathroom, Julian brushed his teeth and his hair, checked his shoes for scuffs, and then adjusted the collar of his button-down. It was blue with thin stripes, not overly dressy but well made. Together with a pair of dark blue jeans and trendy shoes that were a cross between sporty and fancy, the look was precisely what he'd been going for. Casual and yet elegant enough for a Friday night dinner.

For the past two weeks, people had been inviting him over nearly every evening, and since he was too polite to decline, he'd accepted and had to suffer through hours of pitying looks and forced smiles.

Julian had cracked jokes and tried to look as cheerful as can be, but no one was buying it. Regrettably, he wasn't a good actor, and the truth was written all over his face.

This time, though, he was invited to Ella's house for a Friday night family dinner. Not as Ella's anything, just as a family friend. Magnus had mumbled something about Parker having no friends in the village and looking for a partner to play computer games with.

Magnus's intentions, although good, were quite transparent, and the excuse he'd used for the invitation was lame. The guy probably didn't know that those games were played online, and that there was no need for gamers to be in the same room.

Nevertheless, Julian was grateful. It was an opportunity to spend time with Ella without putting any pressure on her. At this stage of the game, even the friend zone seemed appealing. It was better than being on the outside without the ability of even looking in.

Besides, perhaps the friend zone was exactly where he should be.

Ella needed time. This wasn't just another hookup he was going to charm the pants off. She was the real deal, and Julian was in unfamiliar territory.

He knew very little about the intricacies of the wooing and dating game. He'd seen it in movies and had read about it in books, but even though he'd spent a long time among young humans, he hadn't seen much dating or romancing on campus.

It was all about hookups and booty calls, which had suited him perfectly. Romance hadn't been on his horizon, and he'd felt no need to prepare for it.

Perhaps some old romantic films would help him get the gist of it. Going to see a girl in her parents' house was like a trip into a fifties movie. But unlike in the old movies, Julian was on much friendlier terms with the parents than with the girl.

Magnus wasn't officially Ella's father yet, but he was mated to her mother, and he seemed to care about Ella as if she was already his daughter.

Was that how Turner felt about him?

They weren't close, but then Turner had dropped everything to rescue Ella only because Julian was infatuated with her picture.

59

He doubted a real parent would've done that for him, so there was that.

As he reached Ella's house, the shutters were just coming down for the night, but he managed to catch a glimpse of her helping her mother set the table.

Ella was so lovely that she was almost painful to behold.

Parker opened the door before Julian had a chance to knock. "Hey, Julian. Long time no see." He offered him his hand. "Do you want to see my fangs?"

"Sure. But maybe I should come in first. The light is spilling out through the open door."

"Oh, yeah. I keep forgetting about the blackout rules." Parker opened the door even wider to let him in.

"Good evening, Vivian, Ella," he said as he walked toward them. "Thank you for inviting me to dinner."

"I'll tell Magnus you're here," Parker said. "He's in the backyard with Scarlet."

"Hello, Julian." Vivian pulled him into her arms. "I'm so glad you could make it."

"Hi." Ella forced a little smile and looked away.

"Come, sit at the table." Vivian turned to her daughter. "Ella, can you get the wine? It's in the cabinet over the fridge."

"I can't reach it. I'm too short."

"You can climb on a chair."

Julian jumped to his feet. "I'll get it."

As he followed Ella into the kitchen, he wondered whether Vivian had done it on purpose so he and her daughter would have to do something together.

Ella let him in front of her and leaned against the counter as he opened the cabinet's doors.

"Which one does your mom want, do you know?"

"Mom, is there a specific wine you prefer?"

"Could you get one red and one white? I don't care which brand."

"Okay." He pulled out two bottles and handed them to Ella. "Anything else I can get for you?"

For a moment, she just looked into his eyes as if seeing him for the first time, then shook her head. "Thank you, but that will be all."

Strange girl. What thoughts had crossed her mind during that long moment when their eyes had been locked together?

Typically, his nose could supply the missing clues, but not with the strong cooking smells masking the more subtle ones.

"I didn't know what you liked to eat, so I made several dishes to choose from," Vivian said. "There is baked salmon, grilled chicken, and a vegetable curry dish in case you don't eat meat. I know that your mother is a vegetarian."

"I'm an omnivore." Julian spread the napkin over his knees. "And I'm very easy to please. Food wise, at least."

Ella cast him another one of her penetrating gazes. "What are you picky about?"

"Movies, books, music."

"What's your favorite movie?" Parker asked.

"Of all time, or recent?"

"Recent."

"*Avengers: Infinity War.*"

Parker put his fork down. "No way! That's my favorite too!"

Ella rolled her eyes. "Why am I not surprised." She lifted the glass of wine to her lips, but then put it down without drinking any of it.

Julian arched a brow. "You don't like it?"

"It was a horrible movie. Everyone died."

He'd meant the wine, but discussing the movie would keep the conversation going.

"I guess you're right. I'm just expecting a trip back in time or something like that to fix everything. It's a Marvel movie. The good guys have to win."

"I hope so. I love the characters, and Thor is just to die for, but I didn't like how dark that one was."

Thor was to die for?

Was it the muscles?

Julian was going to hit the gym starting tomorrow.

He took a long sip from his wine. "What's your favorite music?"

She shrugged. "I don't have a favorite band or anything like that. I just like what I like. It has to be catchy, though, something I would like to sing along with. What's your favorite?"

"A couple of months ago, I would've said progressive and psychedelic rock, mainly Pink Floyd, but since I moved in with my new roommate, it's classical music. He's a pianist and a very talented one. Listening to him play just soothes my soul. Except for when he plays Debussy."

"Why? What's wrong with the French dude?" Parker asked.

"Nothing. I'm sure many people love him. It certainly takes skill to play his stuff. But I just happen to prefer more melodic, romantic music."

13

ELLA

*J*ulian was a romantic.

Figures.

Just one more thing to make a perfect guy even more perfect. If only she'd met him before Romeo had burst her naïve little bubble and ruined her life.

Sitting next to Julian, Ella fought the irrational urge to go to the bathroom and scrub herself clean. Only, no amount of soap could do that. The taint was on the inside, and she had no business indulging in what-ifs about a pure soul like Julian.

If only he were a little wicked, she could've felt more comfortable with him. Couldn't he be a compulsive shoplifter, or a gambler, or a pothead?

As ridiculous as the thought was, Ella would've loved for Julian to have a vice or two. But she had a feeling that he had never stolen anything, and that he wouldn't know what a joint was even if it hit him in the face.

"I've heard talk about Kian assigning you to the halfway house project," Magnus said.

"You did? I'd only talked to him about it yesterday. But yeah." Julian raked his fingers through his chin-length hair. "He expects me to organize everything, but I don't know where to start. I'm a doctor, not a businessman."

"Who wants coffee?" Her mother came back from the kitchen with a full carafe in hand.

"I would love some. Thank you." Julian lifted his cup.

He had such good manners. Too good. According to her mother he was twenty-six, but he acted much older.

Magnus took the carafe from Vivian and poured coffee into the rest of the cups. "Every big project seems overwhelming until you break it down into a step-by-step action plan. What's the first thing you need to do?"

"Find a suitable place. Not only that, though. Kian expects me to arrange financing for it as well. Turner offered to provide the down payment and suggested we take out a mortgage for the rest. I guess I'll need his help to do that as well because I don't have a clue how to go about it."

"Isn't the clan rich?" Ella asked. "How come he can't just buy the building?"

Julian put his cup down. "I think it's a cash flow problem. Kian tries to keep all the balls in the air. Building this village cost a shitload of money, which severely depleted the clan's cash reserves. Then we've undertaken the huge humanitarian project of fighting trafficking, and with all this going on, Kian still invests in promising technologies whenever the opportunity presents itself."

"What about my ring? That should cover the cost of several halfway houses."

"It hasn't been sold yet, but once it is, we will pay Turner back for the down payment and close the mortgage."

Ella didn't know much about buying real estate and getting loans, but what she did know was that the bank would want to see where the mortgage payments would come from.

"Are you going to charge the girls rent?"

Julian chuckled. "Of course not. Once they have jobs that can pay rent, they should graduate into full independence."

"So how are you going to get a mortgage? The loan officer will want to see where the monthly payments will come from."

And he was raking his fingers through his hair again.

Apparently it was a nervous tick.

"I'm sure the rules are different for a charity." He shook his head. "I'm so out of my element with this. Kian should dump this task on someone who knows a thing or two about running charities."

Not pretending to be a know-it-all was another point in Julian's favor. She liked that he had no problem admitting being lost and confused. It made him seem a bit more human.

Well, the term human didn't apply. Fallible was better.

Ella scrunched her nose. "Have you ever heard of GoFundMe?"

"No, what is it?"

"It's a fundraising platform. When my teacher's house burned down, the school organized a fundraiser, and they collected a lot of money to help her out. I think a lot of people will donate to an important cause like this."

Magnus frowned. "But that's small money. How much would people give? Five bucks?"

"Some will give five, and some will give more, but this can reach millions of people around the globe. I think it would be awesome if a project like this was to be financed by regular people and not some deep-pocketed donors."

"A double-whammy," Julian said. "Raising money and awareness at the same time."

As a plan started forming in Ella's head, tingles of excitement rushed up her spine. "We can make a video of a girl telling her personal horror story. We won't show her face, of course, only a silhouette, and we can even change her voice in the recording. But think what a powerful motivator it would be. I can already imagine the money pouring in."

"You can make several videos," Vivian suggested. "You can even create a fundraiser for each girl featured. It's much more powerful when people see and listen to the person they are helping out."

Ella's excitement was growing by the minute. There were so many possibilities to explore, and the beauty of it was that it was so simple she could do it all on her own.

Not only would she be helping girls who'd gone through hell and deserved every bit of support possible, but she would be repaying the clan for what they had done for her and her family.

"I can shoot videos with the camera on my phone. And I can also post them on YouTube. This can be huge."

Julian shook his head. "I think we should get a professional camera crew to do that. Brandon can help with that."

"Your uncle in Hollywood?" Vivian asked.

"Well, he's not really my uncle, more like a distant cousin, but he is a clan member. He's the one responsible for spreading our message to the world."

Ella frowned. "What message? Vampire and shapeshifter movies?"

Julian chuckled. "Not exclusively. I'm talking about the message of freedom from oppression, equal opportunity, and quality of life for everyone. In order to strive for something better, people need to first know that it exists. For example, a female starship captain in a sci-fi movie demonstrates that women can hold the highest military positions. After seeing enough movies like that, people wouldn't think twice about nominating a woman for a position that was previously thought of as exclusively male. Like the chief of police."

Ella crossed her arms over her chest. "We're not there yet,

but I get what you're trying to say. I'm just wondering what is the best way to showcase our girls without causing them too much grief. I know how hard it is to talk about that stuff."

Crap, she shouldn't have said that. Suddenly, the mood around the dinner table switched from enthusiastic to sorrowful, with everyone but her looking into their coffee cups.

That wouldn't do.

"Don't look so glum, people." Ella lifted her cup and took a sip. "I think this is going to be a very uplifting experience for the girls. The humanity that has turned a blind eye and a deaf ear to their suffering is going to rise up to support them. Personally, I like the idea of millions of individuals acknowledging their silent part in the crimes committed against those girls and trying to buy redemption with their contributions."

14

KIAN

"I know one way that is sure to help me relax," Kian said as they left Merlin's house. "You can come work with me. We will take breaks every couple of hours to make out." He pulled her close against his side. "It's a double whammy. I'll be less stressed, and because we will be having so much sex, we'll have a baby on the way in no time."

It had been fun having her with him in the office. The problem was that neither had managed to get much work done. That was why Syssi had decided to work for Amanda instead.

"Sounds lovely. But we are already making love several times a day, and you know what happened the last time we tried to work together." She chuckled. "All we did was fool around. I don't want to be responsible for single-handedly ruining the clan's business empire."

He leaned to kiss the top of her head. "But we weren't trying to make a baby back then. This would be fooling around with a purpose."

Syssi lifted her eyes to him. "You aren't serious, are you?"

"I kind of am. You have a calming effect on me, and I know

68

that having you around would help me relax. But I also know that this is wishful thinking on my part. You love what you do at the university lab, and office work can't compete with that."

With a sigh, Syssi leaned her head on his chest. "Life is full of compromises, my love."

And wasn't that the truth. At first, right after Syssi had gone back to the lab, they'd been meeting for lunch at Gino's, which was more or less midway between the university and the keep. But pretty soon it became clear that he couldn't take an hour and a half break from his work day, and the daily lunches turned into once a week lunches. After the move to the village, it was more like once a month. They still called each other several times a day, but hearing Syssi's voice over the phone didn't have the same calming effect as having her near him.

He wondered whether the effect was caused by something chemical or was it all in his head? It was a question he might have an answer for pretty soon.

"Did I ever tell you about the virtual reality startup I invested in a while back?"

"I don't think so. Is it a new gaming platform?"

He chuckled. "In a way. In crude terms it's a platform for virtual hookups. People fill out a very extensive questionnaire, listing their ideal partner's attributes and creating a fantasy that they would like to enact. After the software pairs them with the best match in the company's database, a virtual meeting is arranged. Each of the partners is hooked up to a machine, which can be on different continents or in the next room for all they know, and they get to experience a fantasy in cyber world that feels as authentic as any real one."

"Sounds fascinating. Is it up and running already?"

"Not yet. They got stuck with a problem they couldn't solve. I didn't want to lose my investment money, so I sent William to help them with the code. With him on board, I believe they will be ready to start beta-testing soon."

Syssi cast him a seductive smile. "Can we take part in that testing? I can think of several interesting adventures for us to try out." She batted her eyelashes and lowered her voice. "You know I have a wild imagination."

Minx.

He cocked a brow. "Am I not fulfilling all of your sexual fantasies?"

"I meant we should test it together. A joint fantasy. You can be a pirate captain who kidnapped me and is holding me captive, or even better, a space pirate. Or I can be a rich lady on some distant planet who buys you on the slave market and orders you to pleasure her. I'm sure you can see the possibilities."

He'd meant it as a tease, but his imagination hadn't gone that far. Since time moved differently in the virtual world, and a week of experiences could be crammed into a three-hour session, his original idea had been to spend a cyber vacation with Syssi and see if it had the same calming effect on him as being with her physically.

But whatever the scenario, he was going to wait until the beta-testing was done and all the glitches were cleared. Syssi's brain was too dear to him to risk on an experiment.

"We can try it when the company is officially open for business."

"How long until then?"

"It depends on William and on funding. Their original estimated budget was depleted a long time ago. I kept pouring money into it because I believed it was going to be a huge success, but at some point I had to say enough was enough. Now they have no choice but to scrabble for more investors."

"Is it because of the financial squeeze the clan is in?"

"In part. But if that were the only obstacle, I would have sold another company to keep financing the development. The main problem is that the service is going to be expensive. Not only because of the enormous initial investment, but because it's costly to operate. This means that only the wealthy would be able to afford it, and that's a limited market."

"Hmm." Syssi didn't continue, and for a long moment, they walked in silence.

"Does the clan have a controlling interest in it?"

"The founders were not willing to give it up. We have thirty-four percent, and the founders retain sixty-six. Any additional funds they need will be in the form of a loan and not shares."

Syssi stopped and turned to face him. "If the founders are struggling financially, they might reconsider, especially if you promise them creative freedom or whatever else they are afraid to lose."

"They might. But as I said, that's not the only problem. I'm not sure how profitable they will be, and if it's smart for us to keep pouring funds into what seems to be a money pit."

"I have a good feeling about it."

He put his hands on her waist and pulled her closer. "Is it because you're impatient to experience it? I can pretend to be a pirate right now." He waggled his brows. "I'll throw you over my shoulder and take you somewhere I can ravish you. Harrr…"

Laughing, she slapped his chest. "No, silly. Well, yes, that too. But mainly because I have a feeling about it." She lowered her eyes. "Remember Starship Enterprise's holodeck?"

"What about it?"

Star Trek, the old one and the new generation, had been two of the few television series he'd watched. His current guilty pleasure was *Game of Thrones*.

"I kept fantasizing about it. It was a way to experience things I was terrified to do in real life, like skydiving or mountain climbing, or even an open-Jeep safari."

"And sexy pirates?"

"Yeah, that too. But anyway, I would've loved a service like that. I'm sure there are many people like me, men and women, who would love to have a unique experience at least once. A special occasion kind of thing."

"Like a couple's twentieth anniversary."

"Exactly. A way to be young again in a dream world, or rather cyber world. And since everyone is so busy, and time is the most precious commodity, a cyber vacation, even a costly one, might seem like a very attractive alternative to a real one."

"Okay, I understand why you think the company will succeed. But why should I go after a controlling interest?"

"Because a technology like that is a breakthrough, and I believe we should be in a position to defend it and to expand it. Besides, when all the bugs are fixed, we can get a machine or two for the clan's use."

Kian laughed. "It might work for the females, but not the males. Mental biting would not release the pressure from the venom glands."

In addition, because of their unique situation, there was a possibility of being paired with a cousin. Even though it was only virtual, the idea was so abhorrent to them that it would be enough to deter clan members from trying it out. Then again, if they had control over the database, they could ensure that no clan members were paired.

"You don't know that for a fact. It might. If men can ejaculate while dreaming, why not this?"

"Because most men do not, at least not after puberty. But I guess we will find out when we try it."

"You keep calling the startup 'it.' Don't they have a name for the company?"

Kian grimaced. "For now it's called Dream Encounters, but it's only a working title, and I don't like it. It sounds like an advertisement for mattresses."

"Yeah, you're right. That's a sucky name. How about Perfect Match? After all, they are promising to pair people with the best possible partners."

"That sounds like a matchmaking service."

"It does. But in a way it is. People can go on virtual dates, and if they enjoy it, they can request a real life meeting."

Kian chuckled. "I doubt it's a good idea. Imagine finding out that the handsome dude from the fantasy is a middle-aged bald guy with a potbelly. Or that the beautiful young woman who was a tigress in bed is a seventy-year-old grandmother."

Syssi nodded. "That is true. Although it's kind of sad. In their minds they are young and beautiful. But then that's the beauty of a service like that. The mind is free from the body's constraints. The possibilities are endless, and the benefits can be tremendous for people with mobility and other issues. Besides, they can always deny the request for a meeting."

Syssi's enthusiasm was contagious.

Kian wasn't as imaginative as her and therefore hadn't considered all the possibilities. In addition to generating profits, a service like this could improve people's lives, which fell under the overriding umbrella of new technologies the clan wanted to encourage.

"I'll suggest it to the founders when I meet with them."

Kian seldom met with the heads of enterprises he either purchased or invested in. But since this was important to Syssi, and the company was faltering, his personal involvement was needed. He was going to make sure it succeeded.

"And the name too," she added.

"Perfect Match. It has a nice sound to it. It's definitely less cheesy than the Perfect Hookup, although that would be more truthful."

"Don't worry. People will get it." She smiled and put her hands on his chest. "Even though I've already found my perfect match, I can't wait to try out a virtual adventure with you."

"You don't have to." He lifted her up, threw her over his shoulder, and smacked her bottom. "Off to my cabin, lassie. Harrr...."

15

ELLA

*L*ong after Julian had left, Ella was still thinking about him. When dinner was over he hadn't gone home right away, but had stayed to play computer games with Parker.

She'd enjoyed listening to them together, shouting, laughing, poking fun at each other, and teasing like a couple of old friends. Julian had a gift for putting people at ease. He hadn't acted below his age just so Parker would like him. It seemed that he'd been genuinely having fun with a kid half his age.

No wonder Parker liked him so much.

Heck, everyone did, and that included her.

The problem was that right now all Ella could offer Julian was her friendship, while it was quite obvious that he wanted more.

He'd done an admirable job trying to hide his attraction to her, but she'd caught the quick glances he was stealing when he'd thought she hadn't been looking.

It was kind of sweet.

And if Ella were okay in the head, she would have signaled him that she was interested. But she wasn't okay, not by a long shot, and if Julian wanted her, he would have to wait for time to heal her wounds.

When there was a knock on the door, Ella's heart skipped a bit, thinking that Julian had come back, but when she opened the door, she found Okidu's twin brother standing on her doorsteps with a mannequin grin spread over his face and a Saks shopping bag in his hand.

"Good evening, Mademoiselle." He dipped his head and lifted the bag. "Compliments of Mistress Amanda, who sends her best regards along with these items."

"Thank you." Ella took the bag. "And thank Mistress Amanda for me."

It was awkward to say mistress, but Ella was afraid the butler would feel scandalized if she just called his mistress by her name.

"I shall." He bowed. "Good night, Mademoiselle." He turned on his heel and walked down the steps.

"Who was it?" Vivian asked.

"Amanda's butler. Or at least I think that's who he is. He looks like Okidu's twin."

"That's Onidu, and he is indeed Amanda's butler." Her mother pointed at the bag. "What's in it?"

Reaching inside, Ella pulled out a short, dark wig. "Oh, how cool. It's just like her hairdo." She pulled it on her head, tucking her braid under the back. "How do I look?"

Her mom shook her head and grimaced. "Go take a look. If I say something, you're not going to believe me anyway."

Ella peeked into the bag to see what other goodies Amanda had sent. "There is also a ginger-colored wig. I'm going to try both." She glanced at her mother. "Do you want to come with me to my room?"

That brought a smile to Vivian's lips. It wasn't an invitation Ella extended often. After letting her mom tuck her in for the first two days, she'd gone back to her usual 'my room is my castle' attitude.

Standing in front of the vanity mirror, Ella had to agree with Vivian that black wasn't her color. She was too pale to pull it off without putting on a darker foundation, and she had no intention of doing that.

"Try the red. It should suit you better," Vivian suggested.

"Yeah. I like the short style, but I don't like the color." Ella took the black wig off and pulled on the red.

It was a bob with bangs, and it looked cute on her. But since her natural color was light brown with reddish undertones, it didn't change her appearance that much.

The idea wasn't to make her look better, but to disguise her.

"Maybe I should go for bleached blond." She took the wig off. "Or purple."

Vivian followed her out of the bathroom. "You can use the black in the meantime, because it's a better disguise, but you should take Amanda up on her offer for a makeover. I think this was her way of reminding you about that."

"I should, shouldn't I?" Ella sat on her bed. "I need to have my picture taken for my fake driver's license, and I can't do that until I decide on the look I want. And without a license, I can't go anywhere."

Vivian sat next to her on the bed and wrapped her arm around Ella's shoulders. "I'm glad that you want to get out of here, but I don't think you're ready to get behind the wheel and go driving around. I think that you should get out of the house first and mingle with the people in the village. It's so liberating not to have to hide who you are and what you can do."

"Is it? Do you really feel more comfortable here than you did in our old home?"

"There is no comparison. When you start spending time

with the immortals, you'll get what I mean. You'll feel at home like you never have before. These are our people."

Ella smirked. "So that's why I liked Julian so much. Because he's an immortal."

"Oh, I think that in his case, it's more than that."

"He is very handsome, and charming, and kind, and he played with Parker, and he's a doctor." Ella winked. "That last one was for you, since that seems important to you."

Vivian narrowed her eyes at her. "I hear a *but* coming up."

"He's too good for me, Mom, too pure."

"What the heck are you talking about? I'm sure that boy has bedded hordes of women, while you've been with only one man."

"I'm not talking about that, Mom." Ella put a hand over her heart. "I feel like there is darkness in me now. Maybe it was always there, and I just haven't acknowledged it." She lifted a pillow and hugged it to her. "I'm not naïve anymore. I'm constantly on the lookout for ulterior motives, and I no longer believe that people are essentially good. They might think that they are, but they are not."

"That's part of growing up, Ella, not some mysterious darkness lurking inside of you. Heck, I don't trust people either. When Julian came to see me at the dental office with Turner and Magnus, I thought that he'd organized your kidnapping so he and his buddies could swindle me out of every penny I owned."

That was news to her.

"You thought that they were running a scam?"

Vivian nodded. "It was easier to believe in that than the alternative. But when I asked Turner how much your rescue was going to cost me, and he answered nothing, I knew that the situation was much worse than I thought. Compared to what they were telling me, dealing with a bunch of scammers would've been a walk in the park."

Ella could just imagine how devastated and hopeless her mother must have felt. "Oh, Mommy." She leaned her head on Vivian's shoulder. "I'm so sorry for causing you so much grief."

"Don't. It wasn't your fault any more than it was mine. We were both fooled."

"Only Parker wasn't."

Vivian smirked. "Parker likes Julian."

"I like Julian too."

"So what's the problem? Don't you find him attractive?"

She snorted. "I would need to be blind or dead not to realize how gorgeous he is."

"So?" Vivian made a rolling motion with her hand.

This was hard to let out, but her mother deserved the truth even when it was painful. "I can think of him as an attractive guy, and I can see it with my eyes, but I can't feel it on the inside."

"Why not?"

"Because I'm dead in here." Ella patted her belly. "Because I can't feel anything physical for anyone right now. Put a nude Thor in this room with me, and he would stir nothing. I could appreciate his beauty, but there would be no arousal."

Her mother looked so sad that Ella regretted fessing up to the truth. She should have come up with another excuse.

"I wish I could help you, but I don't know how. You should really talk to Vanessa. That's what she does day in and day out. She helps girls get over their traumas."

Ella shook her head. "No shrinks."

"If you want to video the girls under her care, you will have to talk to her."

"Not as a patient."

Her shoulders slumping, Vivian sighed. "Why are you being so stubborn about it? You must realize that you need help."

"I don't. Grief takes its time, and there is no rushing it. Ten shrinks with Nobel prizes can't make it go away, or ease it, or shorten it. I know that from experience, and so do you. And if you're wondering why I'm bringing grief up, it's because I'm mourning my old self. That carefree, naïve girl is gone, and I'm damn sorry to lose her because I liked her."

16

TURNER

*A*s Turner opened the door, the appetizing smells had him lifting a brow. Bridget was cooking?

Or was she just heating up leftovers from yesterday's takeout?

Dropping his briefcase on the counter, he walked into the kitchen and kissed her cheek. "What are you making? Or better yet, why?"

"We haven't had a home cooked meal in a while. I thought I'd throw something together. I'm making curry."

He was surprised she even had the necessary ingredients. It wasn't as if they'd done any grocery shopping lately. With both of them working twelve-hour days, going out to dinner or bringing home takeout made much more sense.

Still, it was a nice change of pace.

Pulling out a barstool, he sat at the counter. "I talked with Sandoval today."

She glanced at him over her shoulder. "About the ring?"

"I didn't bring it up right away, of course. First I hit him up for a donation."

"Did he agree?"

Turner shifted on the stool. "Two hundred and fifty thousand. That's chump change for him, but it will help with the down payment on the halfway house."

"Nice."

"Thank you, I thought so too. After I got him to make the pledge, we talked about his nephew and how things were working out. I let him go on and on about how grateful he was for what I've done for the brat, and I only brought the ring up after half an hour or so of chitchat."

"As a casual aside."

"Precisely. I told him I'm looking for a buyer for it as a favor for a friend who has fallen upon hard times. I added that my friend doesn't want anyone to know that he's selling his dear departed wife's engagement ring, and therefore is asking not to offer it to anyone in Russia."

"Did he buy the story?"

Turner shrugged. "It doesn't matter whether he did or not. It's a matter of appearances. Arturo would never admit to dealing with contraband on the black market. That way he only agrees to help a friend who is helping another friend, and we both come out smelling like roses."

"So he agreed?" Bridget pulled out a bottle of ready-made curry sauce from the fridge and dumped it on top of the vegetables in the wok.

"He said that he might know someone who'd be interested. I need to bring the ring to him, though."

"Is it safe to take something like this to South America?"

"He invited me to his house in Miami. I told him that I need to check with my fiancé."

"When?"

"Next weekend."

Bridget loaded the curry onto two plates and brought them over to the counter. "I'm curious to meet the infamous Arturo

Sandoval, but I don't know if I can take the entire weekend off."

Turner spread his thighs and pulled her between them. "Yes, you can. All the missions for the coming month are scheduled, and thankfully there are no crises to deal with. We haven't gone on a vacation together in a long time."

She leaned into him and wrapped her arms around his neck. "You're right. A weekend in Miami sounds fun. Is it safe?"

"I wouldn't offer to take you if I thought it wasn't."

"Then it's settled." She pushed away from him and sat on the next stool over. "We should schedule time for dates."

He arched a brow. "We go out to dinner at least three times a week."

"Those are not dates. A date is when you dress up and go to a fancy place like By Invitation Only. Or a concert, or a play."

"Don't tell me that you bought a membership in your cousin's snooty restaurant."

"I didn't, but I can have Kian make a reservation for us. I thought that you liked it there."

"I did, but this is not the time for frivolous spending. I could probably afford to get it for us, but I think it would be in bad taste considering the budget cuts."

"No, you're right. That's why I decided not to purchase a membership for us and mooch off Kian instead."

Turner scooped some curry on his fork and put it in his mouth. It wasn't bad, considering that it was made with store-bought sauce, but it wasn't great either.

"It would've been nice to have a gourmet restaurant in the village."

"Maybe one day we will. Callie is thinking about it. But first, she wants to get her degree."

"That's more important than having a restaurant. If Merlin's research is successful and he finds a way to increase fertility, the village might have a bunch of kids who'll need a school and a teacher."

Bridget nodded. "I agree."

She pushed a piece of carrot around her plate. "Speaking of Merlin and his research, how would you feel about joining his program?"

Turner was a smart man, but it took him a moment to process what Bridget had meant.

"You want to have a baby with me?"

"Yes, I do."

"Shouldn't we get married first?"

She eyed him as if he wasn't making any sense. "That's it? I wasn't sure what to expect, but it wasn't a proposal."

Yeah, as usual, his emotional intelligence rivaled that of a brick.

"What do you want me to say?"

She waved her hand. "Tell me how you feel about it. Do you want to be a father? Are you scared? Are you worried that our lives would get messy?"

Taking a deep breath, Turner smoothed his hand over his hair. "I would love to have a child with you, and I would love to actually be there for my child, and not only financially."

"But?"

"First of all, Merlin is only starting out, and we don't know if and when his fertility treatments will work. Secondly, we both work very long hours, not because we need the money, but because what we do is important. I don't see how we can fit a baby into this schedule."

She sighed. "Don't you think I know that? But as you said, it will probably take a long time until Merlin refines his treatments, and there is always a possibility that nothing he does will work. But on the remote chance that the treatments are successful, it takes over nine months for the baby to be born.

That's plenty of time to find a solution. I can train a replacement, and you can downsize a little. Isn't our child worth the effort?"

It seemed that his pragmatic and logical Bridget was taking a leap of faith, and assuming a child was a certainty.

Turner didn't have the heart to burst her bubble. If going to Merlin for treatment would make her happy, he would support her in any way he could.

"I have no problem with giving it a try."

"Remember that you said that." She grinned. "Syssi told me that Merlin's potions are absolutely vile."

He lifted a brow. Was she concerned that her mouth would taste bad when they kissed?

"How much of the potion does she need to drink?"

"She and Kian both have to drink an ounce of it twice a day. Not the same potion, obviously, but she says that they are both terrible."

17

VIVIAN

*A*s Vivian turned into the Sanctuary's parking lot, Ella pulled down the shade and glanced at the mirror. "Do you think I should put on some lipstick? I look like a chemo patient with this black wig."

Vivian parked and reached to get her purse from the back seat. "Here." She handed Ella a red lip pencil. "Dab a little on the outline and then smack your lips. The color is very strong."

Once she was done, Ella examined her reflection again. "Now the shadows under my eyes look even worse. Do you have an eyeliner pencil in there?"

"Yes, I do." She handed Ella a blue one. "Go easy with that too."

The sudden fussing with her appearance belied Ella's nonchalant attitude about meeting with Vanessa.

She'd agreed to come on the condition that all they were going to discuss was her idea for the fundraising project, and she had threatened to walk out if Vanessa tried to psychoanalyze her.

"How do I look now?"

"Gorgeous and barely recognizable."

"Perfect." She smiled. "Let's do it."

Her head held high, Ella walked into Vanessa's office with an impressive show of confidence. It was fake, but Vivian was impressed nonetheless. Her daughter was a fighter.

"Hello, Dr. Vanessa." Ella glanced at the desk as she offered the therapist her hand. "I'm sorry, but I don't know your last name."

"Everyone just calls me Vanessa. No doctor and no last name. Nice to meet you, Ella." She shook the hand she was offered. "Please, take a seat."

"Thank you."

"Your mother told me that you have an interesting idea that you would like to run by me." Vanessa smiled. "She insisted that I should see you as soon as possible because I was going to love it."

Not wanting to steal Ella's thunder, Vivian hadn't told Vanessa what it was about. It was Ella's baby, and if she was allowed to run with it, her sense of accomplishment would do wonders for her self-esteem.

"Are you familiar with the GoFundMe fundraising platform?" Ella asked.

Vanessa nodded. "I am. It's a way to raise money for a friend or a relative. The platform takes care of collecting the donations, but the fundraising is done by the individual setting it up."

"It can be much bigger than that. My idea is to make short videos of the rescued girls telling their stories in their own words. Each video will be about one girl, and we will only show her silhouette. We can even change her voice if you think that's necessary. Then we post it on YouTube, and on Facebook, and ask people to fund the halfway houses for the girls, or share the video, or both."

Vanessa leaned back and crossed her arms over her chest.

"The idea is worth exploring, but I foresee a couple of problems. First of all, I don't know how many girls would be willing to talk on camera, even in silhouette. Secondly, for this to succeed, these videos would need to go viral, and I sincerely doubt that it would happen. People don't like sad stories. Show them pictures of puppies and kittens, and they will share that, but not depressing stuff."

Ella lifted her hand and made air quotes. "Beware. This can happen to your daughter. Save a life. Watch and share."

Raising a brow, Vanessa asked, "And you think a heading like that will motivate people to share a horror-story video?"

"It would motivate me," Vivian said. "If I saw this heading, even before what happened to Ella, I would click on it, watch it, and share it. It could have prevented her ordeal. I might have been more vigilant and investigated Romeo right from the start."

"Yeah, me too," Ella said. "In my gut, I knew that something was off about him. I even told my best friend Maddie, and she agreed with me. But I wanted to believe that he was for real." She shook her head. "I was so naïve."

Vanessa leaned forward. "It wasn't your fault, Ella. He was so convincing that he even fooled your mother, who has much more life experience than you. Good people don't expect others to be bad. They are under the illusion that most people are just as good as they are."

"I guess." Shifting in her chair, Ella tugged on her wig to readjust it. "But back to my fundraising idea. I get what you're saying about people not wanting to listen to harrowing stories. The videos will have to be edited, and the production will have to be done at least semi-professionally. Not too polished, but not too crude either."

Vivian stifled a sigh. Ella had smoothly sidestepped Vanessa's attempt to redirect the discussion toward what had happened to her.

"If you're thinking about bringing in a camera crew, that's not going to work, not even if it's all female. A girl might be willing to talk to you, someone who's gone through a similar experience, but not to strangers, and especially not in front of a group of people."

Ella shrugged. "Originally, I thought to just shoot them with my phone's camera and then do some editing to make sure the girls were not recognizable, but I think I'll need better equipment."

"Do you know how to use a professional recording camera?"

"No, but I can learn. The videos don't have to be movie quality. In fact, it's better if they aren't. People are going to be moved by their authenticity, not their high production value."

"Are *you* willing to tell your story on camera?" Vanessa pinned Ella with a hard look.

As evidenced by Ella's audible gulp, she hadn't considered the possibility.

A long moment passed until she nodded. "I'll hate doing it, but I will. It's important for people to realize that this can happen to any girl anywhere. I don't know how the other girls got lured into a trap, or what their circumstances were before, but I guess some of them were just like me. Middle-class girls from good homes that were tricked by pros."

Vanessa sighed. "There are as many versions of this as there are girls who've been deceived. Every girl's story is different. The common factors are naïveté, wishful thinking, and romantic notions. A new boyfriend who's too good to be true comes with a fantastic offer that's impossible to refuse."

"Hook, line, and sinker," Ella murmured.

E L L A

*V*anessa leaned forward and steepled her fingers. "At some point, you'll have to deal with what you've been through, Ella. Rape is not easy to recover from on your own. I just want you to know that when you're ready to talk, I'm here to listen."

Crap, she'd walked right into the shrink's trap. "I wasn't raped."

Next to her, Vivian shifted in her chair and started fussing with the hem of her blouse.

The traitor.

"Then what would you call what happened to you?"

"I was coerced."

"Isn't it the same?"

"No, it's not. That's like saying that a punch to the face is the same as a slap with a glove."

"Is that how you feel about it? That it was a slap with a glove?"

God, she hated shrinks and the way they turned everything into a question. She'd just said it.

"Yes." Here, that should be the end of it. Unless Vanessa could turn even a yes answer into a question.

"Was it a playful slap with a glove? Or an invitation to a duel?"

Ella snorted. "It was an invitation to a duel alright. Except, I wasn't given any weapons, and my opponent was armed to the teeth."

A victorious smile bloomed on Vanessa's face. "You've just proven my point."

"Well, whatever. I had no choice, and I did what I had to in order to survive. I just want to forget about it."

"When you think back, is there anything you could have done differently?"

Ella rolled her eyes. "Isn't that obvious? I would've never gone with Romeo to New York."

"And other than that?"

"As I said before, I did what I had to do to survive and eventually to escape. I had to make the Russian believe that I wanted to be with him, so he would lower his guard and not keep me in the dark about where we were going and when."

"So you don't regret succumbing to his coercion?"

Ugh, this woman, or immortal, was making her so angry. As a shrink, she sucked even worse than that other one. Was she suggesting that Ella should've fought?

To what end?

Pinning Vanessa with a hard glare, Ella bit out, "Not even for a moment. If I'd done anything differently, I wouldn't be here, talking with you about making videos. I would be married to a mafia boss and pregnant."

The therapist smiled. "That's very good. Many of the girls blame themselves for not fighting harder, but after talking with those who did, they change their minds. He could've starved you, drugged you, even beaten you or forced you physically.

The end result would've been the same. I'm glad you realize this and don't blame yourself."

Would Gorchenco have done any of those things?

Ella didn't think he would've starved or beaten her, but he could've drugged her. It would've been so easy for him to slip a date-rape drug into her drink.

But the worst he could've done was to lock her up and not tell her anything. If he hadn't shared his travel plans with her, the rescue operation would not have been possible.

Crossing her arms over her chest, Ella lifted her chin. "Now that we've had our little chat, I'm sure you can see that I don't need therapy."

"You're doing better than expected. Self-blame and a diminished sense of self-worth are usually the first hurdles to overcome. The second is fear, and the third is mistrust. After such a traumatic experience, it's difficult to interact with people who haven't suffered anything like you have, and even more difficult to have a relationship."

Damn. Vanessa had hit all three nails on the head.

But Ella wasn't going to admit it and give the shrink and her mother more ammunition against her. Hopefully, this had been as close to a therapy session as she was going to get.

It was time for a smooth redirect. "My mother mentioned something about a sewing class she was going to teach. Do you have any other arts and crafts classes here?"

"Yes, we do. Are you interested in joining? It's a great way to meet the girls in an informal setting and get to know them a little. They will be more willing to talk to a classmate."

That sounded like Vanessa's way to trick her into participating, but what she'd said made sense.

"Wouldn't they get suspicious about an outsider joining the class?"

It was Vanessa's turn to pin Ella with a hard stare. "But

you're not really an outsider, are you? You just don't live in the sanctuary. If you want to gain their trust, you can't lie to them."

Sneaky shrink. Did Vanessa think Ella was that gullible?

"I have no intention of lying to them. I'm going to tell them the truth of why I'm here, which is making videos for a fundraiser that will help them transition into independent life."

SYSSI

"*I* missed you all day." Kian put his hands on her waist and pulled her into his body. "The reason I hate Mondays is not work. It's not having you around."

Even though Kian often worked on the weekends, he did it from his home office, and she could be there with him, reading a book on the couch. Or making out on it when he wanted a break, which was quite often. After two days of all that wonderful togetherness, separating on Monday was hard on both of them.

"I can put a couch in your official office, quit my job at the university, and read books all week long. With the occasional interruptions, of course." She waggled her brows.

But even if Syssi were willing to quit her job, which she wasn't, the problem with Kian's official office was that unlike the one at home, Kian was rarely alone in there. People were coming in and out all day long, and the phone didn't stop ringing.

It wasn't the same.

Besides, even though they hadn't been successful in identifying any new Dormants, she loved working at the lab with Amanda.

Eventually they'd have a breakthrough, she just knew that in her gut. And in the meantime, they were collecting important data on paranormal abilities. As far as she knew, no other lab was doing it, probably because there was no funding for paranormal research.

In the past, when the army had been interested in exploring the possibilities of remote viewing and other special abilities, funds had been plentiful. But the subject had fallen out of vogue and was considered pseudoscience rather than science.

Except, proving that paranormal abilities existed wasn't even all that difficult. Most people had at least some extrasensory perception. Like knowing who was calling them before picking up the phone or sensing when someone was looking at them even when their backs were turned. Still, few were willing to explore their abilities, and only when they were strong. Most tried to explain away the inexplicable.

"Sounds like a plan to me." Kian took her lips in a soft kiss. "It would do wonders for my stress level."

"I'm not sure about that. Once your business starts failing because of your neglect, your stress level will skyrocket."

He sighed. "It was a nice fantasy while it lasted."

"Speaking of fantasy. You know what time it is, right?"

"Time to make love to your pirate?"

"First, it's potion time. Then making love."

The concoctions were supposed to make them hornier than usual, but Syssi hadn't noticed any difference. Keeping their hands off each other had always been a struggle, even before they'd started Merlin's dubious fertility program.

Kian grimaced. "Let's get it over with."

In the kitchen, she pulled the two decanters out of the fridge together with two Godiva chocolates.

"Cheers." Kian lifted the shot glass she'd used for measuring the ounce of potion.

"Cheers." Syssi quickly swallowed the vile concoction, and then immediately stuck the chocolate in her mouth. "I really hope Merlin knows what he's doing. I would hate to keep drinking this stuff for nothing."

As he finished chewing his piece of Godiva, Kian pulled a bandana out of his back pocket and tied it around his head.

"Harrr, lassie. It's time for ravishing." He picked her up and carried her to the bedroom, thankfully not throwing her over his shoulder this time.

Her sweet guy was smart enough to know that she would've barfed all over him if he had. It warmed her heart, though, that he'd remembered her fantasy and had even prepared a prop to act it out.

"Oh, no, please don't ravish me!" she pretended to plead.

Taking her seriously, Kian immediately put her down.

"Oh, no, please do!" She laughed so hard that her belly was heaving.

"Make up your mind, lass." Kian picked her back up and kept striding to their bedroom. "I don't have all day." He pulled her shirt off even before they got there.

Gently lowering her to the bed, he kissed her quickly before continuing the act. "What do we have here? A lass dressed as a lad? What kind of a garment is this?" He pulled down her stretchy jeans.

Eyeing her white cotton panties, he put his hands on his hips and leaned forward to inspect them. "That's much better. I was half expecting to find boy briefs." He pulled those down too. "And that's even better than before." Smacking his lips, he dove between her legs. "I need to have me some of that honey to wash the bad taste from my mouth."

"Is that what ravishing is?" Syssi asked innocently.

"That's just the prelude, lass." He flicked his tongue over her sensitive nub.

"Ooh, I like this. Do it again."

"Like this?" He repeated what he'd done before.

"Yes. More."

"Before I do that, there is the little matter of your impudence." He grabbed her by the hips, turned her around, and smacked her bottom. "I don't take orders from my prisoners, is that clear?"

Syssi giggled. "Yes."

His hand landed on her other cheek. "No giggling either."

"Okay."

"And you answer me with a yes, captain." Another smack.

"Yes, captain." Syssi smiled into the mattress.

"And take off your bra. I want to play with those succulent nipples of yours."

This was fun. It had been a long time since they'd played their naughty games, and never like this. She didn't even know Kian could get this playful. Maybe the biofeedback was working, helping him to loosen up and have some fun.

Lifting her bottom up, he licked into her, and all thoughts of biofeedback and anything else flew off. As he alternated licks with light swats, supercharging her arousal, Syssi's hips started gyrating of their own accord.

Her hands fisting the duvet, she buried her face in the soft fabric to stifle her moans, which earned her a couple of harder swats.

"I want to hear every sound you make, lass. Your moans belong to me."

"Yes, captain."

He massaged the small sting away, and then kissed each globe. "Lovely ass you have, lassie. And it's mine too. Mine to spank, and mine to kiss."

Enfolding her with his body, he thrust into her wet folds, eliciting a throaty groan from her. "And that's the ravishing part." He pulled back and surged inside her again.

His arm reaching under her, he found her swollen little nub and rubbed it gently as he kept up a steady rhythm that was enough to have her climbing higher and higher, but not enough to push her over the edge.

He knew her body so well, knew how to bring her to the very precipice and hold her there until she was ready to scream in frustration, but she knew this game just as well. When he finally released her, she was going to fly up to the stratosphere.

As his strokes gained momentum, he grabbed her hip, holding her in place with one hand while the fingers of his other kept massaging, faster and faster until she threw her head back and screamed out his name.

20

KIAN

*A*s Syssi erupted, Kian clamped his lips on her neck and sank his fangs into her soft skin. As always, the double release was so powerful, it felt like he was dying and being resurrected at the same time.

Nothing compared to this, and as impossible as it seemed, the experience not only hadn't diminished with time, but had grown even more earth-shattering.

Kian felt blessed.

He hadn't known that he'd been lacking a vital part of himself until Syssi had entered his life. But now that he was sharing it with her, it was so painfully clear to him that up until he'd met her, he'd been running on empty.

Would the same be true for the child they would hopefully create together? Would he feel the same wonder?

Still buried deep inside his mate, Kian wrapped his arms around her middle and toppled them both sideways. Spooning behind her, he nuzzled her neck, but she was out.

It didn't happen as often as it had in the beginning, but from time to time Syssi still blacked out for several moments after a venom bite.

Knowing how much she loved the sensation of soaring on the clouds of euphoria, he loved giving it to her, which meant waiting patiently for her to come back down to earth.

Sometime later Syssi sighed contentedly. "We should go to sleep like this. I like the feel of you inside of me."

He kissed her shoulder. "I'm not nearly done with you yet, sweet girl."

"Oh, I know." She chuckled. "I can feel you charging up already. I'm just saying later, when we actually go to sleep."

He pulled out a little and then pushed back in, lazy, shallow thrusts that were more about the connection than ramping things up again.

A moment later, he pulled out all the way and pushed Syssi onto her back. "I want to see your face when I make slow love to you." What he really wanted to say was, *when I put a baby inside of you*, but he could make no such claim.

Straddling her, he feasted his eyes on her beautiful face, her gorgeous, smart eyes, and those lush lips that were curved in a coy little smile that was reserved just for him.

He could never get enough of kissing them. Hell, he couldn't get enough of kissing every part of her perfect body.

"Are you just going to stare?" Syssi cupped the undersides of her breasts. "Or are you going to take care of me?"

As his eyes zeroed in on her nipples, the scent of her arousal flared, and the little pink peaks tightened under his gaze. His mate loved it when he paid attention to her breasts, and no lovemaking session would be complete without him pleasuring them thoroughly.

Leaning down, he licked one, sucking it into his mouth, and then took care of the other with his fingers, pinching it lightly and tugging on it in sync with his suckling on its twin.

When both nipples had been properly pleasured, he smoothed his hand down her inner thigh. And as he cupped her between her legs, Syssi moaned and arched up, grinding her core on his palm.

"Come up and kiss me," she breathed.

That was an offer Kian couldn't refuse. Pushing up, he braced on his forearms and cradled her head in his hands.

For a moment, he just gazed into her luminous eyes, still marveling after all this time that she was an immortal like him.

"I love you," he whispered before taking her mouth in a kiss that was all about possession.

Her nails digging into his shoulders, Syssi kissed him back with just as much fervor. Owning him as surely as he owned her.

She was his everything, but even though she was well aware of it, mainly because he told her as much almost every day, she never tried to use her power over him to gain any kind of advantage.

She just loved him back.

"Do you know that I'm the luckiest guy on the planet?"

With a sweet smile, she lifted her head and kissed his lips. "I know. And I'm the luckiest woman." She swiveled her hips under him. "But I'm getting a little impatient."

"Are you now?" He gripped her wrists in one hand and brought them over her head. "What are you impatient for?"

"For you to get inside me and put a baby there."

"Oh, love." He dipped his head and kissed her lightly. "There is nothing I would like to do more, but it's not up to me. Not entirely."

Her eyes hooded with desire, she smirked. "We just need to keep working on it tirelessly."

"Tirelessly, eh?" He pushed just the tip into her.

"Yes, like this, but a little more."

He pushed a little deeper. "Is this good?"

"Almost. But it's still not enough."

He withdrew and pushed in again, going all the way in until he was fully seated inside her. "You meant like this?"

"Yes, please don't stop." Syssi lifted her legs and linked them behind his ass, spurring him on with her heels.

In no time, he was pounding into her, taking her as roughly as she loved being taken while thanking the Fates for giving him the perfect mate.

When Syssi's core tightened around him, and she cried out, Kian's climax was ripped out of him. Throwing his head back, he released a roar that would've been heard by every occupant of the village if not for the topnotch soundproofing of their house.

Panting, he had the presence of mind not to collapse on top of her but to drop sideways.

"Wow," Syssi breathed. "That was baby-making sex."

"Fates willing."

21

JULIAN

"What do you think?" Julian asked.

He'd done his damnedest to sell Ella's idea to the boss. Mostly because he thought it was a good one, but also because it would give her something to do and get her out of the house.

What did she do all day? Think about what she'd been through?

It couldn't be healthy for her to cook in her own juices like that.

And if she needed an assistant, he would jump on the opportunity to be with her in any capacity she was willing to have him.

"I like the idea," Kian said. "Anything that brings donation money and eases our financial burden is welcome."

Bridget pulled out her tablet and opened a page. "After Julian told me about it, I did some research on these kinds of fundraising platforms. There are several of them, with one being the clear leader, but I expect many to pop up in the near future because they are getting so popular. It's a new and fascinating phenomenon. People donate straight from their phones, supporting either someone they know who needs a helping hand or a cause they believe in. I was surprised to find how successful a fundraiser for fertility research was. Apparently, we are not the only ones struggling with the issue. Many humans are as well."

Kian snorted. "Who knows. Maybe Merlin's potions are the answer to our financial difficulties. If they work on us, they should work even better on humans. But that depends on how many would be willing to tolerate the foul taste."

Bridget cast him an amused glance. "I'm not sure about it working at all. But since Merlin tailored it for us, it might not be suitable for humans. In any case, I just wanted you to know that Turner and I are going to start the treatments too, so at least you and Syssi won't be alone in your suffering."

Shifting in his chair, Turner tightened his lips into a thin line. He was either uncomfortable with Bridget talking openly about their conception attempts, or perhaps he wasn't enthusiastic about becoming a father and was only agreeing to it to please her.

Julian wished them luck.

Having a little brother or sister was something he'd never even wished for because it was like wishing for the moon. Now that it seemed possible, he was rooting for his mother and her mate's success.

Hopefully, Merlin wasn't as loony as he appeared, and his potions were not just snake oil.

"We need to discuss logistics and security," Turner said. "For this to succeed, the videos need to be done professionally, but on the other hand, bringing in a professional camera crew and a director to run the show is out of the question."

"What if they are all female?" Bridget asked.

"I wasn't even thinking about the girls' reaction to a bunch of strangers with cameras showing up in their sanctuary. I'm concerned about word getting out. For their safety, we need to keep the location secret. It's next to impossible to get civilians to keep a secret, especially if selling the story can bring them a nice cash reward."

Kian drummed his fingers on the conference table. "What if we have everyone sign non-disclosure agreements with steep penalties for violations?"

Turner shook his head. "Not tight enough as far as safety is concerned. There is too much at risk. My recommendation is to keep the recording in-house. You can get Ella a professional camera and an assistant to handle the lighting."

He glanced at Julian and winked. "I think Julian could do that."

To see Turner wink was so shocking that for a moment Julian just gaped.

"As much as I adore my son, and as sweet as he is, I think a female assistant is a better choice." Bridget cast Julian an apologetic glance. "You can help with the editing, though. It's very labor intensive. I've seen a documentary about filmmaking, and I was astounded that a five-minute end product required hours of work in the editing room. Sometimes even days. I expect you and Ella will be spending a lot of time on that." His mother waggled her red brows.

They meant well, but they made him feel so damn pathetic.

"Do you have a particular female in mind?" Kian asked. "Because if you're thinking about Sylvia, don't. She's just started on another master's degree."

With all due respect to education, Sylvia was taking it too far. The woman was a perpetual student. It was a perfect example of why Turner's suggestion to demand volunteering from clan members had merit.

"I was actually thinking about Tessa," Bridget said.

There were rumors about Tessa having been through some

rough times as a teenager, but Julian didn't know the details. Did his mother know? Had it been something similar to what Ella and the girls in the sanctuary had been through?

"Tessa is a good choice," Kian said. "But she works full time for Eva."

Bridget waved a dismissive hand. "Eva's detective agency is now running less than half the jobs it used to when Eva was active. She is only offering its services to old clients who she doesn't want to lose during her maternity leave. Sharon is too inexperienced for the more complicated field jobs. Nick is only a tech guy, not a detective, and Tessa is an office person. Eva just doesn't have the personnel needed to run more jobs. With the diminished workload, I'm sure she can spare Tessa for a few days."

Turner perked up. "If Eva doesn't need Nick full time either, I can certainly use him."

"I'll ask her," Bridget said.

"Good." Kian tapped his palm on the conference table. "Bridget, you are in charge of talking to Eva. If she can spare Tessa, talk to the girl and see if she's game." He turned to Julian. "If that goes well, explain the arrangement to Ella and coordinate a meeting between her and Tessa."

Julian nodded. "I'll do that. But what about the camera and other equipment as well as training on how to use them?"

"I'll call Brandon and see what he can get us. The equipment can be rented, or we can buy used stuff. We don't need the latest and best for this. I hope he can hook us up with someone to train our new filming crew."

22

LOSHAM

*a*s Losham was escorted into his father's reception chamber, he was unpleasantly surprised to find the brothel's manager sitting across from Navuh and sucking on one of his expensive cigars.

That was a privilege that only Losham had been granted up until now. How the hell had the sniveling Herpon gained such favor in their leader's eyes?

"Greetings, my lord." Losham bowed low. "You wanted to see me?"

He wasn't used to sharing his father's time with another, not even his half-brothers. Losham wasn't a military man, so there was no need for him to attend the mundane field-operation decisions his brothers dealt with.

Usually, the issues Navuh wished to discuss with him were confidential.

Besides, the leader liked to take credit for all of Losham's good ideas, which would have been difficult to do with witnesses. He would have been forced to eliminate them, and that was wasteful.

"Yes. Take a seat, Losham. Herpon came to me with a

problem that I think you can solve for him. I will let him explain."

Even though the man was good at what he did, Losham detested Herpon. He was an underhanded and cunning bastard who had somehow managed to rise in the ranks despite his lowly parentage. He was a crude and offensive fellow, who pretended to be refined in front of Navuh.

Not successfully, though.

Losham doubted his father was fooled by the fake mannerisms, but then Navuh cared about results and not the means to get them.

"The customers are tired of the Eastern Bloc stock we have," Herpon said. "Most of the girls can't speak any English, and those that know a few words would do better using their mouths for something else."

Raising a brow, Losham crossed his legs and leaned forward. "Since when do customers care about the whores' conversational skills? They come here to fuck, not to talk."

Herpon shook his head. "Things are always changing and shifting, and what was good a decade ago is no good now. The more sophisticated customers, those who are willing to pay the most, want to do both. They want a girl they can take out for a drink or to dinner, have a pleasant conversation with, and after that take her to their bungalow and fuck her all night long."

Losham shrugged. "I don't see how I can help with that. You need to discuss this with our suppliers and demand that they bring in a higher caliber stock."

"I did. The answer I got was that girls like that were difficult to obtain, and the cost I've been quoted per specimen was too high."

"I still do not see where I can be of help."

Navuh lifted his hand. "We need college girls, not the runaways and junkies that we usually get, preferably from

English-speaking countries, but other Western Bloc countries will do as well. As long as they are fairly educated and intelligent, we can teach them English in some form of an accelerated program."

Losham smoothed his hand over his beard. "I'm sure we can get educated Russian and Ukrainian girls and teach them English. They are not going to be as costly as those from English-speaking countries because it's not as dangerous to obtain them on the Eastern Bloc and then ship them over here."

Navuh's brows drew tight. "I did not bring you here to hear suggestions and excuses. I want solutions. You are a smart man. I'm sure you can come up with a way to supply the island with the kind of stock our top customers require." He leaned toward Losham and pinned him with a hard glare. "The law of supply and demand states that where there is unmet demand, someone will figure out a way to meet it. If we cannot satisfy these customers, someone else will, and we will lose them."

That was not what the law of supply and demand stated, but in principle Navuh was right.

"Perhaps I can pull warriors away from the drug trade and have them visit local colleges. Most of the men are not big charmers, but they can thrall well enough to have girls come with them. The question is what to do after that."

Navuh waved a dismissive hand. "Even if we have each girl escorted by a warrior and pay for plane tickets for both, we are still going to save a lot of money compared to what we are paying the suppliers now. And the one thing we have no shortage of is men. You can have your pick of the most handsome and charming ones."

That was doable. While posing as a couple on vacation, the soldier could keep thralling the girl through several plane rides and airports. Naturally, Losham would have to come up with a number of different routes and use international airports that didn't employ facial recognition software. Another option was cruise ships. People disappeared from those all the time.

With their natural ability to learn new languages as well as the local vernacular, the men could pretend to be American or British or Australian. It would be easier to lure a girl away from her college friends if the man didn't appear foreign.

"When I'm back in San Francisco, I'll organize several test runs. One way or another, I'm going to get you what you need."

Navuh smiled. "I knew you'd find a solution, my son."

To call Losham 'son' in front of Herpon, getting quality stock for the brothel must have been of utmost importance to Navuh.

Losham pushed to his feet and bowed. "I will keep you updated, my lord."

"Very well. You may take your leave."

23

JULIAN

*B*y the time the meeting was over, Carol's café was closed, but the vending machines still had a selection left over.

Choosing a Danish, Julian inserted his card into the slot, pressed the right number combination, and then watched the wrapped pastry getting grabbed by the mechanical arm and dropped into the receptacle.

"Julian, how are things going for you?" Jackson parked his loaded cart next to the sandwich machine.

Great, he was about to get dating advice from the kid.

No thank you.

"I'm just getting a Danish and coffee and then heading home. Since when are you doing deliveries in the evenings?"

Jackson opened the back of the machine and started refilling the empty rows with new sandwiches. "I've gotten complaints about the machines emptying by seven in the evening. People get hungry, and there is nothing to eat. They have to drive half an hour to the nearest fast-food joint or to a supermarket. So I hired another part-timer to prepare an evening batch."

"At Ruth's?"

Jackson peeked at him from behind the machine. "So it's Ruth's now, eh? Don't let Nathalie hear you say it. It's called Fernando's Café, and technically it's half mine and half Nathalie's. We are equal partners now."

Julian didn't know what business arrangement Jackson had with Nathalie, and frankly, he didn't care. "That's nice."

"How is Parker doing?" Jackson asked. "I haven't seen him since the transition ceremony, and I feel bad about not checking up on him. I'm supposed to be his mentor and all that. But I'm so fucking busy all the time."

"He's doing great. His fangs finally came out, and he would be very happy to show them to you." Julian leaned on the machine's side and crossed his arms over his chest. "Do you play War of the Dragons?"

Jackson lifted his head and looked at him. "Does it look like I have time to play computer games?"

"I meant do you know how to play it? It's an old game, but it's one of Parker's favorites. He'd love it if you played with him."

Pushing his long bangs away from his forehead, Jackson let out an old man's sigh. "In my previous life as a carefree bachelor, I played it."

Julian frowned. "You sound like you're not happy to be mated."

"Are you kidding me? No way! Tessa is the best thing that has ever happened to me, and I thank the merciful Fates every day for her. I just wish I had more free time. I miss hanging out with my buddies, and I miss kicking it with a good video game and a box of lousy pizza."

"I have an idea. How about you and I both go to play with Parker? But instead of lousy pizza, we can munch on your sandwiches and pastries."

Jackson rose to his feet and closed the back of the machine. "Let me check with Tessa. She's babysitting little Ethan so Eva can take a breather. I told her I'd join her there, but maybe she can do without me for the next hour."

As Jackson exchanged texts with his mate, Julian wondered whether Bridget had already spoken with Eva and Tessa about the video project. His mother was a pragmatic lady who didn't postpone until later what could be done right now, so chances were that she had.

"I'm good to go," Jackson said. "Tessa is taking Ethan to Nathalie's and is going to hang out with her until Eva and Bhathian are back."

"Did she tell you anything about the video project Ella came up with?"

"No." Jackson pushed the empty cart behind the café's counter and handed a box filled with sandwiches and pastries to Julian. "What is it about?"

As they made their way to Ella's house, Julian told Jackson about the fundraiser, the videos Ella wanted to shoot, and about Bridget suggesting Tessa as Ella's production assistant.

When he was done, Jackson shook his head. "I'm not sure Tessa would want to do that."

"Why not?" He had his suspicions, but he didn't want to assume anything.

"She likes working for Eva."

"I understand that at the moment things are slow at the agency."

"They are, which means that Tessa can take it easy. She's working on reorganizing files and transcribing the old ones into the computer. When Eva first started her agency, she kept handwritten files."

Julian chuckled. "Turner still does, even though he's several decades younger than Eva. But that's because he's paranoid and doesn't trust cyber encryption. I'm trying to convince him that for the right amount of money he can have an impenetrable system, but he insists that any system can eventually get hacked, and that some information is too crucial to keep anywhere other than in his notes."

"What if someone breaks into his place and steals them?"

"I think he has some form of personal encoding he uses."

Jackson nodded. "So does Eva. She has a shorthand script that she invented, and no one other than her and her crew can decipher it."

"Don't you just love all this cloak and dagger stuff?"

"I love hearing about it, but not living it. I'm not a big risk taker." Jackson chuckled. "I get my thrills from making money."

"Different strokes for different folks."

Jackson was working his ass off, and even though none of it was glamorous or overly exciting, it seemed like he was loving every moment of it.

Julian, on the other hand, didn't feel passionate about anything. Except for Ella, of course, but that was an obsession, not an occupation.

He loved being a doctor, but he wasn't as passionate about it as he'd been at the start of medical school. Money didn't thrill him either, and what Turner did for a living required nerves of steel he didn't have. Besides, strategizing wasn't Julian's thing either.

"When I was a kid, I wanted to be a rock star," Jackson said. "I had fun. Gordon and Vlad and I even got some gigs of the non-paid variety. It didn't take long for me to realize that performing wasn't a good way to make money, and that I needed to find something else. Still, if not for Bhathian introducing me to Nathalie, I might not have discovered my entrepreneurial streak so early in the game."

"I'm glad that you found your groove. I'm still looking for mine."

Jackson frowned. "You're a doctor, dude. There is nothing nobler than that. You can save lives, or at least improve them."

"That's why I chose to be one. But reality kind of slapped me in the face. I'm too empathetic to work with humans because it's torture for me to absorb all that suffering and worrying and grief. And with Merlin here, I'm not really needed in the village. Kian dropped an assignment on me that I'm unqualified for, mainly because I have the time to do it."

"What's the assignment?"

"He wants me to find a place that can be turned into a halfway house for the rescued girls, and also to come up with the financing for it."

Jackson cast him a sidelong glance. "So that's what the fundraising is for?"

"Among other things. If it succeeds, we can have more than one halfway house and help many more girls get back on their feet."

"I'll talk with Tessa. If all she needs is a little nudge in the right direction, I'll encourage her to do it. But if she's really reluctant, you'll need to find another assistant for Ella. Carol would've been fantastic, but she already has too much on her plate."

Jackson thinking of Carol as a suitable replacement for Tessa made it clear to Julian that Tessa's past involved something similar to what Carol and Ella had gone through.

Not that the experiences were comparable.

Carol had been abducted by Doomers and tortured by a sadist. In comparison, Ella's ordeal had been much less traumatic. Except, Carol was a resilient immortal and as far from naïve as it got, while Ella was a very young human girl, who hadn't been exposed to evil until that scumbag Romeo had trapped her, luring her away from home and delivering her into the clutches of a sex trafficker.

ELLA

*a*s Ella strolled along one of the many trails meandering through the sanctuary's grounds, she was surprised at how eerily quiet everything was. Usually, nature was full of sounds, leaves rustling in the wind, bugs buzzing, birds calling, crickets chirping, but the landscape around her was static and quiet as if it was a backdrop in an indoor filming studio.

"That's because you're dreaming." Logan appeared at her side. "But I can fix that for you." He snapped his fingers, and suddenly, they were surrounded by all the sounds that had been missing before.

"How did you do that?"

He tapped her temple with his finger. "I just activated your imagination. You weren't working hard enough on your scenery." He looked around. "Although I have to admit that it is pleasant enough, I would make it greener, and maybe add a brook. More trees would be nice too."

As he was about to snap his fingers again, Ella lifted her hand to stop him. "You've got a hell of a lot of nerve to give me crap about my landscape after not showing up for nearly two weeks. Besides, this is as green as it gets here. This place is a memory, not something I created in my imagination."

Logan took a quick look around before returning his eyes to her. "My apologies." He bowed with exaggerated flair. "Did you miss me?"

Ella shrugged. "Not really. I've been busy."

His dark eyes widened almost imperceptibly. "Doing what?"

"Oh, this and that. But I'm going to be very busy soon enough."

He waved a hand. "Don't keep me in suspense. Tell me what you're planning. Perhaps I can be of help."

"I doubt it. I'm organizing a fundraiser to help girls who were rescued from situations similar to mine." She pinned the specter with a hard gaze. "Unless you want to make a donation, that is. I'm sure a rich mercenary warlord like you can afford to spare a few thousand for a good cause."

It was silly to scold a specter, but on the other hand, it was fun to act as if she could be so brave and outspoken facing the real Logan, telling him what she thought of him straight to his face.

"As you can imagine, I'm not a philanthropist, but I would do it for you." His eyes went to her mouth. "You could auction your lips, and I'd bid for a kiss from you."

"Dream on, perv. I'm not kissing you, no matter how much money you pledge to the cause."

He pouted, pretending offense. "Why not? I'm handsome, and I know for a fact that you're attracted to me because I'm in your head."

There was no point in lying to herself, which talking to Logan essentially was. Her subconscious probably needed to sort this out.

"I don't know why I am. It must be some chemical reaction.

Did you put on a pheromone imbued cologne the one time we met?"

"I did no such thing. It's just my natural magnetism." He waggled his brows.

"It's not working on me, so you may as well stop it."

He didn't like her answer, and with his smile and fake charm momentarily gone, Logan looked just as scary as he had in her first and second dream encounter with him.

"You're such a hypocrite, Ella. Are you telling me that you wouldn't sacrifice one little kiss to get thousands for a cause that's so dear to you?"

Well, when put like that, he had a point.

Except, giving even one kiss to Logan was dangerous. To raise money for the halfway house, Ella was willing to auction her kisses to complete strangers, but not to Logan.

"That's because I don't like you, and I don't trust you. You're really bad, and I doubt you'd be satisfied with one kiss."

He laughed. "True on both counts, but oftentimes naughty girls like bad boys to take charge and steal more than one kiss."

"I'm not naughty, and I'm too smart to fall for a bad boy again. I was stupid once, and I paid dearly for that. I'm not going to repeat that mistake with you."

Logan rolled his eyes. "You had sex with Gorchenco, who loved you and cherished you, and you're making a big deal out of it. Only a spoiled American girl would make such a huge fuss about such a trivial matter."

Ella frowned. No way was this her own thought.

"Are you in my head, Logan? Because that wasn't me talking."

He smiled. "Are you sure?"

She was about to answer that yes, she was absolutely sure, when Logan started fading into mist, and then with a hand wave and a wink he disappeared.

Jerking awake in bed, Ella sucked in a breath. Had the actual Logan been invading her dreams?

She shivered at the thought.

It didn't make sense, though. Even if Logan was a telepath and could communicate with other telepaths from afar, Ella had put up extremely strong mental walls, and she knew they held up while she slept because her mother couldn't penetrate them no matter how hard she tried.

The simpler explanation was that the words she'd put in dream Logan's mouth were probably what she thought the real Logan would say, and not her own subconscious thoughts. That was why what he'd said had sounded so foreign and offensive to her.

Her mind had just reminded her why she'd found the real Logan so repulsive in the first place. This was precisely the kind of reasoning he would use.

Shaking the bad feeling away, she decided not to let the dream ruin what was going to be a great day.

Later this morning she was meeting with Brandon, the clan's media specialist, and Tessa, Jackson's fiancée, for a crash course in operating professional recording equipment.

If Tessa was half as nice as Jackson, the two of them were going to get along great.

What a charmer that guy was. He'd won over everyone in the family, including her brother, her mother, and the dog. Ella was so glad he'd been chosen as Parker's initiator. According to the clan's tradition, that meant they were honorary brothers, which was so cool.

Not for the first time, Ella wondered how her mother was going to be initiated. It didn't make sense for her to fight an immortal male, and as far as Ella knew, immortal females' tiny fangs were only for show.

But every time she tried to steer the conversation in that direction, either Magnus or Vivian would change the topic.

It must be something really bad for them to act so evasively.

Which was another reason to finally start leaving the house and mingling with other immortals. Jackson had told her that Tessa used to be a human, so maybe she could ask the girl what was involved in a female Dormant's activation.

25

TESSA

*A*s Ella walked into Kian's office, Tessa smiled and got up. "Hi, I'm Tessa." She offered the girl her hand.

Ella was just as ethereally beautiful as Jackson had described her. Looking away from that angelic face was hard. No wonder Julian had fallen for a mere picture of her. She was short, but not as short as Tessa, and Ella was more full-figured —not fat, and not skinny, kind of average.

But then, with that face, Ella didn't need anything else to call attention to herself.

That beautiful face, however, was probably what had gotten her in trouble in the first place. People didn't realize that sometimes beauty could be more of a liability than an asset for a girl. Especially when it was as striking as Ella's.

Shaking Tessa's hand, Ella smiled. "It's nice to meet you and thank you for agreeing to do this."

She seemed nice, friendly, but also reserved.

Sadly, Tessa was well familiar with that guarded look—the one worn by those who'd been hurt and had lost their naïveté and innocence. For many years, the same expression had been staring at her from the mirror. And if not for Jackson, it still would be.

She smiled back, trying to look as friendly and as welcoming as she could. "My pleasure. When Jackson came home last night, he was so excited about your idea that I had no choice but to get swept away by his enthusiasm. When my guy gets like that, he can convince Eskimos to buy ice from him."

"I've noticed. Your Jackson is so charming and charismatic."

Tessa was about to say something nice about Julian when the door banged open, and Brandon walked in with a stack of boxes tall enough to hide his face.

"Let me help you with that." She took two from the top.

Ella took two more.

"Thank you." He dropped the rest of them on the conference table and handed Kian an invoice. "That's all the equipment Ella and Tessa are going to need, except for the background paper roll. I ordered it online, and it should be arriving tomorrow."

Tessa cast Ella a puzzled glance, but apparently Ella didn't know what he was talking about either.

"Hello, Ella." He shook her hand. "Welcome to the clan. I'm glad your story had a happy ending."

"Thank you."

He shook Tessa's hand next. "How are Eva and the baby doing? I haven't seen them since little Ethan's party."

"They are both doing great. And Ethan is not so little anymore. He's such a cute, chubby baby."

"Give Eva my regards, would you?"

"I will."

Brandon was one of a small group of immortals not residing in the village. He kept his penthouse in Hollywood and was apparently too busy to come and visit more than once in a blue moon. The only reason Tessa even knew him was that Eva had introduced them at Ethan's party.

Kian looked at the invoice and shook his head. "Professional equipment used to be expensive. You're telling me that you bought everything for under a thousand bucks?"

The media specialist chuckled. "When was the last time you purchased a camera, Kian? The eighties?"

"More or less. I didn't have much use for one."

"A lot has changed since then, and with the explosion of blogging, the market became much less niche. Mass production always lowers costs."

"That's good. So other than the paper roll you've mentioned, this is everything they will need?"

"Yes. The white background paper is for the silhouette shoots, but the girls can learn all they need to know about filming that from YouTube."

He pulled out his phone and turned to them. "Give me your phone numbers, and I'll text you a list of links I've prepared. Watch the videos, and if after that you still have questions, you can call me. But I doubt it will be necessary. All you need to know is on YouTube."

With that done, Brandon put his phone back in his pocket and pushed to his feet. "It was a pleasure to see you, ladies, but now I have to run."

And off he went.

Ella looked at the door closing on Brandon's back and shook her head. "If he wasn't going to show us anything, he could've just ordered the stuff online and sent it here."

"YouTube," Kian bit out. "He wants you to learn everything from YouTube? I don't understand why he even bothered to come."

Tessa had a feeling she knew the answer to that. Brandon

had been curious about Ella and wanted to see her in person. Maybe he thought that he could steal her away from Julian?

The rumors claimed that Ella was not showing any romantic interest in the handsome doctor, which meant that pretty soon all the sharks would start circling around the unattached Dormant, and Brandon had probably decided to beat them to it.

Except, if that was his intention, teaching Ella in person would have better served his agenda.

Maybe he didn't like what he saw?

But that didn't make sense either, and not only because Ella was so beautiful. She was a Dormant. That was enough to make her a coveted prize.

"Brandon seems like a busy guy," Ella said. "It would've been a waste of his time to show us something that we can learn from YouTube. And he was nice enough to compile a list of videos for us. We should be fine, right, Tessa?"

"I hope so. I don't know anything about cameras. Do you?"

Ella shook her head. "I only ever used my phone. But I've learned to do many things from YouTube videos. I even fixed a problem with my computer after watching a guy explain what to do step by step. And trust me, other than turning it on and typing on the keyboard, I know nothing about it." She eyed the pile of boxes. "Let's each grab a few and take them to my house. We will have to come back for the rest."

"You don't need to carry anything," Kian said. "I'll have Okidu bring all the boxes to Ella's house. You can go ahead and start on those videos."

26

ELLA

"*D*o you like it here?" Tessa asked as they left the office building.

Ella waved a hand at the greenery. "What's not to like? It's like a little piece of heaven here."

In her previous life, she might have found the village boring, especially since it seemed like the only place to hang out was the café. But the new Ella appreciated the reclusiveness and serenity.

Tessa pushed a strand of her straight bleached-blond hair behind her ear. "It's safe. I've never felt as safe as I feel here. If not for Jackson dragging me out of here from time to time, I would never leave. But he likes to go out to clubs, and bars, and movies, and I don't want to be the drag that keeps him from having a life."

It sounded like Tessa was a lot like Ella. The new one. Not the old one. The old Ella would have loved to hang out with Jackson at all the places Tessa had mentioned. Not as his girl-friend or anything, but perhaps with a larger group of friends. Even though the guy was gorgeous and charming, she wasn't attracted to him.

Besides, Jackson and Tessa were practically married.

Except, Ella would not have been interested in him even if he were available. He was a pretty boy, but a boy nonetheless. And anyway, dating was the furthest thing from her mind. If she ever felt like going out with anyone again, it would be with Julian.

The question was whether she would ever be ready for that.

Maybe things would change after her transition, and the transformation would be more than physical. Perhaps a third version of Ella would emerge, one that was better and stronger than the first two.

"Can I ask you something?"

Tessa cast her an amused glance. "Depends on what it is."

"It's okay if you don't want to answer, but I can't get anyone to tell me how female Dormants transition. I know that Dormant guys have to fight an immortal male, but I can't imagine a woman fighting one of them, and as far as I know, female immortals don't have venom in their tiny fangs."

Eyes widening in surprise, Tessa nearly stumbled over a crack in the paving stones. "You've been here for two whole weeks, and no one has told you what's involved in transitioning yet?"

Ella shook her head. "Every time I bring the subject up, someone manages to steer the conversation to another topic. Is this a taboo subject?"

Hands on her hips, Tessa looked up and sighed. "No, it's not. But I know why no one wants to tell you."

"Does it have anything to do with what happened to me?" Ella asked in a hushed voice as they resumed walking.

"Yeah, it does. But they are making a mistake by hiding it from you. You may not like it, but you should know." Tessa stopped again and faced Ella. "To produce venom, immortal males have to either get aggressive or aroused. They bite during fights with other males and during sex with females."

Ella's hand flew to her neck. "Ouch. That's nasty."

"Not really. The venom is a powerful euphoric and aphrodisiac. It hurts for about two seconds when the fangs break your skin, but after that, it's unimaginable bliss and the best orgasms of your life. Not a bad trade-off."

"Isn't it dangerous, though? If it's used for fighting, it must be potentially lethal."

"It's not. Because the venom production in each situation is triggered by different hormones, its composition is different."

"Do they always bite, or only sometimes?"

"Biting is the same as ejaculating for immortal males. They can refrain if they must, but it's difficult."

Now it was Ella's turn to stop in her tracks. "So, if Magnus is biting my mom, which I must assume that he does, how come she didn't transition yet?"

"They must be using condoms. To induce transition, the venom bite must be combined with insemination."

Great, so if she wanted to transition, Ella would have to have sex with an immortal male and also chance getting pregnant.

It seemed like she wasn't transitioning anytime soon.

"I see. Thank you for telling it to me straight. I don't know why my mom thought that I couldn't handle it. It's not like I'm a blushing virgin and can't talk about sex."

Come to think of it, when Julian had told her the truth about himself, the clan, and her being a Dormant, he'd evaded her questions on the subject too. But then he might have been embarrassed to talk about it with a girl he hardly knew.

Her mother had no such excuse. Before, they used to talk freely about sex.

Tessa smiled, but it was a sad smile. "Don't be angry at her.

Her intentions are good. She and Magnus probably assume that because you were violated, any mention of sex will bring you grief, and they don't want to hurt you. What they don't realize is that it's even more hurtful to be treated like a victim."

It seemed like Tessa had more in common with her than Ella had initially suspected. "You sound as if you're talking from experience."

"Unfortunately, I am. Not many people know that about me, so don't tell anyone. I hate to be regarded with pity. I'm telling you only because you understand how I feel."

"I do. And your secret is safe with me. I wish no one knew about what happened to me either. Pretending to be normal would have been so much easier."

"I'm glad we see eye to eye."

The question was how come Tessa got to keep her ordeal a secret, while everyone in the clan knew about Ella's. "I'm guessing that the clan didn't rescue you. Otherwise, everyone would've known about you like they know about me."

Tessa shook her head. "Eva, my boss, saved me. I owe her my life. She killed the scumbag who'd bought and abused me, she took me in, and she gave me a home and a job. But as I said before, this is between you and me. Don't tell anyone."

It sounded as if Tessa's ordeal had been much worse than Ella's. At least Gorchenco had not abused her.

"Your boss must be a kickass lady."

"Oh, she is." Tessa perked up. "You have to meet her. But it's not like she's doing any ass-kicking recently or planning to return to it anytime soon. Eva has a cute baby boy, and she is wholly dedicated to being a mother."

"I'm happy for her. I'm sure it's more fun taking care of a baby than killing scumbags."

Tessa chuckled. "For you and for me, almost anything

would be better than going after scum, but I'm not sure about Eva. I think she's secretly itching to get back to work."

"What exactly is her work? I was told that she can hook me up with prosthetics to change my features. I need to have my picture taken for my fake documents."

"Eva is a detective. Mainly, she's done corporate espionage, but she's also gone after cheating spouses. Elaborate disguises are her specialty. That's why she has taken it upon herself to provide movie-quality makeup to clan members, including prosthetics, for their licenses and other documents. My friend Sharon has taken over the detective work, but she's still a rookie, so Eva doesn't send her out on anything too dangerous or difficult."

The more Tessa told her about Eva, the more fascinating the woman sounded. "I'd love to meet her. Can you check with her when is a good time for her to hook me up with prosthetics?"

Tessa pulled out her phone. "It would be best to go see her when Bhathian is there, that's her husband, so he can take care of the baby while she's busy. This evening work for you?"

"Sure. But first, we need to unpack the equipment, watch a few YouTube videos, and familiarize ourselves with how everything works."

Tessa waved a dismissive hand. "That shouldn't take us more than a couple of hours."

27

JULIAN

"Is this it?" Yamanu poked his head out the window and regarded the building Julian had parked in front of. "Not much to look at. It's a dump."

"That's because you have no imagination." Julian killed the ignition. "A new coat of paint, some more trees in the front, and it will look great."

Yamanu got out of the car and waited for Julian to join him. "It's like putting makeup on a pig. It's not going to make it pretty."

"If we are using animal analogies, then the one about not looking a gift horse in the mouth is more appropriate."

Yamanu slapped his back. "Can't argue with that, mate. How come Kian is being so generous, though? I thought money was tight."

"He bought this old hotel a while back and was planning on erecting a new one in its place. But the city dropped an unexpected obstacle in his path, and they did it after the plans for the new hotel were almost done. The pencil-pushers came up with some crap about it being a historic building because someone no one has ever heard about had stayed there once in the late thirties, and therefore it had to be preserved."

"Kian should have sold it as is."

"No one would've bought it after it was declared a historic building. And instead of waging battle with the city bureaucrats, Kian decided to donate it and take a tax write-off."

Yamanu looked at the broken windows and shook his head. "Lucky us."

It was ironic that after all of his posturing about the halfway house project being Julian's baby, and expecting him to find a location and the financing for purchasing it, Kian had ended up taking care of it.

Now it was up to Julian to make it work.

Inside the building, the situation was even worse. Between the peeling paint, rotted through carpet, and broken windows, the structure seemed suitable for only one thing. Demolition.

Yamanu opened the gate of the ancient elevator. "Just to bring it up to code will require massive work. I don't think one elevator is enough for a building this size."

"There are two staircases. One interior and a fire escape in the back. That's good enough."

"Are you sure?"

"I checked."

A grimace on his handsome face, Yamanu turned in a circle. "At least the neighborhood is decent."

"And it's close to the village."

"Twenty-five-minute drive, and it's not a heavy traffic route, which is the biggest plus." He rubbed his huge hands together. "Let's see the rooms. If they are okay, then the rest can be worked on."

Julian eyed the ancient elevator. "I suggest we take the stairs."

Hesitantly, he put his foot on the first stair, and the next, and the one after that, but the staircase ended up being surprisingly sturdy.

The carpet covering the corridor was in better shape than the one in the lobby, but not good enough to stay.

As Julian opened the door to the first room, he was surprised that it was still furnished. Given the broken windows on the lobby level, he'd been sure that vandals had either stolen or destroyed everything.

Yamanu went over to the narrow four-poster bed and gave it a shake. "Sturdy. We can use it." Next, he checked the nightstands and the writing desk. "I'll be damned. We can use all of it. The mattress needs to be replaced, but other than that the furniture is good quality."

"Let's check the bathroom." Julian opened the door.

It was tiny, with a pedestal sink, an old-fashioned toilet, and a charming claw-foot bathtub.

"What do you think?" He turned to Yamanu.

"Looks good. The question is whether the stuff works. Do you know if the water is connected?"

"I think so." Julian twisted the faucet knobs. "Water pressure is fine. The heaters are not on, so it's cold. We will have to check those too."

The toilet flushed, the faucet in the bathtub worked, and the tub drained adequately.

Yamanu lifted his eyes to the ceiling. "No leaks either."

"How much do you think we will need for remodeling?"

Yamanu shrugged. "No clue, buddy. This is not my area of expertise. Dealing with idiot bureaucrats, however, is. I'm surprised Kian didn't ask me to take care of this problem for him."

"Does he usually?"

"When it's something ridiculous like this, then yeah."

Interesting. It seemed that Kian had changed his mind

about financing the halfway house and had donated the building even though he could've salvaged the situation with Yamanu's help.

Why hadn't he just come out and said it?

There had been no need for him to make it look as if he had no choice and was forced to donate the building.

"We need a name," Yamanu said. "A halfway house has a negative connotation. How about Chateau Clarice?"

"Who's Clarice?"

Yamanu shrugged. "No one I know. It just sounds nice."

"If it's going to be Chateau anything, it should be Chateau Bridget."

"I like it. But both are a mouthful. It needs to be something simple and generic, like The Grove or The Orchards."

"Or The Palms. Because of the two palms up front."

"That's good. The Palms it is."

ELLA

*E*va was awesome.

A fierce, unapologetic, master of disguise, defender of the weak, and a killer of scumbags.

This was who Ella wanted to be when she grew up.

Maybe not the killer part, she didn't know if she had it in her, but a kickass woman who inspired respect and a healthy amount of fear.

And according to Tessa, this was Eva at her mellowest.

Sitting in Eva's living room and sipping on virgin margaritas, the three of them had let go of all pretenses and laid it all out, but only after swearing to take the secrets to their graves, of course.

Tessa shook her head. "I can't believe you were an active vigilante during the years I worked for you. I thought that Martin was the only scumbag you killed."

Eva smirked over the top of her margarita glass. "If I got caught, I didn't want my kids to get in trouble."

Tessa cast Ella an amused glance. "She's talking about Sharon, Nick, and me. She's always treated us like we were her kids. We loved it but thought that she was a little nuts. We didn't know that she was old enough to be our grandma."

"It must've been so hard for you to keep your immortality a secret." Ella put her glass on the coffee table. "Always on the run. You're so brave."

Eva shrugged. "I did what I had to, but it was also in my nature. When I joined the DEA, I didn't know I was immortal. I just wanted to fight the bad guys. At the time, I believed drugs were the worst problem, so that's what I wanted to fight. If I'd known about human trafficking back then, I might have chosen a different path. Except, there is no agency that deals with that. And that's a shame. After rescuing Tessa, I started looking into it, and that's how my vigilante days started."

After hearing Tessa's story, which she was sure was a highly diluted version of what had really happened to her, Ella could totally sympathize with Eva's motives for assassinating traffickers.

It made Ella feel guilty for the self-pity she'd allowed herself to indulge in. Poor Tessa had been to real hell, but she didn't pity herself. She counted herself lucky for getting out alive, and she'd even managed to fall in love.

"You are both so brave, each one in her own way. I feel humbled."

Eva waved a dismissive hand. "You're brave too. The way you handled the Russian was perfect, and you did it without any prior training, relying only on your instincts. But still, if it makes you feel safer, I can kill him for you. Not right now, but in a couple of years when I'm back to work."

Ella almost choked on her virgin margarita. "Thank you," she croaked after the coughing fit had subsided. "That's a very generous offer, but if I wanted Gorchenco dead, I would've let Turner's team do it. I specifically asked that they spare him, which complicated my rescue."

"I understand," Eva said. "You're young and soft. But if I hear that he bought another girl, he's dead."

"He won't. That's not how he is. I was a special case."

Eva shook her head. "He took what wasn't his for the taking. That's bad. But it's your choice to forgive him. However, if he does it again to someone else, I'll deal with him when I'm ready. But if he comes searching for you, the Guardians should take him out, and you shouldn't try to stop them. You shouldn't live in fear."

Ella loved Eva's bluntness, and she loved even more that the woman didn't regard her or Tessa as victims.

On the contrary, it seemed as if Eva felt closer to the two of them than she did to others. It was kind of a weird symbiosis. They were kindred spirits, with Eva on one end as the savior, and Tessa and Ella on the other end as the saved.

"I need to change the way I look. When you say prosthetics, what exactly are we talking about?"

"Movie makeup." Eva emptied the rest of her margarita and took the glass to the sink. "But that takes a lot of time and skill. It's not something you can just slap on in the morning." She came back with a box of cookies. "A makeover will work better. When Tessa had hers, it gave her confidence a nice boost, am I right?" She glanced at Tessa.

"Yeah, it did. Before that, I had mousy hair, and I wore kids' clothes. Subconsciously, I wanted to look like a kid and not a woman, so no one would approach me. I don't think anyone seeing me now would recognize me as that girl. Which also boosted my confidence and made me less fearful. Before the makeover, what I was most afraid of was Martin's brother coming after me."

Ella reached for a cookie. "I don't have a confidence problem, and I'm not particularly fearful either. I just made one really big stupid mistake."

"Stop beating yourself up over that," Eva said. "You're eighteen, that's still a baby. Your mother should've been smarter, though."

"But I tricked her. I told her that I was staying at my friend Maddie's."

Eva smirked. "You see, that's the difference between your mother and me. I would not have bought that story and would've been immediately suspicious. Vivian needs coaching."

"Not really. I'm not going to do anything stupid like that ever again. She has nothing to worry about."

"But she does worry, and that's why she's not going for the transition, which she should do sooner rather than later."

"Why? What's the rush?"

"Your mother is not getting any younger, and the transition is more difficult the older the Dormant."

"I'll talk to her." About this and about keeping important details from her.

Her mother should've told her about how Dormants were turned, and that age was a factor. Ella shouldn't have learned it from Tessa and Eva, whom she'd just met that day.

"Anyway, back to the makeover," Eva said. "Since gaining confidence is not important to you, we should go for the most drastic transformation possible. Are you okay with it making you look worse rather than better than you do now?"

"A hundred percent." Ella pointed to her face. "This is what has gotten me in trouble. I'm sick of people gawking at me, and I don't want to be a target."

Eva smirked. "What I have in mind will not solve the gawking problem. How do you feel about going Goth?"

"Ugh, black hair looks really fake on me. It's not going to work."

"I was thinking more along the lines of pink, or maybe purple."

"Then we should wait for my mother to transition because when she sees me with pink hair, she's going to have a stroke."

Tessa frowned. "But you need to change your appearance to get your picture taken for your fake documents."

"I was just joking. My mom will have to deal with it. When can we do it?"

"Let me check with Amanda." Eva reached for her phone. "She'd never forgive me if we do it without her."

"Right. She told me the first day I got here that she's the one I should turn to."

The answer to Eva's text came right away.

"She says that she's free on Saturday, and that we should meet up either in her house or yours."

29

VIVIAN

"Mom, I need to talk to you," Ella said as she entered the house. "In my room, if you don't mind."

Vivian put her book down. "Did something happen at Eva's?"

"Nothing happened, I just want to talk to you in private." She motioned with her head toward Parker. "Girl talk."

"Oh, okay." Vivian pushed to her feet and followed Ella to her room.

"What is it, sweetie?" she asked after closing the door.

"When were you going to tell me about how female Dormants are turned?"

With a sigh, Vivian sat on the bed. "Did Eva tell you?"

"No, Tessa did."

"What did she tell you?"

"That it involves sex with an immortal male and getting bitten." Ella threw her hands in the air. "Did you think I couldn't handle it? We used to talk about everything, Mom. Nothing was taboo. I don't want to lose this together with everything else I've lost because of one stupid mistake."

As Ella's chin started quivering, Vivian felt like crying herself. "Come here, baby. Sit with me." She patted the spot next to her on the bed.

Sitting down, Ella leaned her head on Vivian's shoulder. "Talk to me, Mom. Like we used to."

Her arm around her daughter's shoulders, Vivian kissed the top of her head. "It's more than just sex for the immortal guys. And I didn't think you were ready to hear that yet."

"I might not be ready for sex, but I'm ready to listen and learn."

She was right, and Vivian felt stupid for keeping this from her. "When an immortal male induces a female Dormant, it's a big deal for him. For her too. He's not supposed to do that unless he is sure that she's the one for him, and he is the one for her. If the connection isn't there, he's supposed to step aside and let another immortal take his place."

"So, let me get it straight. In order to transition, I'm supposed to fall in love with an immortal male before we have sex, and he has to fall in love with me?"

"You can have sex. In fact, you should do it before you decide if he's the one, just with protection."

"Yeah, Tessa told me that the venom works together with semen to induce transition."

"The romantic involvement was the reason I didn't tell you. I knew you weren't ready for that. Or for the sex."

"I'm not."

"You know that Julian is completely infatuated with you and thinks that you're his one, right?"

Ella's eyes widened. "Why? He doesn't even know me. I know he likes me, and I like him back, but we talked for what, one hour, two?" She rose to her feet and started pacing. "That's not enough for anyone to fall in love. It's this." She circled her hand around her face. "That's all he and everyone else sees. Not what's inside." She pointed to her chest.

"Perhaps you should allow him to get to know you, and you get to know him. Physical attraction is what brings a couple together in the first place, not some intellectual or metaphysical connection. But if they are lucky and discover that they also like the person inside the attractive cover, then love can bloom. It's not going to happen without spending time together, though. That's why I think you should give Julian a chance and go out with him. He's a very nice guy, and thanks to him you're free. Not that it's a reason to date him, but maybe it's just another reason to give him a chance."

Plopping down on the bed, Ella covered her eyes with her arm. "Maybe I should. I don't know. Julian is so handsome, and he seems so sweet, but what the heck can he see in me other than my face? He's eight years older than me, and he is a doctor. We have nothing in common. I wouldn't even know what to talk to him about."

"You did fine over dinner. And you've started this whole thing with the fundraiser idea. You can talk to him about that. Don't sell yourself short, Ella. You have a lot more to offer than your pretty face."

As Ella lifted her arm off her eyes, there was a cunning look in them. "If I go out with Julian, would you start your transition?"

"What does that have to do with anything we've talked about?"

"Eva said that you're waiting for me to get better before you attempt it, and that the longer you wait, the more difficult it will be. I don't want you to endanger yourself because of me."

"Oh, sweetie. That's not the only reason I'm dragging my feet about it. The truth is that I'm scared."

"You're scared because you think that you'll be leaving Parker and me alone."

"Well, that too. But I also don't want to die just when I've found happiness again."

Bracing on her forearms, Ella pinned her with a hard stare. "You're not going to die, Mom. Stop being such a pessimist. Fate didn't bring you and Magnus together just so you could break his heart."

Vivian grimaced. "As much as I would like to believe that, I don't put much faith in fate."

"At least promise me that you'll give it some thought."

"I will."

"For real?"

"Yes, for real."

30

ELLA

"*Mom*, can I do the dishes tomorrow? I'm going to be late for archery practice with Carol."

Ella rolled her eyes. Parker and his excuses. He'd probably eaten dinner slowly on purpose so he could get out of doing the dishes.

"Sure, sweetie. Say hi to Carol for me."

As usual, her mother had fallen for it. Or maybe not. Poor kid was braving growing fangs, which Magnus had confirmed hurt like hell, so he deserved a little slack.

"Ella, do you want to come and see me shoot arrows?" Parker asked. "Last time, I hit the bullseye eight times out of ten."

He'd asked her to come with him to the gym several times already, but the place was teeming with immortals, and Ella hadn't been ready to interact with them yet, so she had declined.

Except, it had been a good day so far, and meeting Tessa and Eva had been not only fun but uplifting and encouraging as well. Even Brandon, the clan's media specialist who she'd expected to be intimidating, hadn't made her feel uncomfortable. He hadn't looked at her with pity in his eyes, and he hadn't leered either. At most, he'd shown mild curiosity.

If everyone reacted to her like Brandon had, she could handle new introductions.

"Okay. I guess it's time I met the famous Carol."

"You could've met her at the café on day two," Vivian said. "But you didn't want to come."

"I will, the next time you go. I think I'm ready to meet people."

Her declaration was met by three happy faces and a thumbs up from Magnus.

Ella's heart swelled a little.

Her family.

As long as they didn't push her too hard, thinking that they were doing it for her own good, it was nice to have her own cheering squad. It was on the tip of her tongue to tell them that she loved them, but that would've led to a mushy moment with hugs and tears, and Parker was running late.

Besides, it would've weakened her just when she was finally feeling strong.

"Come on, Parker. We need to get moving if you want to make it on time."

On the way to the pavilion they didn't encounter anyone, and as they exited the elevator on the gym level, Ella braced for some awkward hellos and fake smiles. Not everyone was as cool as Brandon.

But there was no one in the corridor either.

"Where is everyone?" she asked.

Parker pointed to one of the doors. "Most people are in the classrooms, taking self-defense lessons, and some are in the gym and in the shooting range. But don't expect them to stop their exercise routine and come say hi to you."

"I would appreciate it if they didn't," she murmured under her breath.

"Back home, you used to be friendlier."

Crap. She'd forgotten about his super hearing. "That's because I knew all of our neighbors, and I worked in a diner, where I had to be friendly, or I didn't get tips."

"Maybe you should get a job at the café? Wonder told me that it was the best and quickest way to get to know everyone."

Ella ruffled his hair. "I don't think they are hiring."

"You can ask Carol. Or I can ask Wonder tomorrow. I'm going to her house to study."

Ella smirked. Wonder was pretty and sweet, and Parker had a crush on her, which the girl was utterly oblivious to despite it being obvious to everyone else.

Upon entering the shooting range they kept walking past the firearms booths and continued to another hall, where a lone figure was shooting arrows from a very cool-looking bow and hitting the bullseye every time.

"Wow. She's good," Ella whispered, so as not to break the shooter's concentration.

"That's Carol, and she has noise-canceling headphones on, so you don't need to whisper."

The woman released one arrow after another, hitting the target's center every time without fail and making it look so easy and effortless that Ella was tempted to try archery herself. Except, she was sure that it wasn't as easy as it seemed. Unlike a firearm, a bow required muscle power.

Parker waited to approach Carol until the target retracted and the electronic scoreboard flashed her impressive results.

Taking the headphones off, Carol shook out her curly hair and turned around with a big smile on her face. "Ella, finally I get to meet you."

She handed the bow and headphones to Parker, then

146

walked over and offered her hand to Ella. "I'm Carol." Tugging on Ella's hand, she pulled her into a tight embrace.

For a small, curvy woman, Carol was incredibly strong, and as the air was squeezed out of Ella's lungs, she tapped the immortal on her back. "I can't breathe."

"Oh, I'm sorry." Carol let go. "I forgot that you're still a fragile human." Pursing her lips, she gave Ella a thorough once over that thankfully didn't hold even the tiniest trace of pity. "A situation which should be rectified as soon as possible."

Ella tilted her head in Parker's direction. "I'm not in a rush."

"Right." Carol smiled and turned to him. "Ready to start your practice?"

He lifted the bow up in the air, already assuming victory. "Can't wait."

"Let me program the target sequence for you." She walked over to the control screen and typed a series of instructions. "Put the headphones on."

Parker arched a brow. "Why? It's not noisy in here."

"As I've told you before, it helps with concentration, which is the most important component in your skill set." She turned to Ella, including her in the explanation. "When you shoot, you need to be in the zone, and that means the outside world has to disappear while you're at it. Once it becomes second nature to you, you'll be able to slip into that state even with distractions. But until then, use headphones during practice."

"Yeah, I get it." Parker put the bulky things on and reached into the arrow bag, pulling the first one out.

For several moments they watched him shoot, and as he finished the first round, Ella gave him the thumbs up. "I thought he was boasting, but he's really good," she told Carol.

"I know, right? He has a natural talent for it." She turned and motioned to the row of chairs lined up against the wall. "We can be more comfortable watching him from over there."

She waited for Ella to sit down. "I'm here mostly as a supervising adult. It's rare that I need to adjust his form. At the rate Parker is going, Brundar will have to take over his training soon."

"Who's Brundar?"

Carol arched a brow as if Ella should've known that. "He's one of the head Guardians and the clan's weapon master, which probably makes him the best in the world."

"If he's so good, why would he want to waste time on my kid brother?"

"Training a new prodigy is a privilege. Besides, everyone likes Parker. I'm sure that even stoic Brundar won't be able to resist his charm."

That was good to hear. Apparently, her little brother was becoming the darling of the clan. She just hoped it wouldn't go to his head. It would be a shame if Parker turned into a self-entitled brat.

"Are you also training to become a Guardian?" she asked. "I know that you're running the café and that you're teaching a self-defense class. That's already a lot."

Carol chuckled. "I'm a busy, busy girl. Doesn't leave much energy for hunting. But perhaps it's a good thing."

Despite her mastery with the bow, Carol looked so delicate and sweet that Ella couldn't imagine her shooting arrows at living things.

"Hunting? Like in animals?"

Laughter bubbled out of the immortal's chest. "Some claim that all men are animals. So yeah."

With that angelic face, there was no way Carol was a killer. Not of animals and not of people.

Ella shook her head. "I don't get it. I'm sure you don't mean that you're an assassin."

Snorting, Carol slapped her thighs. "Aren't you just

precious. When immortals talk about hunting, we usually refer to hookups. I don't know whether you've noticed, but we are a highly sexed bunch, and since most of us don't have mates, we have no choice but to seduce humans for casual sex. That's why we call it hunting."

Ella glanced at Parker, making sure he still had the noise-canceling headphones on. "Julian told me about the mates problem. I hope more Dormants can be found for all of you."

He hadn't told her, however, about the highly sexed part, and since she hadn't interacted with clan members much, Ella didn't know whether Carol was exaggerating or not.

"I hope so too. But until then, a girl has to do what a girl has to do, and this girl likes to hunt—men, that is. Animals, not so much. But I'm starting to realize that I'll have no choice if I ever want to go on the mission I've been training for."

"Now you've lost me completely. You said you're not a Guardian and not training to become one, right?"

This time it was Carol who glanced Parker's way before answering. "I have a special set of skills that makes me perfect for a particular secret mission, but my trainers are not going to clear me for it unless I prove that I can be ruthless. And the way they expect me to prove it is by killing an animal and then cutting out its heart."

Ella grimaced. "That's awful. Are you actually considering doing it?"

"I want to go on that mission. I figured that I can kill something nasty, like a coyote. Sometimes at night, I can hear a pack of them howling as they attack some poor animal and its horrible squeals as it's torn apart. At those moments, I don't have any qualms about getting a rifle and taking them out."

"It's just nature. If they don't hunt, they don't eat."

"I know. Still, I think they are horrible, and I have no

problem killing at least one to prove that I can be a badass." She narrowed her eyes at Ella. "Which I totally am."

There was a determination in that beautiful cherubic face, and even though Carol was teasing, Ella could sense the steel in those blue eyes that on first impression had looked so guileless.

"Oh, I believe you. You don't have to prove anything to me."

A sweet smile replaced the hard stare. "You're smart. Most people just look at the exterior and think that I'm soft, which is actually one of my biggest assets. No one expects me to be dangerous."

"Are you?"

Carol shrugged. "I'm not a soldier or an assassin, if that's what you mean, but I can make one hell of a spy."

Ella arched a brow. "Is that what your mission is about, spying?"

"Yeah. But other than providing proof of my ruthlessness, some technical issues are preventing it from getting approved."

"Can you tell me about it, or is it a secret?"

31

CAROL

*T*o buy herself a moment, Carol tucked an errant lock behind her ear. Her mission wasn't general knowledge, and the fewer people who knew about it, the better. But no one had told her it was a secret either, probably because it was self-explanatory.

The head Guardians knew about it, as did Turner and Bridget, and obviously Kian. But so did Robert. And if it was okay to tell an ex-Doomer about the plan then why not Ella?

Except, maybe it hadn't been okay to tell Robert?

But what the heck. Something about the girl tempted Carol to share her secrets. Could it be the eyes?

Looking into them, Carol could understand Julian's obsession with Ella's picture. Ella's gaze reminded her of Edna's, just without the age-old wisdom and without the judgment.

With that accepting and understanding expression on her angel face, she must have people pouring their hearts out to her all the time.

But there was more to why her gaze was so compelling. Ella's eyes were intense, penetrating, soul searching. Either that, or the girl was just very short-sighted and in need of corrective lenses.

"Do you wear glasses or contacts, Ella?"

"No. Why? Do I squint?"

"Not at all. In fact, now that I think about it, you don't blink much at all. Did anyone else ever notice that about you?"

Shaking her head, Ella blinked twice in quick succession as if to prove Carol wrong. "Sometimes, when I concentrate really hard, I forget to blink. It's kind of like holding my breath. But it doesn't happen often. I guess I was so excited to hear about your secret mission that I forgot to blink. Can you tell me anything at all about it?"

"I can tell you some of it, but it has to stay between the two of us. I'm starting to think that too many people know about it already."

"Like who?"

"Kian, naturally, some of the Guardians, Eva, Turner, probably Bridget too. My ex-boyfriend, who happens to be an ex-Doomer."

Ella's eyes widened. "I thought the Doomers were the clan's enemies."

"They are. But there are exceptions. Dalhu, Amanda's mate, is one, and Robert, who is now happily mated to Sharon, is the other."

"Eva's Sharon?"

"That's the one."

"If you don't mind me asking, how did two Doomers become part of the clan?"

"Dalhu left the Brotherhood because he fell in love with Amanda. Robert did it to save me from his sadistic commander."

Ella recoiled. "Do I want to hear this story? Or more to the point, do you want to tell it?"

Shrugging, Carol glanced at Parker who seemed to be getting tired. "What happened to me isn't a secret. The entire clan was mobilized when I was kidnapped. It was just a dumb misfortune. I happened to be in a club's parking lot when a bunch of Doomers showed up. They grabbed me and brought me to their sadistic commander who tortured me for information."

She smiled sadly. "I played the ditsy blond part so well that he believed I had no idea where the clan's headquarters were. But then he tortured me just for fun."

Looking paler than a ghost, Ella put a hand on Carol's arm. "I'm so sorry."

Carol released a shuddering breath. "It was a dream come true for the sadist—an indestructible fuck-toy he could whip and rape as much as he pleased because by the next morning she was as good as new."

Why the hell was she telling this young and impressionable girl all of this?

People knew the dry facts about her abduction and about Robert helping her escape, and they also knew that she had been tortured for information that she hadn't revealed. But Carol hadn't talked with anyone about what had actually happened to her. Not like she was doing now.

Perhaps enough time had passed and talking about it didn't bring the memories to the surface as it had in the beginning, or perhaps it was the special something about Ella that was pulling the words out of her throat.

Now that she'd started, though, Carol felt compelled to keep going. "No matter what he did to me, my body would heal by morning, but my mind would've eventually snapped if not for Robert. At first, he brought me powerful painkillers to help with the suffering, and eventually he helped me escape just before the clan attacked the place and freed the other girls that had been imprisoned with me."

Carol closed her eyes. "I was afraid that with me gone, the sadist would go for the human girls. None of them would've survived that level of cruelty. But the attack went well, Dalhu killed the sadist, and all the girls were freed."

"Dalhu? The ex-Doomer?"

"Yeah. By then, Kian was over his initial mistrust of Dalhu and took him along because he was an insider and therefore could be helpful in anticipating his former comrades' moves. Dalhu, who held a grudge against the sadist, was delighted to be the one to cut off his head."

Ella nodded. "Remind me to thank him personally for that. What happened with Robert, though? How come you two broke up?"

"For a while, I tried to repay Robert's kindness by being his girlfriend, but at some point, I realized that letting him go so he could find his true love would be kinder."

"Sharon."

"Right. It didn't happen right away, and it required some matchmaking on Amanda's part, but they found each other and the rest is history." She smiled. "I was so happy. You can't imagine the guilt I felt for kicking him out. Everyone thought I was such a colossal bitch for doing that."

ELLA

"You did the right thing. I can imagine how much courage it took to break things off with Robert and face everyone's scorn, and I'm sure it wasn't easy either. People are stupid. They should've realized that you were doing it for his own good, and you should be proud of yourself for having the guts to do it."

"I am. Screw what everyone else thinks."

"Amen to that." Ella raised her hand for a high five, which Carol returned, thankfully moderating the force of her slap.

The woman was so incredibly brave. Ella couldn't imagine what Carol had been through, and the truth was that she didn't want to. The images Carol had painted in her head were enough to cause nightmares.

Twice in one day, Ella had heard stories so much worse than hers. First Tessa's, and now Carol's. Which made three things abundantly clear to her.

First and foremost, this kind of shit happened a lot, and it claimed numerous victims. The village was a small community, and if three out of its female residents had fallen victim to despicable evildoers, then it was a widespread phenomenon.

There could be even more women who'd been wronged but who hadn't told anyone about it.

Secondly, both Tessa and Carol were such bad asses. Carol even more than Tessa. If the entire clan had been mobilized to rescue Carol, then everyone in the village knew she'd been violated, and yet no one thought of her as a victim. On the contrary, they were considering her for some super-duper secret spy mission that she was uniquely qualified for.

And thirdly, Ella was done feeling sorry for herself and hiding in her room. She was going to be like Tessa and Carol. She would hold her head high, look everyone in the eye, and be a badass like those two.

How did the saying go? That which doesn't kill you makes you stronger?

Tessa and Carol were proof of that, and so was Ella.

Since she wasn't dead, not for real anyway, it meant that she was stronger now than before what had happened to her.

As the buzzer announced the end of the session, and Parker's last target retracted, he took off his headphones and looked at the scoreboard. "Awesome. I improved on my last score." Turning around, he grinned from ear to ear.

Ella clapped her hands. "I'm impressed."

"Do you want to go another round?" Carol asked.

His eyes widened in delighted surprise. "Could I?"

She got up and walked over to the control screen. "You're on a winning streak. I'll give you another short session. Four targets."

"Thank you."

Ella hoped that Carol was giving Parker extra practice time because she wanted to talk about her mysterious mission. That was how their talk had started, but it had veered off in other directions that had been no less illuminating.

When Parker put his headphones back on and lifted his bow, Carol sat down next to Ella. "We have fifteen minutes."

"Are you going to tell me about the mission?"

Carol tucked a lock of hair behind her ear. "So, you know who the Doomers are, right?" When Ella nodded, she continued. "Their base is on some uncharted island in the middle of the Indian Ocean. Not even Dalhu and Robert can tell us where it is because they fly people in and out of there on planes with no windows and everyone is searched for tracking devices. Anyway, other than serving as their home base and training grounds, the island is also a high-class resort for the rich and the perverted."

She smiled at Ella. "It's trafficking taken to the next level. As far as we know, they buy girls from suppliers rather than carry out the abductions themselves. The place is a giant brothel that serves the Doomer army as well as some discriminating clients. My idea is to get in there as one of their victims and do two things."

She lifted one finger. "One is to collect information for the clan." She lifted another one. "And the second is to sow the seeds of rebellion. If I can seduce a high-ranking Doomer and have him fall for me, I'll have a good start."

That was the craziest idea Ella had ever heard, and she couldn't understand how anyone was even considering it.

"Are you nuts? Do you know what they will do to you? And how in hell are you going to start a rebellion even if you get some top-level Doomer to fall for you?"

Carol smirked. "I may not look it, but I'm a pro. I love sex, and I have no problem with multiple partners. And as far as having someone fall in love with me and do everything he can to please me?" She rolled her eyes. "I've done it so many times. Men are incredibly easy to manipulate, and I'm an expert at it. I know I can start something."

Ella swallowed hard. What had Carol meant by that? Was she a pro at sex? Or was it more than that? And what did any of it have to do with killing animals and cutting out their hearts?

Then it hit her. Carol had to be capable of killing, and the animals were just the test.

She leaned closer and whispered in Carol's ear. "Does Kian want you to assassinate their leader?"

"Navuh?" Carol pursed her lips. "That's actually not a bad idea. He is the glue that holds the Brotherhood together. I doubt any of his sons would be able to do that with him gone. But no, Kian doesn't want me to kill Navuh. He wants me to incite someone else to do it." She sighed. "But unless we find a way to sneak some form of communicator into the island, Kian won't approve the mission. That's one obstacle. The other one is an extraction plan in case things go wrong. Unless he has solid solutions for these two problems, it's a no-go. And of course, there is the little detail of me proving that I'm capable of killing if the need arises."

"Can you? I mean when it's not a coyote?"

Carol nodded. "I'll kill in self-defense and to defend others. I only have a problem with killing for no reason."

Ella pinched her brows between her thumb and forefinger. "If the island is a resort, then I'm sure they need staff for cleaning and cooking, right?"

"Yeah. They do. The girls they bring over there are given a choice. They can work in the brothel and enjoy lavish accommodations and lots of perks, or they can do the menial jobs, sleep four to a room, work sixteen-hour shifts, seven days a week, and get no perks."

"So, if you want, you can work in housekeeping, right?"

Carol waved a dismissive hand. "I'm a trained courtesan. And anyway, how am I supposed to seduce a high-ranking Doomer while working in the kitchen?"

Well, that answered the question about what Carol's specialty was.

"Actually, I was thinking about myself. I can't do the courtesan stuff, but I can clean and cook."

Carol regarded her with a puzzled expression. "What on earth are you talking about?"

"I'm offering a solution to your communication problem. My mother and I can communicate telepathically from anywhere in the world. If I'm on the island and she's here, your problem is solved."

Leaning, Carol hooked a finger under Ella's chin. "That's so sweet of you to offer, but hell would freeze over before anyone would allow an innocent like you on the Doomers' island. You think that with a face like that you'll be given a choice? And besides, I'm quite sure that pretty kitchen maids and room attendants are not given the option to say no on that island."

"What if I'm not pretty? What if I make myself look ugly?"

Carol laughed. "You can try, but even if you succeed, there is no way you're going. Forget I ever told you anything about it."

"Why? Why is it okay for you and not for me?"

"Because, my sweet Ella, you're an eighteen-year-old human girl who's slept with maybe two or three guys. I'm an immortal who is nearly three hundred years old, and I can fill a couple of phone directories with the names of men I've bedded."

LOSHAM

"I have the list of properties you asked for, sir." His laptop tucked under his arm, Rami stepped out into the backyard. "Would you like me to print them out for you?"

Losham put down the shot of whiskey he'd been sipping on and sat up. "First, let's see what you've found."

"Very well." Rami put the laptop on the table, opened it, and then sat down on the chair across from Losham. "Here you go, sir." He turned it around. "I made a page for each property, including pictures and prices."

"Excellent. Thank you, Rami."

Scrolling through the list, Losham smirked. Navuh might have lowered his position (from the mastermind of global intrigue, Losham had been reduced to a pimp and a drug lord), but by doing so, Navuh had lost his best advisor's loyalty.

Not that he'd been overly loyal before.

The simple truth was that Losham was well aware of his limitations. He might be brilliant, but he lacked Navuh's charisma to inspire and lead. That was why he'd never entertained leadership aspirations or wasted his time on plotting a revolt against his father.

Losham had been satisfied with being Navuh's right-hand man and charting the Brotherhood's course in the background. The game—the planning and scheming and seeing it all come to fruition—was the part he enjoyed.

Navuh's global agenda was less interesting to him.

Come to think of it, it wasn't all that important to Navuh either.

Or maybe it was.

Navuh was a complicated man. Sometimes it seemed as if he was indeed striving for world domination, and sometimes it seemed as if he was using this far-fetched goal as propaganda aimed at solidifying the Brotherhood and ensuring the warriors' loyalty and dedication.

It was the classic 'us versus them' motivator that never failed to work on groups of people large and small.

Losham, however, had left that train and boarded his own.

He was still going to supply the island with the high-quality female stock Navuh had tasked him with acquiring, and he was still going to run the drug trade to provide funds for Navuh's ambitious plans.

But in addition to all that, he was going to accelerate the accumulation of his independent wealth.

The house he'd bought for himself in the hills overlooking San Francisco Bay had appreciated more than twenty percent in less than a year. That was a staggering rate of return.

It seemed that in the United States, and especially in the Bay Area, the best way to build wealth was through real estate.

The funds he'd been allotted to provide accommodations for the new stock of warriors arriving shortly were not going toward renting apartments for them. He was going to use the money to buy a multi-unit property instead, and house them there.

But investing in real estate didn't mean that Losham had

given up on reclaiming his previous position. While the properties he bought were making him money, he was going to search for hot spots around the globe and make strategic plans that would appeal to Navuh.

After all, instigating wars was always a profitable business for the Brotherhood, and if Navuh's top priority was filling its coffers, then he would be open to suggestions.

Providing the idea was good enough, Navuh might even reassign Losham to a more lucrative spot, like Lokan's post in Washington, and put Lokan in charge of the drug and prostitution operations.

Except, it seemed that his much younger half-brother had gained Navuh's trust, leapfrogging over Losham to the position of Navuh's favorite. To get booted out, Lokan would have to incur Navuh's displeasure, but that wasn't likely to happen.

The cunning son of a bitch had always managed to avoid shit sticking to him.

Losham, on the other hand, had been responsible for several recent blunders, and even though he'd covered them up flawlessly, Navuh must have found out somehow. That was probably why Losham was elbows-deep in human refuse, while Lokan was hobnobbing with Washington's movers and shakers.

But perhaps getting assigned Lokan's post wasn't all that desirable.

Moving to Washington would mean leaving the comfortable arrangement Losham had in San Francisco, specifically the lovely house overlooking the bay and his relative independence. Politicking in Washington would also mean more frequent meetings with his father back on the island, which would ruin Losham's illusion of autonomy.

Even dealing with muck was preferable to that.

"I like this one." He turned the laptop around to show Rami. "I want to see it. Please arrange for a viewing with the realtor."

His assistant swallowed. "I know you've told me to ignore asking prices, sir, but we don't have the money to purchase it. Where are we going to get ten million dollars to pay for it?"

"Mortgage, Rami. The building has twenty-two units. We only need eight to house the thirty warriors I've chosen. We rent out the rest and pay the mortgage with the proceeds."

The story Losham had sold Navuh was that the warriors would need good- quality accommodations, and because they had to pose as humans or even students, they had to reside in a building near the university where other students rented apartments. Those were costly.

Navuh hadn't even batted an eyelid. He'd let Losham have his pick of the best-looking warriors, and then from that selection to narrow it down to those possessing a good command of the English language and reasonable charm.

To capture top-quality females, Navuh had agreed that they needed the most attractive males the island had to offer.

Nevertheless, the bunch would need coaching. Used to either paying for sex or thralling for it, the men were not skilled in seduction. Losham might have to hire someone to teach them.

"The warriors will be pleasantly surprised to be assigned such luxurious accommodations," Rami said.

Compared to what they were used to, the apartments in the building he planned to put them in were indeed luxurious, even if four men shared a two-bedroom two-bathroom apartment.

It was no less than what he'd promised them.

To ensure the best selection, Losham had to whet their appetites, and the accommodations were the least of it. Instead of grueling training in the tropical island's unbearable heat and humidity, the men would be seducing women and traveling with them around the globe on so-called romantic vacations.

After he'd dangled that bait, Losham had no shortage of volunteers. The men had fought each other to be chosen for the "Acquisition Squad."

E L L A

Breakfast is ready, Vivian sent.

Ella replied, *I'll be out in a minute.*

Usually, she and her mother made an effort to limit their telepathic conversations when around other people, but with the excellent soundproofing of the house, the only two ways to communicate through closed doors were phone to phone or mind to mind.

These houses should've come with an intercom system.

Shuffling her feet and yawning, Ella got to the kitchen. "Good morning." She sat at the counter next to her mother.

Vivian cupped her cheek. "You have dark circles under your eyes, sweetheart. What happened? Did you have bad dreams?"

Leaning into her mother's hand, Ella sighed. "I did, but not about what you think. I talked with Carol yesterday, and she told me some things from her past. It was very disturbing."

That wasn't the only reason Ella hadn't slept much, though. After waking up with Carol's screams of agony still echoing in her head, she'd spent the rest of the night thinking about the island and the hundreds or maybe even thousands of girls who would never leave it alive.

She kept agonizing over how terrible it was for them—spending their lives in servitude of one kind or another with no possibility of ever having a family of their own or fulfilling any of their dreams.

Slavery should not be tolerated.

It was irrational, but Ella couldn't help feeling guilty. She was free, while they had no chance to ever be. Those girls' only hope was Carol, provided that she could somehow infiltrate the island and cause a revolution before it was too late for them.

The plan was so crazy that even Ella, who didn't know much about anything, realized that it was more a fantasy than an actionable mission. She'd spent hours trying to come up with something better, but none of her ideas were good.

Well, what did she expect? Smarter people than she had pondered the problem, and she thought to outdo them?

"Do you want to talk about it?" Vivian whispered while casting a quick look at Parker's open door. "After breakfast, we can go for a walk."

Ella shook her head. "Carol asked me not to." She looked at the coffeemaker. "I'm not hungry, but I'd love some coffee."

Vivian poured what was left in the carafe into two mugs and handed one to Ella. "I know that she was rescued too. But I don't know any of the particulars. I have a feeling that it was nasty, though. Carol is usually so upbeat and easy-going, but the moment that subject comes up, her expression turns deadly." Vivian chuckled. "In a blink of an eye, the sweet angel turns into a cold-blooded killer. It's scary."

"Yeah, I don't blame her. And by the way, she wasn't rescued by the clan. One of the Doomers couldn't stand her torment and helped her escape before the clan had a chance to organize a rescue. But she wasn't the only prisoner held there, and they ended up saving a bunch of human girls. So, it wasn't a waste."

Vivian put her coffee mug down. "I know that part of the story. But did she tell you where she was held?"

"No."

"The sanctuary. I just love the poetic justice of it. When the clan freed the girls and eliminated the Doomers, they burned the old monastery that had served as the Doomers' base to the ground. Later on, Kian bought the property, and the clan built the sanctuary for rescued girls in the same spot where others were imprisoned."

Ella wasn't sure how she felt about that.

The place must have absorbed tons of dark energy, and even though the building was new, that darkness might still linger there. If it did, the sanctuary wasn't a good place for healing.

"What are you frowning about?" Her mother pressed a finger between Ella's eyebrows. "You'll have wrinkles."

"I don't think either of us needs to worry about those. Immortality comes with many perks."

Avoiding Ella's eyes, Vivian lifted her mug and took a long sip before answering. "I hope it will take care of the wrinkles I already have. And the freckles. I would love to get rid of those too."

It seemed her mother had given transitioning some thought. "Did you decide when you're going to start working on your transition?"

A smirk lifting the right side of her lips, Vivian cast Ella a challenging look. "We had an agreement. You and Julian have to start dating first, and then I'll wait a couple of weeks to see how it's going."

"This is blackmail, Mom. What if we start dating and it's a disaster? Once Julian gets to know me, he's going to realize that we have nothing in common and that he's way out of my league."

Vivian lifted two fingers. "Two weeks, Ella, no less. And at least three dates each week. Total of six."

"Fine." Ella took her mug to the sink and rinsed it out before putting it into the dishwasher. "But he has to ask me first."

"Oh, he will."

Pointing a finger at her mother, Ella glared. "Don't you dare tell him to do that. And tell Magnus not to say anything either. It has to come from him without any prompting."

"He's not going to ask if you don't signal him that you're interested."

"I will smile and bat my eyelashes." Pursing her lips and crossing her eyes, Ella demonstrated how she was going to do that, making Vivian laugh.

"I guess I'm going to stay human." Vivian shook her head. "Magnus is going to be so disappointed."

"Blackmailer." Ella wagged her finger. "I'm going out for a walk."

"Do you want company?"

Ella wanted to do some more thinking, but she didn't want to insult her mother. "Maybe some other time. I want to give running a try."

Any mention of running would dissuade her mother from joining. Vivian liked to stroll, not even fast walk.

"Have fun."

Out on the pathway, Ella started with a couple of minutes of brisk walking, then jogged for a couple of minutes before slowing down to a fast walk again.

Carol had said that the two main obstacles preventing her from executing the plan were communication and a means of escape.

The communication part would be a non-issue if Ella could convince Kian to let her accompany Carol, and extraction shouldn't be that hard if humans visited the resort part of the freaking island all the time.

All the clan needed to do was to find those humans and either bribe them or thrall them to take Carol with them when they left. It wouldn't be easy, but it didn't seem impossible.

As that line of thought brought up a forgotten memory, Ella stopped in her tracks. Gorchenco and Logan had talked about an island. Logan had asked the Russian whether he would be visiting it again, and Gorchenco had answered that he wasn't going anywhere without Ella. Then Logan had said something about Ella's beauty being appreciated over there, and that had gotten the Russian pissed.

Could they have been talking about the Doomers' island?

Gorchenco was definitely rich enough to afford it, and he liked exclusive, high-end things, which no doubt included the paid company he sought.

If the clan followed Gorchenco around, he might just lead them to the damn island.

Her first instinct was to turn around and tell her mother, but that was something the old Ella would have done. The new Ella headed in the opposite direction.

KIAN

*A*s someone knocked hesitantly on his door, Kian frowned. Usually, he could tell who it was by the signature mix of their emotional makeup, but not this time.

Except, strangers didn't just come knocking on his door.

It took him a moment to realize that the slight anxious scent was human and not immortal, which meant that the knocker could be only one of two people, Vivian or Ella.

"Come in," he called out.

The door opened slowly, and Ella poked her head inside. "I hope I'm not interrupting anything, but there is no receptionist up front, so I had no one I could ask. Do you have a moment?"

"Sure." He didn't. But if the girl had braved seeking him out it must be important. "Please, take a seat." He motioned for the chair in front of his desk.

"Thank you." She sat on the very edge. "There were no signs on the doors either, but I figured the corner office would be yours." She smiled. "And I was right."

"It seems so. How can I help you, Ella?"

"I spoke to Carol yesterday, and she told me about the Doomers' island." Ella lifted a pair of worried eyes to him. "She told me about the mission she's training for. I hope she won't get in trouble for telling me because it's not her fault. Sometimes I have this weird influence on people. They feel compelled to tell me their secrets. I thought I was imagining it, or that I was just easy to talk to, but I'm starting to think that there is more to it."

The girl was rambling on, probably because she was nervous. But if what she was saying was true, it was good to know that he had an asset like her at his disposal.

She kept going. "I don't know. It still might be nonsense." She waved a dismissive hand. "Anyway, after Carol told me about the mission and the problems with it, I figured that the communication one could be easily solved if I joined her on the island. The telepathic connection between my mother and me is not location bound. I can transmit any information Carol needs me to."

Kian was shaking his head vehemently, but Ella ignored him and kept on going.

"So, then I thought about the extraction problem. It shouldn't be too difficult to find some of the men who visit the island regularly, and either bribe them or thrall them to get Carol out if needed."

"Even if that was on the table, which it is not because you are never setting foot on that island, the clients don't arrive on their own planes. They are flown there in windowless aircraft, and every piece of luggage is carefully checked. No one can smuggle Carol out."

"Are you sure that they check the luggage upon departure? Because it would make more sense if they checked it upon arrival to make sure that there were no trackers. They have no reason to check on the way out. The visitors are all filthy rich, so it's not like they are going to pilfer anything. And Carol is small. She can fit in a suitcase."

The image of Carol folded into a suitcase brought a smile to his face. "You're very imaginative, and I'll take what you've said under consideration. But I'm afraid we are not anywhere near an acceptable risk margin."

Syssi should have heard this. She would've been proud of how politely he'd phrased his refusal. Normally, he would have just said that the idea was ridiculous and that no way in hell was he going to allow Ella on the island. This was progress.

Except, it didn't work.

Ella narrowed her eyes at him. "I'm so sick of everyone treating me like a breakable doll. I'm a survivor, and I have a special skill no one else has. Are you just going to waste it because you think of me as this fragile girl who needs to be protected?"

The girl had guts. He had to give her that. Not many people dared glare at him or challenge him to a verbal duel.

Should he take her down a peg?

Nah. Let her keep her spunk. Right now, it was probably what was keeping her from falling apart.

"I know that you are strong and brave, but you're still a very young human, Ella. Compared to us, to Carol, you are extremely fragile."

Slumping in her chair, Ella nodded. "I get it. As long as I'm human, all of you are going to keep me in bubble wrap." She looked up at him, the spark of defiance burning in her eyes. "I want to help those poor girls. But since you're not going to let me do the most helpful thing I have to offer, I can at least help out with some information. I'm pretty sure Gorchenco visits that island. I heard him talking about it with someone. If you can track him or maybe even thrall him to assist you, he can lead you to its location."

That was indeed a good piece of information, but not as useful as Ella thought it was. Finding men who visited the island wasn't all that difficult. The problem was that just like Dalhu and Robert, they were clueless about its location.

Not wanting to disappoint Ella, he nodded. "Gorchenco isn't easy to follow, but we will give it a try." He raked his fingers through his hair. "To tell you the truth, I've given up on that plan. I just don't have the heart to tell Carol. It's too risky, and the benefits are iffy at best. With all due respect to Carol, it was a crazy idea to think that she could start a revolt. And we are not strong enough to launch an attack, nor do we want to. For better or worse, the Doomers and we are all that's left of our people. Even though they are my enemies, I'm not going to seek their annihilation."

Fuck, why had he told her that when he hadn't told anyone else?

Maybe there was something to Ella's claim about people feeling compelled to tell her their secrets.

"What about all those girls?"

"My heart goes out to them, but there isn't much I can do about it. Their suffering was what prompted me to even contemplate the insane idea of planting Carol on the fucking Doomers' island."

Pinning him with those big soulful eyes of hers, Ella asked, "Isn't there another way?"

"The only way to end the Brotherhood's reign of terror and free the girls they enslave is to start a change from inside the organization. That's still the best approach. The big question is how to do that. I've been wracking my brain trying to come up with a more viable idea. Unfortunately, I don't see how it can be done. My hope is that unrest will eventually start naturally."

Surprising him, Ella snorted. "Yeah, right. Their leader has managed to stay in power for the past five thousand years. He must know every trick in the book to subdue rebellion before it even starts. Either that or he has complete mind control over his people."

"I can't argue with that."

"So, what do we do, nothing?"

Reaching across the desk, he patted her hand. "You seem to be the kind of person who thinks outside the box. Maybe you can come up with a fresh idea?"

Taking his teasing seriously, she nodded. "I will come up with something. I know that Gorchenco is the key to unlocking this puzzle. I just don't know how yet."

"Why do you think he is the key?"

She put her hand over her heart. "Even though he wronged me, I knew Gorchenco shouldn't die because there was some important task he still needed to do. I have a strong feeling that this is it."

"Feelings are subjective, Ella. You can't trust them."

"Sometimes that is all you can trust. I'm not a normal person, that's quite obvious given the telepathy, and when I have a strong feeling about something, I shouldn't ignore it. I've learned that the hard way."

36

ELLA

*T*he polite goodbye Ella had forced as she'd left Kian's office had taken a monumental effort.

Glad that there was no one around to see her stomping along the pathway, she decided to take the long way home to cool off.

Kian had basically blown smoke up her ass with all that crap about never really intending to send Carol to the island. He'd treated her like a child. Had he thought she'd fallen for his fake assignment?

Right, as if he was ever going to listen to any of her ideas even if she managed to come up with something brilliant.

Not that she had a freaking clue.

For that, she needed much more information about the island and its safety protocol, as well as any other information that could be useful. Which meant picking the two resident Doomers' brains. Dalhu and Robert.

Hopefully, Carol maintained a good relationship with her ex and could introduce them. Dalhu might be easier, though. Ella could visit Amanda, using the makeover she'd been promised as an excuse, and try to get Dalhu to talk.

Eh, who was she kidding?

Why waste time on it?

An ancient and powerful immortal like Kian was not going to take the advice of an insignificant young human. The only thing she had going for her was the telepathic connection to her mother.

A two-way radio of apparently limited usefulness.

Because if Kian wouldn't allow her anywhere near danger, he sure as hell wouldn't allow her mother either, which meant that gossiping and talking through closed doors was all their telepathy was good for.

Well, that and communicating while being held captive by a Russian mobster, but that wasn't going to happen ever again.

Except, would Kian still refuse their help if both Ella and Vivian were immortal?

After all, he'd been willing to use Carol, so why not them?

One thing was clear. As long as they were weak and breakable, there was no chance of anyone being willing to even consider using their unique ability. Bottom line, they both needed to transition.

Not a problem for Vivian, but a big problem for Ella.

She didn't want to think about anything sexual, let alone do it. But maybe that was because sex equaled the Russian in her head. Perhaps the way to get rid of those nasty memories was to replace them with good ones?

How had Tessa done it?

She'd been even younger than Ella when she'd been violated, and she had been treated much worse. How had she managed to let Jackson touch her?

The guy was gorgeous and charming, a real prince, but so was Julian, and still Ella couldn't think about getting intimate with him without a major freak out. Time was supposed to take care of that, but Ella didn't have the patience to wait.

Pulling out her phone, she texted Tessa. *Are you busy?*

I'm at work, but I can take a break. What's up?

I need to talk to you. Can you meet me at the playground?

I can be there in fifteen minutes.

Awesome. See you here.

Asking Tessa to drag up a past which she obviously preferred to remain buried wasn't fair, but Ella desperately needed advice.

She would start with a few gentle questions and see if Tessa was willing to talk. If not, she'd drop the subject and pretend that she wanted to talk about the practice video they were going to shoot later that evening.

With no one using the playground, Ella sat on one of the swings and pushed back with her legs. It had been ages since she'd been on one. Starting a slow rhythm, she closed her eyes.

"Having fun?" Tessa sat on the other swing.

"In fact, I am. I had forgotten how much fun swings were."

"Yeah, me too."

"I'm sorry for dragging you out of work."

Tessa waved a dismissive hand. "There isn't much to do. I'm transcribing old files into the computer. There is no rush on that. What did you want to talk about?"

Ella decided to start with what she thought was an easier topic. "Did you know right away that Jackson was the one for you?"

"Not at all. First of all, he is several years younger than me. Secondly, he's a god, and I'm a plain Jane. I couldn't see us together. Never mind that I was emotionally and physically closed off. I have no idea what he saw in me. I was dressed in kids' clothes, on purpose, and I did my damnedest to impersonate a mouse."

"Did Jackson know right away that you were the one for him?"

Tessa nodded. "He was so sweet and so patient with me. At first, I couldn't stand being touched at all." She chuckled. "Jackson must've had the worst case of blue balls in the history of men. But he suffered through it for me."

"How did you manage to get over it?"

"Slowly and with a lot of patience on his part, and sheer determination on mine. I wasn't willing to let the scumbags who'd hurt me win. I was sick of feeling weak and scared all the time. So, I joined a Krav Maga class and really got into it. It gave me confidence, and some of it spilled over into my relationship with Jackson."

Tessa sighed and let her head drop back. "I remember being afraid that he'd lose patience and leave me. Then I was worried that maybe I would never be ready and thought that I should leave him because it wasn't fair to him. Jackson is such a sensual guy. It's not just about sex with him. He likes to touch me all of the time." She smiled. "Now I love it. I could not imagine life without him."

By the time Tessa was done, Ella had tears in her eyes. The love that girl shared with her fiancé was epic.

Ella wanted it too.

Could Julian be her Jackson?

Although her situation was vastly different than Tessa's had been, there were a lot of similarities between their stories too.

Tessa had thought that she wasn't good enough for Jackson, and Ella thought the same about Julian, but for different reasons. It wasn't about her not being pretty enough, it was about being less in every other area. She wasn't as smart, and she wasn't as good, and she wasn't as pure.

She was contaminated by darkness.

"Did you ever feel tainted?" Ella blurted out before thinking better of it. It was such an intrusive question.

"Of course. How could I not have? I think every victim feels that way."

"Do you still feel it?"

Tessa nodded. "I was touched by evil. I've seen it, I've tasted it, I've been immersed in it. I don't think I'll ever feel clean again. I envy those who have never been touched by it. Not because of the suffering that they've been spared, but because they can't really internalize the evil that's out there. I wish I never knew it existed."

37

JULIAN

*J*ulian buttoned up his dress shirt and straightened the collar, which refused to stay put. Should he button the shirt all the way up?

Nah, it made him look like a dork. It would've been okay with a tie, but that was too dressy for a family-style Friday night dinner. Magnus, who was a fancy dresser, hadn't worn one the other Friday.

Maybe two open buttons were better than one?

He popped another button, but that revealed too much chest. Would Ella find it hot? Or would she think he was a slob?

Probably the second one.

It was back to where he'd started, with one button open and a collar that flopped on the right side.

He could get another shirt or pull out the iron. If he could find it. Did he even own one? His dress shirts were the kind that supposedly didn't need ironing because who had time for that?

Right. He was obsessing over nothing. The shirt was fine.

His beard was neatly trimmed, his hair was combed back but not slicked, and he was wearing his best-fitting pair of jeans.

His looks had never been a problem. If Ella didn't find him attractive, a straight collar was not going to change that.

What did she find attractive?

Grabbing a wine bottle, he headed out the door. He could think while walking to her house.

Should he try to be more amusing? Maybe she appreciated humor?

Or maybe the opposite was true, and she was attracted to the silent, brooding types?

Except, Julian didn't want to pretend to be someone he was not. She either liked him the way he was, or she didn't.

Perhaps the simple answer was that she found him too old for her, and he couldn't really fault her for that. The eight-year difference would become a non-issue when they both got older, but at this time in their lives, it was huge. Especially since he'd spent most of those eight years furthering his education.

That gap was probably bothering her too.

In fact, he should be bothered by it as well, but he wasn't. On the plane after her rescue, he'd done all the talking while Ella had tried to keep her eyes open, and the only time he'd actually had a conversation with her had been last Friday over dinner.

He'd found her just as engaging if not more so than any of his fellow students at medical school. She was smart and eloquent, and her idea for the fundraiser demonstrated that she had the capacity to think outside the box.

Fates, he wanted her.

He wanted those beautiful big eyes of hers looking at him with more than just gratitude and friendship. He wanted her to gaze at him with adoration. Lust too, but that was too much to expect after what she'd been through.

Stifling a sigh, he knocked on her front door.

"Julian." Vivian opened the way with a smile and pulled him into a quick one-armed hug. "Come on in. Dinner will be ready in a minute."

"Thank you for inviting me." He handed her the wine bottle.

"It's our pleasure."

"Hi, Julian," Parker said. "Do you want to play a bit before dinner?"

"No time, buddy." Magnus got up from the armchair. "Go wash up." He offered Julian his hand. "I heard that you've found a place for the halfway house."

Shaking Magnus's hand, Julian chuckled. "Not me. Kian. It was an old hotel that he bought with the intention of demolishing it and building a new one, but the city declared it as a historical building, so all he could do was remodel it, which wouldn't have been profitable. Instead, he decided to donate it to the charity and take a tax write-off."

"Whatever works." Magnus clapped him on the back. "Is it habitable?"

"It needs some work."

As a door down the hallway opened, Julian turned his head in that direction. With the rest of the family all in the living room, it could only be Ella.

His heart skipped a beat or two when she entered.

"Hello, Julian." She walked over to where he was standing next to Magnus and offered him a sweet smile. "I heard that you've been busy."

For a moment, he was too stunned to answer.

Could it be that she'd dressed up and put makeup on for him?

It was nothing fancy, just a long, curve-hugging skirt and a loose sweater that exposed one bare shoulder, but it was enough to cause his tongue to stick to the roof of his mouth.

When he finally found his voice, it was to blurt, "Busy?"

"Yeah, with the new place for the rescued girls."

"Oh, that." He raked his fingers through his hair. "It needs a lot of work. Yamanu and I named it The Palms because we didn't want to keep calling it the halfway house, and there were palm trees up front."

He was rambling like an idiot.

She tilted her head. "Is the name still negotiable?"

"It is. Until we officially open."

"I'll think of something more original. By the way, I would love to see it. Is there a chance you can take me there?"

Julian wasn't the only one surprised.

Parker gaped, Vivian grinned and nodded enthusiastically, and Magnus regarded Ella with narrowed eyes.

"I would love to."

She put a hand on his arm and smiled. "Thank you. When can we go?"

Up close, Ella's feminine scent was doing all kinds of things to him, none of which were okay given present company. And that was without her emitting even a whiff of arousal.

"Whenever you want." He forced a smile. "If you'll excuse me, I should wash my hands before dinner."

Ducking into the powder room, Julian closed the door behind him and ran a frustrated hand over his face as he leaned against the wall.

He hadn't imagined it. Ella had been coming on to him. She was subtle, but he had enough experience with girls wanting to start something to recognize it for what it was.

Usually, though, he was much better at controlling his reactions. A hand on the arm shouldn't have given his dick and fangs ideas.

Yeah, he'd been as smooth as a porcupine in a balloon shop.

Lifting his head, he glanced at the mirror. Not surprisingly, his eyes were glowing.

The long abstinence must have been the culprit. Julian wasn't as sexually driven as some of the older immortals, and he could go for prolonged periods without, but this had been a really long stretch.

In fact, he hadn't been with anyone ever since he'd met Vivian and had gotten obsessed with Ella's picture. It hadn't even been a conscious decision on his part. He just hadn't been in the mood for hunting, which was understandable given how worried he'd been for her.

Still was.

Nothing in his life could've prepared him for handling that kind of stress. Up until Ella, the only times Julian had felt anxious were during finals. Unlike Kian or Turner or even his mother, Julian hadn't accumulated the set of tools necessary to deal with catastrophes.

But now that it was all over, and Ella was safely home, Julian's sex drive had not only returned, but it was demanding compensation for missed time.

he arched a brow. "What other crazy ideas are you referring to?"

Crap. She'd been thinking about Carol infiltrating the Doomers' island and starting a revolution, but she wasn't supposed to talk about it. Julian might know because he was Bridget's son, and maybe even Magnus knew because he was a Guardian, but her mom and Parker didn't and shouldn't.

Waving a dismissive hand, Ella snorted. "Where do I start? The government hiding debris from alien spaceships and alien bodies in Area 51. Hidden alien bases under the ocean floor. Atlantis submerged but still functioning. Should I go on?"

JULIAN

*O*nce coffee had been served and dessert eaten, there was no more reason for Julian to stay.

He was about to thank his hosts and leave, when Parker asked, "How about a game now?"

"Sure."

Thank you, Parker.

The good news was that he'd gotten to talk some more with Ella. The bad news was that he'd either misunderstood her friendliness as flirtation or had blown his chances by not responding to it right away.

After those initial coy smiles and resting her hand on his arm, Ella hadn't done anything to indicate her interest. But maybe if he stayed a little longer, he'd have a chance to correct his mistake.

If he'd made one.

Julian still wasn't sure that he hadn't imagined Ella's subtle come-on.

"After I'm done with the dishes, I'll come to watch you." Ella got up and started clearing the table.

Damn it, he should've offered to do that.

"Let me help." Julian picked up the largest serving platter and followed Ella to the kitchen.

She waved him away. "Go play with Parker. I'll be done in a few minutes."

"Can't do that." He winked. "My mother would box my ears if I don't help."

That got a laugh out of her. "I don't think Bridget can reach your ears, let alone box them." She looked him up and down. "Your father must've been tall."

The compliment combined with the appreciative once over had Julian's ears heat up for the first time in forever.

He cleared his throat. "I've never met him, but my mom used to have a thing for tall guys." He chuckled. "And then she fell for Turner. Go figure."

A thoughtful look in her eyes, Ella nodded. "Turner is very handsome. And he has those incredible pale blue eyes that make him look so intense. I can totally understand what she sees in him. He's a born leader."

Why the hell had her appreciation of Turner made him so jealous?

Maybe Ella was into short, intense guys?

The leader types.

Was he a leader?

Julian wasn't sure. He was competitive, and excelling at school had been important to him, but he'd never felt the need to lead anyone.

Deciding it was best not to respond with something that would make him sound defensive or worse, arrogant, Julian opted to make a quick exit. "I'll get the rest of the dishes while you load the dishwasher."

"Thanks."

Magnus stopped him. "I'll help Ella finish up. Parker has been waiting all day to play with you."

"He has? Then I guess I should go."

It would give him time to calm down from the unexpected jealousy spike over Turner of all people.

"Ready to play?" He sat on the bed since Parker occupied the only chair in the room.

"Here." The kid thrust a controller into his hands. "It's the same game we played with Jackson."

"You played with Jackson and then with me. Jackson and I never played against each other."

Parker closed one eye as if that was going to help him remember. "Yeah, you're right. But you know what I mean." He smirked. "Get ready to lose again."

"Not going to happen, kid. I've been practicing."

"Since Wednesday?"

"Aha."

"We will see about that." Parker started the game.

After each of them had decided on an avatar and a weapon of his choice, it was time to battle it out.

Julian had been joking about practicing, but once he'd gotten the gist of the game, his competitive streak kicked in, and he forgot all about wanting to let Parker win.

His lead in the game didn't last long, though. As soon as Ella joined them and sat next to him on the bed, his concentration was blown, and he barely managed to keep going without dying in the game, which would've ended that round.

Her nearness, her scent, it was scrambling his brain, and sitting on the bed wasn't helping either. He had the insane impulse to drop the controller, push her back on the mattress, and kiss her like she'd never been kissed before.

It was good that the girl was still human and couldn't hear his heart racing. To his ears, it sounded like a locomotive was accelerating inside his ribcage.

Parker, however, didn't suffer from his sister's limitations.

The moment the game ended, with him the winner, of course, he turned off the console.

"Hey, aren't you going to give me a chance to win the next round?"

"Next time you come over I might let you win." Parker put his controller on the charging station. "I promised Magnus that I'd go swimming with him after dinner. See you later, guys."

The kid couldn't hide the smirk as he grabbed his swimming trunks and left the room, closing the door behind him.

Ella frowned. "I didn't hear them making plans to go to the pool."

Not knowing what to say, Julian shrugged. "Maybe it was a last minute thing." He lifted the controller and offered it to her. "Do you want to play?"

"I'm not big on blood and gore. Out of all the games Parker plays, I only like *Minecraft*." She smiled. "I guess boys are more into the shooting and killing games."

He lifted a brow. "That's a sexist remark."

"But it's true. I bet you also like watching war movies. I can't stand them. They make me so sad."

"But you like Marvel movies. Those are pretty violent."

"It's different. I know there is nothing real about them. But I hated *Infinity War* because it was so dark. Movies about real wars always make me think about the poor soldiers, and how scared they must've been, and then I think about the families grieving for those who didn't make it back."

As Ella's eyes misted with tears, Julian was taken aback. It took him a moment to realize why such a mundane conversation had made her so sad.

Her father had died in the line of duty.

Fighting the impulse to pull Ella into his arms and kiss her pain away, Julian pushed to his feet and offered her a hand up. "Would you like to go for a walk with me?"

"I would love to." She smiled and took his hand.

As an electric bolt zapped his hand, and from there traveled to his groin, Julian quickly pulled Ella up so her eyes wouldn't be level with the erection straining his jeans.

"Perhaps you should put on something warmer. It's chilly outside." A big puffy coat that covered her from head to toe would be great.

She chuckled. "It's not that cold, and I'm already wearing a sweater." She threaded her arm through his and leaned against him, causing the locomotive in his chest to go into hyper speed. "And if I get a little chilly, you can warm me up."

Damn.

ELLA

You can warm me up?
Had those words actually left her mouth? Where had they come from? Some cheesy movie or romance novel?

Ella didn't know who was more shocked by them, she or Julian.

While the guy almost stumbled over his own feet, her cheeks flamed with embarrassment.

"Just kidding. I should get a warmer sweater." She pulled her arm out of his.

"Don't." He caught her elbow. "If you get cold, I'll wrap my arm around you. If that's okay with you."

Lifting her head, she braved a look at his eyes and took a step back. "Your eyes are glowing."

"Don't mind them. It's an immortal thing. When you transition, yours will glow on occasion too."

Way to throw gasoline on her already flaming cheeks. There was only one way she could transition, and it would probably involve the tall and handsome guy holding on to her elbow.

She wondered what shone brighter, her cheeks or Julian's eyes.

Covering her embarrassment with a chuckle, she pulled her elbow out of his grasp. "That's a useful trick. I was afraid we'd get lost walking in the dark, but your eyes can illuminate the trail."

Out in the living room, she found her mother sitting on the couch with a book.

"Julian and I are going out for a walk. Are you going to be okay here by yourself?"

Vivian grinned. "Of course, sweetheart. Have fun."

"Thank you for dinner," Julian said. "Everything was delicious."

"I'm glad you liked it. Goodnight, Julian."

"Goodnight, Vivian."

It was weird to hear him call her mother by her first name, but then the age difference between them wasn't that great. Julian was only ten years younger than Vivian.

"I can't believe that all of this started with you hitting on my mom," she said as they took the stairs down to the walkway.

Julian pushed his hands into his pockets. "Vivian is a knock-out, and she looks a lot like my childhood idol, Kim Basinger. But if she told you the rest of the story, you know how she responded to my clever come-on lines."

"By showing you my picture. I'm so sorry about that. I don't know what possessed her to do that. Usually, she's a chill mother who doesn't pull embarrassing stunts like that."

In the dark, Julian's eyes seemed to be glowing even brighter as he looked at her. "I'm grateful beyond words that she did that. If not for that picture and my promise to try and get you an audition, there would've been no rescue. The only reason I called your mother was because Brandon found a part for you."

She'd heard the story, but with a different spin. Her mother was positive that Julian had fallen in love with that picture, and that was why he'd mobilized his clan to save her.

Could Vivian have been wrong?

Maybe Julian had done it just because he was a nice guy?

If that was the case, then she was wasting her clumsy flirting efforts on him. Perhaps she should seek another immortal for her transition?

The idea was enough to make her gag.

Julian was the only one she could envision herself getting intimate with. Not right away, she wasn't ready for that yet, but maybe she could follow Tessa's advice and start with something easy. Like a kiss.

He seemed like the kind of guy who could be patient and would not assume that she was ready to hop into bed with him after one little kiss.

On the one hand, she wanted to have with Julian what Tessa had with Jackson—a slow build-up of trust and passion that would erase the taste of her bad experience and replace it with something wonderful. On the other hand, though, she wanted to turn immortal as soon as possible, so dragging things out was not going to be helpful in that regard.

Still, she had to start somewhere, and she was pretty sure she could handle a kiss. The question was how to let Julian know what she wanted.

Maybe flattery would work?

If she let him know that she found him attractive, maybe that would be enough?

Threading her arm through his, she leaned her cheek on his bicep and sighed. "You are so handsome, Julian. I bet you have many girls chasing you."

Had that sounded as lame as she thought?

Given the puzzled expression on his face, it had. "Thank

you for the compliment, but I'm a little confused. Until today, you've shown no interest in me."

"I wasn't ready."

He arched a brow. "And now you are?"

"I'm trying to figure it out. I thought…" She couldn't look into his eyes and shifted her gaze to a spot on his shirt. "I thought that maybe we could start with a kiss," she whispered.

Hooking a finger under her chin, Julian lifted her face, so she was forced to look at him. "There is no rush, Ella. Don't get me wrong. I would love to kiss you, but I don't want you to do anything before you're ready. Take all the time you need." He chuckled. "And don't worry about all the other girls who are supposedly chasing me. They can't catch me because I don't want anyone but you. I will wait for as long as it takes."

Was he the sweetest guy, or what?

Except, he'd misunderstood her clumsy attempt at complimenting him as her worrying about losing him to someone else if she didn't hurry. It was a concern, but she hadn't thought of it at that moment.

"It's not that. Well, not only that. You're a gorgeous, sweet guy, and to top it off you are also a doctor. It doesn't get any better than that, and I'm not sure for how long you can fight off the temptation my competitors are no doubt throwing at you. I would be a fool to ignore that. But that's not the main thing I'm concerned about."

Crap, if she admitted why she was rushing, Julian might feel that she only wanted to use him as a catalyst for her transition. She did, but that wasn't the only thing she needed him for.

Ella wanted to have with Julian what Tessa had with Jackson, but she didn't know how to get from here to there.

"What are you concerned about?"

"I need to transition, Julian. I will feel so much safer once I do, and maybe all of you will stop treating me like I'm made from glass. I have a special talent the clan can use, but Kian won't let me do anything that even smells of danger because I'm human and breakable."

She should've stopped talking the moment his expression soured, but she'd been on a roll, and her mouth had just kept on flapping.

No longer mellow, the softness gone from his eyes, Julian looked scary when angry.

Suddenly, she was very aware of how much bigger than her he was, and how much stronger. Except, she didn't really fear him. Even when angry, Julian would never do anything to hurt her.

The worst he could do was walk away from her.

"Don't be angry with me," she whispered.

JULIAN

*F*ates, he was a fool.

He should have known better than to fall for Ella's coy smiles and her compliments. If her sudden interest in him had sounded too good to be true, it was because it was.

Like a stupid teenager, he'd gotten all excited about the prospect of a kiss from her. She wanted to transition. That was the only reason for her flirting. He was a means to an end.

"Don't be angry with me," she whispered, her eyes pleading for him to understand.

And just like that Julian's anger went up in smoke.

How could he be mad at her?

Ella wasn't a sophisticated temptress who was out to get him. She was a young girl with limited experience, who was scared and hurting and sought to get over both by becoming an immortal.

It was true that she needed him to transition, and right now she might not realize that she needed him for much more than that, but with a lot of patience, guidance, and persistence, he could prove it to her.

"I'm not angry." He smoothed a finger over her cheek.

Her eyelids drooped a little as she leaned into his touch. "A moment ago you looked mad."

"I was a little disappointed, that's all."

"Why disappointed?"

There was no guile in her eyes as she looked up at him. She really didn't know.

"I think it's natural to want to be desired for who I am and not for what I can do for you."

"Oh." A pink hue colored her pale cheeks. "I just let my mouth flap without thinking. The way I said it made you think that I came on to you only because of the transition."

He shrugged. "It's okay. I understand. If I were in your shoes, I might have done the same thing."

"You don't understand anything, Julian." She shook her head and started walking again.

He followed, afraid that she'd gotten offended and was leaving him without even saying goodnight.

Except, Ella found a bench and sat down with an exasperated sigh. "It's my fault. I didn't explain myself right."

Relieved that she was still talking to him, he sat next to her. "Do you want to give it another try?"

"I don't know." Lifting her feet, she tucked them under her long skirt and hugged her knees. "I'm all over the place. One moment all I want to do is hide in my room and never come out, and the next one I feel like I'm ready to take on the world."

Without thinking, he wrapped his arm around her shoulders and kissed the top of her head. "How about finding a middle ground between the two? Hiding in your room is obviously not a solution to anything, but instead of taking on the whole world all at once, how about taking one step at a time?"

She looked up at him and waved her hand. "But that's exactly what I've been doing. The fundraising idea was the first step. It got me out of the house. I met Tessa, and Eva, and

Carol, and I even went to talk to Kian about another idea I had."

That was a surprise. Ella was showing more spunk than he'd expected from her. Kian was an intimidating guy, and to approach him with an idea took guts.

"Care to share your idea with me?"

She shook her head. "It's not important. Kian would never allow a human girl to do what I proposed."

Now he was really curious. "I would like to hear it anyway."

"I can't tell you."

"Can't or won't?"

"Can't. It involves information I was asked to keep a secret. I can check if it's okay to tell you, but until I get permission, I can't."

"Understandable."

It also explained her sudden rush to secure an immortal male for her transition.

He rubbed her arm. "Is that why you flirted with me? Because Kian wouldn't allow you to do that thing you wanted unless you were immortal?"

As she lowered her head onto her upturned knees, the pink color in her cheeks deepened into a peachy red. "That was part of it."

He waited for her to continue, but when she didn't, he asked, "What's the other part?"

A long moment passed until Ella answered with a question of her own, "Do you like me, Julian?"

"Of course, I do. Isn't it obvious?"

Without lifting her head off her knees, she shook it lightly. "My mother is convinced that you have feelings for me that are more than just friendly. But I think she just wants it to be true because you're such an awesome guy. How can you have feelings for me if you don't know me?"

She was right and explaining it without sounding like a romantic fool was going to be tough. But maybe he should just swallow his ego and tell her the truth?

"It started with the picture. You're very beautiful, but I don't think that was why I reacted so strongly." He put his hand over his heart. "I felt as if the eyes gazing at me from that picture were trying to tell me something. I could almost hear you calling me, asking me to find you, to help you. I know it doesn't make sense."

He chuckled. "Even though I believe that aliens and UFOs are real, I'm not prone to flights of fancy. I thought I was going nuts. But when I called your mother to tell her about the audition Brandon arranged for you, and she told me that you were missing, everything suddenly made sense. I was meant to meet your mom. I was meant to help save you. And I was meant to be your mate."

ELLA

*E*lla shook her head. "I asked if you liked me, and you didn't really answer that. You talked about fate and meaning, but that could all be a coincidence. It's quite a leap to jump from that to being my mate. I would think that love should come first. But how can there be love if we don't know each other?"

Raking his fingers through his hair, Julian released a puff of air. "I realize how it must sound to you. Coming from the human world with human attitudes and expectations about what brings two people together, you probably find me irrationally romantic, or just foolish. But immortals, and by that I mean Annani's clan, believe in fated true-love mates—two people who are meant to be together and bond for eternity. It's what every immortal, male or female, yearns for, but only a few get lucky enough to be blessed with a true-love mate. I believe you are mine. Now all I have to do is convince you that I am yours."

As if she needed convincing. The guy was perfect.

Her cheek still resting on her upturned knees, she looked up at him and smiled. "It's not going to be a hard sell, Julian."

"You're not in love with me."

"And neither are you with me. With all that talk about fated true-love mates, I'm still waiting for you to tell me that you like me."

"Of course, I do."

"Why? Is it this face?"

He smoothed a finger over her heated skin.

She'd been blushing so much that her face was warm even when she wasn't embarrassed.

"Yes, you have a beautiful face, but that's not the only reason."

She waved a hand. "Do tell. I'm eager to hear what you can possibly know about me after spending about eight hours together, half of which I was asleep for."

Lifting his arm off her shoulders, he leaned back and crossed his ankles. "You're a fighter. Right after your rescue, when I expected you to be wary of all males, you followed me to my hotel room and asked to borrow my clothes. I was flabbergasted. Then when I told you about who and what your rescuers were, you listened calmly and accepted my explanations without going into panic mode or denial. I like that you're not impulsive and that you are logical and think with your head and not your heart."

So far so good. Everything he'd said was not only true, but things she prided herself on. The only time she'd failed to think before acting was with Romeo, and it was never going to happen again.

"There is more," he said. "Your fundraising idea is absolutely brilliant. You're a creative thinker. I also think you're a wonderful sister and daughter, which speaks volumes about your character."

It was embarrassing to hear him say all those nice things

about her, and Ella's knee-jerk reaction was to make fun of it. "Hey, you make me sound so good that I want to marry me."

He waved a hand. "There you go. Now you know how I feel about you."

"Just so you won't get disappointed when you find out, I'm also argumentative, opinionated, and I don't do well with authority. On the positive side, I try to be polite, I don't cuss much, and I'm not a big spender."

Grinning, Julian returned his arm around her shoulders. "Sold. I'm ready for the altar."

Yeah, the question was whether she'd be able to tolerate more than his arm around her shoulders and a kiss to the top of her head. As good-looking and charming as Julian was, Ella was attracted to him in her head, but her body remained on neutral.

If she had never felt the stirrings of desire before, she would've thought nothing of it, but she had.

For freaking Romeo of all people, and then for Logan, who might have been even worse.

What was wrong with her?

Did her body respond only to dangerous, evil men?

Julian hooked a finger under her chin. "I was expecting a smile, not a frown. What's the matter, did I make a bad joke?"

As if she was going to tell him that he didn't excite her or share her suspicions with him as to why her body's response to him was so lackluster.

Except, it might have nothing to do with him and everything to do with what she'd been through. It was as if a comfortable numbness had settled upon her, blocking any sexual yearnings she might have normally felt. It was safe inside that numb blanket, but it was also unsettling.

This wasn't her.

It wasn't normal.

It was the same as hiding in her room, only instead of getting her sense of security from walls made from wood and plaster, she was deriving it from walls made of emotional and physical indifference.

"Ella? Can you answer me?" He sounded impatient.

She hadn't realized how long she'd been lost in thought while staring blankly at his handsome face. "Who's rushing things now, Julian? All I wanted was a kiss, and you've taken it all the way to the altar."

"You think you're ready for a kiss?" He arched a brow.

"Only one way to find out."

Crossing her fingers, Ella hoped that Julian's kiss would awaken some of her dormant arousal, but she was willing to settle for none provided that it didn't evoke repulsion.

If it did, she was going to swallow her pride and take Vanessa up on her counseling offer because it would mean that there was something very wrong with her.

The glow in his eyes intensifying by the second, several expressions passed over Julian's face, but his hesitation didn't last long.

Moving faster than she'd thought possible, he lifted her onto his lap and tucked her close to his hard body.

She was trapped, his arms feeling like iron bands around her, and yet there was no fear, only breathless anticipation.

43

JULIAN

*I*t felt incredible to have Ella's body nestled against his chest, his arms wrapped around her and holding her tight. But she was tense and knowing that she wasn't aroused even in the slightest dampened Julian's excitement.

Up close, there was no way he was missing it, and given the plethora of other scents Ella was emitting, he knew she wasn't an anomaly like Turner who didn't produce any emotional scents at all.

Julian's nose and his empathic ability made it easy for him to read her emotions. She was a little anxious, a little worried, and more than a little sad, but she was also determined.

But what was she determined about?

Getting the kiss she'd asked for?

If she wasn't attracted to him, why did she want him to kiss her?

Maybe she hoped the kiss would awaken her desire?

The situation was entirely unfamiliar to him, and therefore utterly confusing, not to mention disappointing.

Usually, the women Julian hooked up with were eager for him, their arousal unmistakable. And as long as he found them even moderately attractive, that unique feminine scent was enough to turn him on. In its absence, his initial arousal dissipated.

It seemed like he was a different kind of animal than most of his immortal brethren and even his human counterparts. His first response to an attractive female was the same as any other heterosexual male's, but unless she responded with clear sexual interest, his arousal would fade away.

Perhaps it was good that he was wired like that. Exercising patience was not going to be a problem for him.

His palm gently cradling the back of Ella's head, he brushed his lips over hers. That tiny contact was enough to send a zap of electricity straight to his deflated arousal, awakening it and shattering his theory of only a moment ago.

Leaning away, he gazed at her face.

Her eyes closed, she parted her lips and darted her tongue out to moisten them.

Experimentally, he took a long sniff and there it was—a faint scent of feminine arousal. It seemed like his body had sensed it before his nose could confirm that it was there.

"My beautiful, sweet Ella."

She smiled without opening her eyes and relaxed in his hold, her body losing some of the rigidness. He should remember to use terms of endearment with her.

Apparently, Ella liked it.

"I've wanted to kiss those lush lips of yours for so long." He smoothed a finger over the bottom one. "Your cheeks." He smoothed a finger over one and then the next. "Your eyes." He dipped his head and kissed one eyelid and then the other.

With each little touch, Ella seemed to loosen up some more, and he debated whether to keep going with what appeared to be working so well or to give her the kiss she wanted.

"Your skin is so soft," he murmured.

Wrapping her arms around his neck and pulling him down, she solved his dilemma. "Kiss me, Julian. I'm not going to break."

The next time he touched his lips to hers, Julian was bolder, flicking his tongue over the seam and coaxing her to open for him.

As she parted her lips, the scent of her arousal flared, and that was all the encouragement he needed.

His hand tightening its hold on the back of her head, he took her mouth, sliding his tongue inside and tangling it with hers in a slow and deliberate dance of discovery.

It wasn't the way he normally kissed. But being attuned to Ella's every response, he realized that the urgency his other partners had responded so well to needed to be tempered for her.

As he drew back, Ella pulled him back down and kissed him, thrusting her little tongue into his mouth.

Julian's first instinct was to deny her access, but then he remembered that there was no need to hide what he was. She knew about his fangs. The question was whether she remembered to be careful around them.

"Watch out for the sharp tips," he murmured against her mouth.

In response, she cupped his cheek and twirled her tongue around one fang, and then around the other, sending shivers up his spine. But more than the intense pleasure of his fangs being licked, he was turned on by Ella taking the initiative and the growing scent of arousal she was emitting.

When she let go of his neck and slumped in his arms, he resisted the impulse to kiss her again.

He needed to take cues from her.

Until she felt completely safe in his arms, he was going to stifle his need for dominance and let her dictate the pace.

"Oh, wow," she said after a long moment. "Talk about butterflies. That was a kiss for the memory book."

Julian would've been puffing his chest out and strutting like a peacock if not for his empathetic and olfactory extrasensory perception. The kiss had aroused Ella, but for some reason, the strongest emotion she was experiencing at the moment was relief.

What was she relieved about?

That he had finally kissed her?

That he hadn't pushed for more?

Or maybe for being able to get excited over a kiss?

Should he ask her?

Normally, revealing his superhuman abilities was not an option, which had provided an excellent excuse for using them to his advantage with his partners none the wiser. But that loophole didn't apply to Ella.

Other than exercising patience, Jackson's advice had been to build up trust first, which meant that Julian couldn't keep his extrasensory perception a secret from Ella because it gave him an unfair advantage.

"I sense your relief," he said.

"I am relieved. But how did you know? Am I that obvious?"

He tapped his nose. "Immortals can smell emotions. When you're this close, the scents that you emit tell me a lot about what you're feeling. I'm also slightly empathic."

She narrowed her eyes at him. "Does it mean that I can't keep any secrets from you?"

"I can't read your mind." He chuckled. "And frankly, being able to read your emotions confuses me more than it educates me. Like right now. I don't know what's the connection between a hot kiss and feeling relieved. I would expect arousal, elation, appreciation for my incredible kissing skills, maybe even a little bit of adoration, but relief?"

Shaking her head, Ella laughed. "You're honest, I'll give you that." She cupped his cheek and looked into his eyes. "I like that."

His gamble had worked. Ella seemed to appreciate his humorous self-aggrandizing that was actually meant to be self-deprecating. "I'm glad. But you're evading my questions. Why relief? Were you afraid my breath was going to stink?"

She took him seriously. "Of course not."

Averting her gaze, she sighed. "Ever since my rescue, I've felt numb. I would look at you and think how gorgeous and attractive you are, but my body didn't follow my brain. There were no tingles, and I was afraid that the numbness was permanent, and that I'd never feel normal again. Or even worse, that I'd feel repulsed by any kind of intimacy."

She lifted her gaze to him. "I bet your sense of smell has already told you that my fears were baseless. It felt wonderful to be kissed by you and to kiss you back." Lowering her eyes again, she whispered, "I'm relieved because now I know that I can make new memories to replace the old ones. Maybe plenty of the good kind will erase the bad."

Julian frowned. Ella sounded as if all of her prior sexual encounters had been terrible. Had there been others who'd mistreated her before Gorchenco?

"I'm sure not all of your memories are bad. Before that scumbag lured you into a trap, you must've had some good experiences."

She shrugged. "Romeo was my first serious boyfriend, and I enjoyed kissing him, but now that I know it was all fake, the memory of those kisses disgusts me."

Julian was starting to get a really uncomfortable feeling.

If Romeo had been Ella's first boyfriend, and kissing had been all that she'd done with him, then she'd been a virgin when Gorchenco had taken her.

Fates, it was bad enough to be coerced into having sex with a man she hadn't wanted. It was ten times worse to have had her virginity taken in such a despicable way.

"Julian? Why are your fangs getting longer?" She pointed at his mouth. "And they are dripping something."

Damn, his venom glands had been activated, but not by arousal.

"I'm going to kill that son of a bitch with my bare hands, and I'm going to do it slowly."

Stiffening in his arms, Ella tried to back away. "Uhm, Julian? Didn't anyone tell you that Romeo is dead? I think Turner beat you to it."

Using his hand, he wiped the venom drops away. "I meant Gorchenco. He deserves to die for what he did to you."

44

ELLA

*J*ulian's fangs were so long by now that he looked like a saber-toothed tiger. And the venom dripping from them was gross. Getting all worked up over a dead issue, he was ruining the memory of that wonderful kiss.

"That's a bit overdramatic, don't you think?"

"The bastard took your virginity."

She stifled the need to roll her eyes. It was her virginity, not his, that had been taken. He had no right to get so angry.

"I know, and I think I have the right to be more pissed about it than you. But he doesn't deserve to die over it. If you get the chance and it makes you feel better, you can beat him up for me."

Heck, if Julian were gay, she would have suggested that he coerce the mafioso into unwanted sex with him. That would be very sweet revenge.

An eye for an eye kind of thing.

But thankfully, Julian was into girls, or rather one girl. Ella.

A small smile lifted one corner of Julian's lips, making him look comical. A smiling tiger. "If I can beat him up within an inch of his life then I accept your offer."

"Nah-ah." She shook her head. "He's too old for that and might die from heart failure. We still need him."

"What?" Julian hissed.

"He used to vacation on the Doomers' island. Now that he's a widower, I'm sure he's going to visit it again. I told Kian about it. Gorchenco can lead them to the island, provided they can find a way to track him."

"How do you know that?"

"I heard him talking with someone about it. When Carol mentioned the kind of resort the Doomers run on their island, I made the connection."

"Finding rich bastards who fulfill their perverted desires on that island is not difficult. Placing any sort of tracker on them, that's the hard part."

"Oh."

Kian hadn't mentioned that, letting her believe that she was being helpful.

The jerk.

He was treating her like a kid.

"So, do I have permission to pound him to the ground?" Julian smiled his grotesque fanged smile that did nothing to detract from how gorgeous he was.

"No. I have a gut feeling that the Russian is going to be instrumental in something. If not in finding the island, then in something else. He needs to live a while longer."

"I don't understand, but it's your call."

"It is." She pushed off his lap, and he let her go. "I should be getting back. My mom is probably worried about me."

They both knew that wasn't true, but it was a polite way to say that she wanted to go home.

The kiss Julian had given her was incredible, but his later

215

angry outburst was tiring her. It didn't matter that it wasn't directed at her. It was negative energy she was still too frazzled to handle.

"I'm sorry," he said at the door to her house. "I'm usually a much mellower guy." He took her hand. "I care about you, Ella. Your pain is my pain."

No, it wasn't.

Julian was an immortal male who was not only stronger than most human males but who could also get out of sticky situations by thralling his assailants. He didn't know how it felt to be small and defenseless with only her wits to aid her, or having to make terrible compromises in order to survive or protect his loved ones.

Still, it was nice of him to say that.

Stretching up to her toes, she kissed his cheek. "I had a lovely time, Julian."

"Me too. How about I take you out sometime? Like on a proper date?"

"I'd love to, but unless you invite me to the village café, I can't. Not until I'm given a makeover. I don't feel safe going out as me."

He nodded. "I'll wait then. Because we will have no privacy in the village café. You have no idea how quickly rumors spread through here."

"Okay." She smiled. "Goodnight, Julian."

"Goodnight, Ella." He lifted her hand to his lips and kissed the back of it.

Crap. That brought back bad memories.

Yanking it out of his clasp, she blurted, "Don't do that."

"Kiss your hand? Why?"

"I'll tell you some other time. I'm tired, and I want to get in bed."

He looked so hurt. "Okay. Goodnight, Ella."

"Goodnight."

Forcing a smile, she opened the door and went inside, letting the smile drop as soon as she closed it behind her.

Thankfully, there was no one in the living room. Tiptoeing to her bedroom, she opened the door as soundlessly as she could and closed it just as gently.

Letting out a whooshed breath, she plopped down on the bed and closed her eyes.

The evening had been a success, but it had been exhausting as well. She'd pushed her boundaries, which was good, and it hadn't backfired, but she'd also overestimated her resiliency.

A lot of residual crap still lingered inside of her. It was sticky and disgusting, and she wished she could just cough it up like phlegm and flush the toilet.

Except, mental discomfort wasn't as easy to alleviate as a physical one. She had a trick for that, though. If she closed her eyes and imagined a pleasant scene, the emotional phlegm would feel less suffocating.

What should she imagine though?

The stroll with Julian had been very pleasant, she could start with that, but instead of it being under the evening sky, she could change the scenery and make it a sunny day on the beach.

Smiling, she imagined the sun kissing Julian's light brown hair, highlighting the blond and gold strands interwoven in between the browns. His eyes would look so blue because his pupils would be pinprick-sized and not overtake his irises like they did at night. He would be smiling, but his fangs would be fully retracted.

With a contented sigh, she let herself drift off into the fantasy, letting the dream unfold on its own.

The scene was so real that she could actually feel the warm

sand under her feet, and as a bigger than usual wave broke onto the shore, the cold water lapped at her toes.

It was a glorious day, made even better by walking hand in hand with a gorgeous guy.

She leaned on his arm and sighed. "I love walks on the beach, Julian."

"Who's Julian?" Logan asked.

Gasping, she yanked her hand out of his. "None of your business."

"A new boyfriend?"

For some inexplicable reason, she didn't want to share Julian with Logan even though he wasn't another entity and was just part of her psyche. For the sake of sanity, it was easier to think of him as separate from herself.

"I said that it was none of your business. Can you go away? You're intruding on my dream."

He arched a brow. "Isn't this our beach?"

They were walking along the boardwalk, the same one he'd transported her to before. But it was her beach, not theirs. The same one she used to hang out at with Romeo.

Maybe she should find a new dream beach. This one had too much bad juju.

"It's not our beach, and it's not even mine. Go away. I was enjoying someone else's company until you popped in and replaced him."

Why the heck had it happened, though?

Ella had no idea. She hadn't thought about Logan in days.

"That Julian fellow?"

She shrugged.

His dark features darkened even more, and the sun that had been shining bright a moment ago was suddenly obscured by rain clouds. Scary Logan was back, and apparently his mood was affecting their dream environment.

"Are you having sex with him, Ella?"

Even though he terrified her, she regarded him with a sneer. "Really? You think I'm going to answer that?"

With a snakelike hiss, he grabbed her by the back of her neck. His fingers digging painfully into the soft flesh, he smiled with a pair of fangs very similar to Julian's. "You don't let anyone other than me touch you, Ella. You'll be very sorry if you do."

"Let me go!"

Surprisingly, he released her. "We are meant for each other, Ella. No one can give you what I can."

"And what's that? A missile launcher? I don't need anything from you, Logan."

As he smiled, his fangs were almost back to normal. "We will see about that."

Ella jerked awake and bolted upright.

What a creepy dream. Julian must have scared her with his venom-dripping fangs and his anger more than she'd realized because now she'd given Logan his fangs.

Except, hadn't Logan had fangs and glowing eyes in the first dream she'd had about him?

Ella scrubbed a hand over her face.

This was bad.

She hadn't known about immortals back then. Could it have been a prophetic dream?

Or was Logan an immortal just like Julian? Except, unlike Julian, he was an evil one.

"No fucking way!"

Suddenly it all made sense. Logan was a Doomer. That was why he had fangs in her dreams, and why he and Gorchenco had been talking about the Doomers' freaking island.

Since she hadn't known about fanged immortals before her rescue, she couldn't have given fangs and glowing eyes to dream Logan. Which meant that somehow he was getting inside her head while she slept.

Could thralling be done long distance?

That wasn't likely.

Even Yamanu, the clan's secret weapon, had distance limits. He could cover a large area, but he needed to be there. That's why they'd flown him to New York for her rescue mission. If he could've done it from the village, he wouldn't have gone.

But then none of the clan members could communicate telepathically like her and her mother either, so different and unknown abilities existed. Logan could have the special ability to penetrate dreams.

What was she going to do?

Could he see the village through her eyes?

Was she endangering everyone by being there?

Should she tell someone?

45

ELLA

*A*fter spending half the night freaking out over Logan's possible identity, Ella had managed to pass the second half in dreamless sleep.

By morning, the entire episode seemed silly.

Fangs and glowing eyes were a trope used in every book and movie about vampires and demons, and she'd watched and read quite a few of those. The *Twilight* saga alone, which she'd watched twice, once with Maddie and another time with her mother, could explain dream Logan's appearance.

The island with its secret resort coming up in a conversation between two powerful, rich, and dangerous men shouldn't be taken as proof that Logan was a Doomer either.

Probably every mafia boss, arms dealer, warlord, and drug lord had visited the exclusive brothel at one time or another, and she wouldn't be surprised if some of the high-ranking politicians were its clients as well.

She'd learned a thing or two from Gorchenco.

Power was corruptive, and politics, although legitimate, was a nasty business in which only the most brutal and unscrupulous reached the top, regardless of their so-called ideological leanings. Corruption and the thirst for power didn't care about party lines.

Still, it was possible that Logan was indeed a Doomer, but Ella wasn't going to run into Kian's office and tell him about her dream encounters. She could only imagine his response.

He would probably suggest that she visit with Vanessa and get her head checked.

Before she did anything rash, she was going to wait for the next dream visit and test Logan. If she asked him a question to which she couldn't possibly know the answer, and what he said checked out, then she'd have proof that he wasn't a product of her mind but a separate entity.

But even that wouldn't prove or disprove that he was a Doomer.

Logan could be a human with special abilities, and maybe even a Dormant.

One thing she was going to make sure of, though. Every dream encounter from now on was going to happen on "their" beach. Just in case he was a Doomer, she wasn't going to show him her real surroundings and give him clues as to the village's location. Also, she was going to be very careful not to mention anything about Doomers or immortals because that would give her away too.

Luckily, up until now, nothing about immortals had been mentioned in their dream encounters. To make sure, she'd gone over every word they'd ever exchanged.

When her phone buzzed, she snatched it off the charging station, hoping it was a text from Julian, but it was from Amanda, reminding her that today was the big day.

Ella was finally getting her makeover.

The good news was that her mother together with Magnus and Parker were going shopping and would be gone most of the day.

Vivian wasn't going to be happy about the changes Ella intended to make, and it was best she didn't see the work in progress, but was presented with the completed project. Other than lamenting Ella's pretty hair, there wouldn't be much her mother could do after the fact.

When the doorbell rang two hours later, Ella was alone in the house, with only Scarlet for company.

"Hello, darling." Amanda sauntered in with a big duffle bag slung over her shoulder. "I hope you don't mind, but I decided to make it a girls' get together."

Ella had been expecting Carol and Eva to join, but not Tessa and another woman she didn't know.

"This is Sharon," Eva introduced her assistant. "Sharon, this is Ella."

"Hi." Sharon offered her hand. "I couldn't resist seeing Eva's magic in action."

Eva shook her head. "I told you that you were going to be disappointed. This is Amanda's show. I'm here only as an advisor."

"Where do you want to do it, Ella?"

Good question. Hair coloring was messy, and Ella didn't want to chance staining any of the nice furniture or the rug in the living room.

"Can we all squeeze into my room?"

"Sure." Amanda waved a hand. "Girls, grab a couple of chairs and let's go."

"You go ahead," Carol said. "I'm going to make us virgin margaritas."

Amanda grimaced. "Why virgin?"

"Because Eva is breastfeeding, and Ella is only eighteen."

"That doesn't mean we all have to suffer."

Sharon patted her shoulder. "It's only ten-thirty in the morning. It's too early for alcohol."

"Oh, well. I guess virgin it is."

Carol headed to the kitchen, Sharon and Tessa each grabbed a chair, and the five of them filed into Ella's room, with Scarlet closing the procession and promptly jumping on the bed.

Amanda patted the dog's head. "Since you're a girl too, you're allowed. But you need to behave."

Scarlet wagged her tail.

"I see that we have an understanding."

Putting her duffle bag down on Ella's desk, Amanda started taking stuff out. Several boxes of hair color, four different brushes, two pairs of scissors, a hair dryer and a hair curler. Next came up a bottle of shampoo, a conditioner, and miscellaneous other hair treatments Ella could only guess the use of.

"I also brought several outfits for you to try out once we are done with the hair and makeup."

Eva lifted a rectangular box. "I brought several colored contact lenses. You can change your eye color every day of the week if you want."

"I've never worn contact lenses."

Eva waved a hand. "You'll get used to them. And anyway, you only need to put them in when you go out."

One hour later, Ella looked into the mirror and could hardly recognize herself. "My own mother could pass me on the street and not know it was me."

Amanda had bleached her hair, colored it pink, cut it short, and then spiked it using tons of hair glue. Smokey-eyes heavy makeup framed her new amber colored eyes, and her brows grew to twice their size thanks to some specialty brow product that mimicked real hairs. Her face had been primed and contoured, giving her a hollow-cheeked appearance.

"What do you think?" Amanda looked at Eva.

"Couldn't have done it better myself."

"I have some fake piercings for you to try on," Carol said. "They look so real I'm tempted to play with them myself."

"Why fake?" Tessa asked. "Ella can have fun with real piercings as long as she is still human. When she transitions, the holes will close."

"I prefer the fake ones." Ella reached for the box. "They don't hurt."

First, she put in big hoop earrings, then she added a removable nose ring, and lastly she stuck a glue-on fake diamond on top of her new bushy brow. "I look like a pink goth."

"That was the idea," Amanda said. "Now let's move to the wardrobe." She pulled a pair of shredded black jeans out of her duffle bag.

"Be careful when you put them on. There are more holes in them than fabric."

She hadn't been kidding. And they were really tight too.

Next was a black T-shirt with some band name printed in pink lettering on the front.

"That's so awesome." Ella turned this way and that in front of the mirror. "I look like such a badass."

"You do, darling. But I'm not done." Amanda pulled out a pair of monster boots from her bag. "Put them on."

They were six inches high, but since they were basically chunky platforms, Ella had no trouble walking in them. They must've been expensive. The leather was soft, and they weighed very little considering how bulky they looked.

"I love it."

"Now the bangles." Amanda handed her a bunch of bracelets made from various materials.

"Anything else?" Ella asked after putting several on each wrist.

Amanda shook her head and smiled. "I think my work here is done. What do you think, girls?"

"Unbelievable," Tessa said. "That's even more drastic than my makeover."

Eva nodded. "I agree. No one is going to recognize you, Ella."

Looking in the mirror, Ella liked what she saw. The question was whether Julian would too.

"What do you think will happen if I go out into the village looking like this? Am I going to trigger the intruder alert?"

"You might." Tessa chuckled. "You'll have to reintroduce yourself to every person you meet."

Sharon shook her head. "I'm worried about your mother. She's going to faint seeing you like that."

"I can handle my mom. After the initial shock, she'll get used to it, especially since this makeover is supposedly for my safety."

"Supposedly?" Eva asked. "I thought that was the entire purpose of this."

"It was. But I like the new look. It's so drastically different from the good-girl-next-door one I was ready to get rid of. It makes me feel cool, like an individualistic badass who is not scared of anything. The only thing I'm missing is a tattoo." She arched a brow at Amanda. "Any chance you do those too?"

Amanda laughed. "No, darling. Tattoos don't hold on immortals."

"Bummer."

"You can have a fake henna one," Carol offered. "It will hold for a couple of months. Where do you want it?"

"On my face." Ella smoothed her hand over her left cheek. "A vine that will start around the eye and continue down to my neck."

"That's going too far," Eva said. "You don't want to encourage close inspection of your features, and a facial tattoo will make people want to take a closer look."

There was some logic to that, although she already looked weird enough to attract attention, but at least it would be for a different reason than before.

She was no longer as pretty, which was precisely what she'd wanted to achieve with the makeover. Her beauty had brought her nothing but trouble.

The only thing she was worried about was Julian's reaction.

"Any of you know where Julian's house is? I want to surprise him with my new look."

Tessa cleared her throat. "Maybe you should text him first and let him know that you're coming."

"Yeah, that's a good idea," Sharon said. "And include a selfie with your text."

Amanda, on the other hand, smirked like a she-devil and wrapped her arm around Ella's shoulders. "Let me show you how to get there."

46

JULIAN

*A*s the piano playing abruptly stopped, Julian lifted his head from the article he was reading and glanced at his roommate.

"Are you expecting a visitor, Julian?" From his bench, Ray had a good view of the path leading to their house. "Because someone is walking this way."

"Who is it?"

"No one I know, but she's hot."

Ray didn't hang out much with other immortals, but he could probably recognize each of the village's residents. The only newcomers were Vivian and Ella, whom he might've not met yet.

Hot could apply to both mother and daughter. Except, neither had a reason to come visit him.

Suddenly worried, Julian got up and rushed to the door, yanking it open and leaving his visitor with her hand up in the air ready to knock.

"Hi, Julian."

He gaped. "Ella?"

The voice was the same, the body shape was the same, but

that was it. The disguise must've been Eva's work. The transformation was so complete that he would not have recognized Ella on the street. Even her unique personal scent was barely accessible under the heavy perfume she had on.

Brown contact lenses with a tint of amber covered her blue eyes, and her hair had been cut short, colored bright pink, and spiked. Two large hoops pierced her ears, a much smaller one was threaded through her nostril, and a fourth one through her brow.

The tight black jeans, black punk-rock T-shirt, and monster shoes made her look much thinner and taller.

Despite the godawful getup, she was still beautiful, but he'd loved her old, softer look and hated the new, edgy one.

Smirking, she turned in a circle. "Do you like?"

He rubbed a hand over his face. "It will take some getting used to."

Her smile faded, but then she shrugged. "It's good to know that you're honest. May I come in?"

Damn, he'd kept her on the front porch instead of inviting her in.

"Of course." He threw the door open.

"Hello," she said to his roommate. "I'm Ella."

"Ray." He got up and offered her his hand. "I don't know what you looked like before, but this is hot."

She beamed at him. "Thank you."

Barely managing to stifle the growl that had started deep in his throat, Julian coughed.

Ella pulled her hand out of Ray's and turned to Julian, handing him the plastic bag she'd brought with her. "Your clothes. I totally forgot to return them. I'm sorry it took so long. But better late than never, right? They are washed and ironed, so you can put them right back in your closet."

Apparently, when embarrassed, Ella talked a lot.

"You ironed my socks and boxer shorts?"

That wrested a smile out of her. "Just the T-shirt and the sweatshirt."

"Do you iron all of your T-shirts?"

She scrunched her nose. "I do. Is it weird?"

"Not at all. I do that too," Ray said.

Liar.

The dude was supposed to be his friend, or at least stick to the bro code. It wasn't cool to flirt with his roommate's girlfriend.

Glaring at him, Julian motioned to the couch. "Would you like to sit down, Ella?"

She shifted from foot to foot. "In fact, I came here to take you up on your offer to go out. I've been cooped up in this lovely village for far too long, and I need to do some shopping. But I don't have my fake driver's license yet, and I'm also afraid to go out by myself, so I thought you could take me."

Probably feeling awkward about initiating their date, Ella was rambling on, the scent of her embarrassment overpowering the stinky perfume.

Shopping was a great idea.

He was going to buy her a lineup of good smells and ask her to throw out the hippie patchouli or give it back to whoever had thought it was a good scent on her.

"Let's go." He grabbed his phone, his wallet, and his car keys off the kitchen counter.

She glanced at his feet. "Don't you want to put shoes on first? And maybe exchange your sweatpants for jeans?"

"Yeah." He raked his fingers through his hair. "I should, shouldn't I?"

Smiling, she nodded.

"Do you want to wait here? It will only take me a minute."

"If you don't mind, I would like to see your room." She

stuck her hands in the back pockets of her torn jeans. "I want to see if you are really as tidy as you claimed to be."

For a moment, he had no idea what she was talking about, but then he remembered the hotel in New York. When he'd hesitated to invite her to his room, she'd assumed he was embarrassed about it being messy.

"By all means." He motioned for her to go ahead of him.

Later, he should thank his mother for insisting that he always make his bed. The habit was so ingrained in him that he couldn't leave his room in the morning unless everything was in its place.

"Very masculine," she said as he opened the door for her. "And tidy. I'm impressed."

He noticed her looking at his motorized reclining armchair. "Take a seat." He motioned to it. "I'll be out in a moment." He ducked into the walk-in closet and closed the door.

Changing into one of his nicer pairs of jeans, he heard Ella engage the recliner's motor, and a moment later her contented sigh.

Julian smiled. Ray could laugh all he wanted about his old-man chair. The thing was the most comfortable seat in the house.

As if sensing that someone was thinking of him, Ray resumed his playing, no doubt in an effort to impress Ella.

It worked.

A moment later Julian heard the chair's motor engage again and then his bedroom door open. Ella's chunky boots clanked on the hardwood floor as she walked toward the grand piano in the living room.

Grabbing a button-down off the hanger, Julian pushed his feet into a pair of loafers, saving the time it would have taken him to put on socks, and tackled the buttons on his way to the living room.

He found Ella leaning with her elbows on the side of the piano and gazing at Ray with open admiration.

"Ready to go?" Julian asked.

She nodded and waved at Ray. "See you later."

His roommate stopped playing. "Pop in anytime. I'm home most days, practicing. Maybe next time you could stay a little longer and listen to one piece from start to finish."

"I would love that. You play beautifully."

47

ELLA

*T*he first ten minutes of the drive were unnerving. As soon as the self-driving mechanism engaged and the windows turned opaque, Julian sat back and crossed his arms over his chest.

He was brooding, and the compliments she'd paid Ray could be the only reason for it. Julian seemed to have a jealous streak and Ella wasn't sure how to feel about that.

With her limited dating experience, she didn't know if that was true of most guys, or just the possessive and controlling types. Julian didn't seem like one, but she'd been wrong before.

Well, that was why they were going on an actual date. They were going to talk and get to know each other, and she was going to pay close attention to any telltale signs of character flaws that were unacceptable to her. She didn't expect perfection and was willing to overlook one or two annoying habits, maybe even more, but some things were not negotiable.

A little jealousy was fine, she wouldn't want a girl to flirt with Julian either, and so was a little possessiveness, but not control. The moment he started to demand that she do or not do things, she was going to walk away from him no matter how attractive Julian's total package was.

Heck, she was willing to settle for a much more modest package deal in exchange for a respectful and easy-going attitude.

Like Magnus's.

Observing him interact with her mother and her brother was warming Ella's heart. The guy somehow managed to balance everything perfectly. He was easy-going and accommodating, helpful and respectful, but he wasn't a pushover.

He had what she thought of as a good alpha vibe.

Magnus often took charge, but it was seldom about him. His primary concern was taking care of the people he loved and being the pillar of strength they could lean on.

That was what Ella wanted from a partner, or mate, as the immortals called it. Hopefully, Julian could be that person for her.

But that was putting the cart in front of the horse, or as Amanda would say the eyeshadow before the foundation.

He cast her a sidelong glance. "You know that those piercings will close once you transition."

Chuckling, she removed the hook from her nostril. "These are fake piercings. The one on my brow is glued on."

"Why use them at all? They don't help to obscure your features."

"It's for the total effect. Like the nails." She wiggled her fingers. "Metallic blue nail polish just goes with the Goth look."

He cast her another glance just as the windows started to clear. "I'm getting used to the pink hair. It's actually not so bad."

"I've heard better compliments, but as I said before, I appreciate the honesty."

As the computerized voice announced that self-driving was going to disengage in thirty seconds, Julian put his hands on the steering wheel. "That's good because I'm a terrible liar."

"Tell me what you hate the most about my new look."

"Easy. The contact lenses and the eyeshadow because I love your eyes so much. But that's also the best part of the disguise. Your eyes are very distinctive." He reached with his fingers and smoothed them over her cheek. "I also don't like those dark smudges on your face. They make your cheeks look hollow. I like your softness."

"So, you're okay with the hair?"

He glanced at her again. "Yeah. It's cute."

Cute wasn't what she was going for, but she could live with that. "I'm only going to put in the colored contact lenses and heavy makeup when I go outside the village. The only thing you're going to see is the hair, which you're okay with."

Tapping his fingers on the steering wheel, Julian shook his head. "If you enjoy the new look, you shouldn't change it on my account. I'll get used to it. You're beautiful even when you impersonate a Goth fairy."

That was so sweet of him to say. "Thank you. But I don't like makeup, and I really don't like contacts. They irritate my eyes."

"What did your mom say about all that?"

"She didn't see me yet. The three of them went shopping."

"I hope you called her and told her that I'm taking you to the mall. She'll be worried if she comes home and you're not there."

Arching the brow with the fake piercing in it, Ella tapped her temple. "Did you forget about this? I don't need to call or text my mom. I sent her a mental message." She chuckled. "It will be so funny if we bump into them at the mall and my mom doesn't recognize me. She'll get mad at you for going out with some other girl."

"Then we should go to a different mall. I don't want to be there for the showdown."

"Chicken."

"You bet I am."

Cute. She liked that he didn't mind belittling himself, even if only teasingly. With his many attributes, Julian could've been a pompous ass, but he wasn't, not even a little.

She wondered how it was possible. Bridget probably had a lot to do with it, raising Julian to be modest and not boastful.

"You keep surprising me," she said.

He glanced at her with a cocked brow. "Me? I'm the most boring and predictable guy."

"You've just proven me right. Those are precisely the kinds of things I would not have expected a guy like you to say."

"What do you mean by a guy like me?"

"You know what I mean. Your good looks alone would make any human guy strut around like a peacock and expect girls to drop their panties as soon as they saw him. But you're also a doctor, and most of them are the most pompous people I've met. They think that they know everything."

Pushing his fingers through his hair, Julian grimaced. "The panty-dropping thing I've been guilty of, I admit that, but it just happened whether I expected it or not. And as to knowing everything, I'm well aware of my limited knowledge. Even in my own profession I still have a lot to learn, and I certainly don't know much about other disciplines."

He waved a hand. "For example, if this car broke down, I wouldn't know how to fix it. On the other hand, I know that I can learn almost anything I put my mind to."

"Almost? What can't you learn?"

"Quantum physics. I just can't wrap my mind around it. And believe me, I've tried."

"Perhaps you just need a good teacher. Did you try learning about it from books?"

"Books and recorded university lectures. I still don't get it."

Fiddling with the frayed edges of her jeans, Ella was reminded of something the Russian had told her. "I hate to bring him up, but Gorchenco told me that you should always hire professionals to do what they are trained for. You need to find a good teacher and pay him. That will be the fastest way to learn a difficult subject."

Julian's hands tightened on the steering wheel. "I don't want to take anything from a morally corrupt, evil man. Even if it's good advice."

That wasn't smart. Julian was letting his emotions cloud his judgment. As much as she resented the Russian and detested what he'd done to her, Ella wasn't going to ignore the things she'd learned from him.

48

JULIAN

"I'm sorry." Ella gave him a lopsided grin. "I know that shopping for clothes is torture for guys."

She wasn't sorry at all, and she hadn't bought that much either, but she sure as hell had spent hours going from store to store and trying things on.

Julian took the latest shopping bag from her hand. "Ready to call it a day?"

"Yeah, my feet hurt and my eyes are burning. I can't wait to take the contacts out. But I had fun. Thank you." She looped her arm around his neck and pulled him down for a quick kiss. "You're a prince for letting me drag you around all day long."

Transferring all the shopping bags to one hand, he wrapped his arm around her waist and kissed her back. Just a quick peck on the lips because they were in a crowded shopping mall and getting aroused was out of the question. "I had fun too."

They'd eaten an early dinner in one of the mall's restaurants, and after that Ella hadn't made too much of a fuss when he'd insisted on buying her perfumes, especially when he'd told her how much he hated the patchouli smell she had on.

It had been a good day.

Hell, it had been great.

Nothing had been said, but they were officially a couple. Ella's acceptance of his gift had been the final proof of that.

She'd been relaxed with him, comfortable as if they'd been dating for a year and not just one day, and the longer they were together, the better it got.

Was that what being fated for each other felt like?

Or maybe it was just his inexperience with actual dating, and that was how everyone felt? Or at least those who found someone they really liked?

He was trying hard to keep some emotional distance and not let his obsession with Ella cloud his judgment, but what he was discovering was better than the fantasy, and the very real and down-to-earth Ella was much more than what he'd built up in his head.

Like her crusty sense of humor, which was increasingly surfacing the more comfortable she got with him. Julian hadn't expected to like it so much, but it was refreshing being with a girl who wasn't afraid to express herself without worrying about making a guy think that she was sweeter than cotton candy.

She also liked to touch and be touched, which suited him perfectly because he craved the closeness and implied familiarity. They'd been holding hands or having their arms wrapped around each other throughout the day. He especially loved the way she'd leaned her head on his arm or thanked him for doing that or this with a smile or a peck on his cheek.

The truth was that he was looking forward to many more days like that, shopping with her, carrying her bags, and giving his opinion about the things she wanted to buy. Being a couple was so much better than prowling for hookups and spending his days alone.

"You're just saying that." Ella's eyes smiled as she threaded her arm through his. "Admit it. You've been suffering valiantly."

"How about I prove it to you? I'll take you shopping tomorrow too."

She laughed. "I think I spent enough money today. I need to find a job before I go on another shopping spree."

"Guardians are paid very well. I'm sure Magnus can afford it." They exited the mall and headed for his car.

"It's not a question of whether he can afford it or not. I don't want to spend his money. I want to have my own."

He opened the passenger door for her and dropped the bags on the back seat. "Magnus thinks of you as his daughter," he said as he turned the ignition on.

"That's very sweet of him, but I am not. And even if I were his daughter, I would've felt bad about mooching off my parents instead of working for my spending money."

"What about when you go to college? The clan will pay for your tuition, but you'll need spending money."

She shrugged. "I can work part-time."

Julian frowned. He hadn't considered it before, but there was a very real possibility that Ella would choose an out-of-state college.

If she did, he would have to follow her there because there was no way he was letting her out of his sight.

Just thinking about it felt like a vice was closing around his heart.

"What's the matter, Julian? It suddenly feels as if the temperature in this car has dropped ten degrees. Did I say something to upset you?"

He reached for her hand, remembering at the last moment that she didn't like it kissed. Was it something that reminded her of Gorchenco?

Instead, he threaded his fingers through hers and just held

it, resting their conjoined hands on her thigh. "I hope you're going to choose a local college. Now that I found you, I can't fathom being without you."

"Oh, crap." She pulled her hand out of his and reached for her eye. "Why did you have to make me emotional? Now my eyes sting, and I have to take the freaking contacts out, and I don't know how to do that. Eva didn't show me how."

"I'll pull over and help you."

Searching for a place to park, he spotted the vacant lot of a closed-for-business mattress store.

He parked, killed the engine, and turned to Ella. "Let me see." He cupped her chin and lifted it. "Your eyes are red."

"They feel as if I polished them with sandpaper. Can you take the contacts out?"

"Ouch." His own eyes teared as his empathy kicked in. "Look up and open your eyes wide."

"Yes, doctor."

Since Ella didn't expect him to move so fast, the first contact was easy. She didn't even have time to blink before he got it out.

"Oh, wow. It's such a relief."

He caught her hand, stopping her from rubbing the eye. "It's going to itch much worse if you get makeup in it."

"Right. Can you get the other one too?"

"Look up again."

"Yes, sir."

This time, she blinked before he could pinch the contact out. "I'll either have to hold your eye open or show you how to do it yourself."

"You do it. I'm scared to do it myself."

Her trust melted his heart.

Holding her eye open, Julian quickly pinched the contact,

got it out, and let go. "All done." He kissed her lips. "Should I kiss the boo-boos away?"

"Yes, please."

He gently kissed one eyelid, and then the other, not caring about the shadow he was getting on his lips. If it made her feel better, he would lick the makeup off them, but he doubted she was willing to go that far.

"You don't happen to have tissues in here, do you?"

He shook his head. "I don't get sick. But I can drive to the nearest pharmacy and get you some."

"No, that's okay." She bent down and lifted the bottom of her T-shirt to her eyes, exposing a very tempting midriff.

It wasn't flat, and Ella didn't have the muscles of someone who exercised regularly, but her skin looked so soft and creamy, and her slightly rounded belly was cute and feminine.

Once she was done wiping the makeup off, she glanced up at him. "I probably look like a raccoon."

He couldn't lie. "A raccoon that got punched in both eyes, or an escapee from a zombie movie."

"Great." She covered her eyes with her palms. "I will have to spend the rest of the drive like this."

"Don't be silly." He pulled her hands away from her face. "No one is going to notice."

A slight scent of fear wafted off her. "There are traffic cameras on the way. Without the contacts, I'm exposed to facial recognition software."

"Would sunglasses help? I have a pair in the glove compartment."

"I don't know if regular sunglasses would do the trick."

As she looked at him, Ella's worried blue eyes stood in stark relief against the backdrop of the dark makeup smeared all around them.

"I have an idea. You can lie down on the back seat and cover your face with the sweatshirt you bought."

"What if the police stop you?"

"I'll thrall the cop to think you're a dog."

"That's nasty, but I like it."

49

ELLA

*a*wake even though it was after midnight, Ella rubbed a finger over her lips, the phantom memory of Julian's goodnight kiss still lingering despite the long hot shower she'd taken after he'd walked her home.

Her mother had been so ecstatic over their date that she hadn't made a big fuss about the pink hair, or the raccoon eyes, or the Goth clothing and monster boots.

Vivian was okay with whatever got Ella out of the house, especially with Julian.

She should've gotten a tattoo at the mall. It had been a missed opportunity to do something wild and not get an earful from her mom about it.

Turning to her back, Ella stared at the ceiling.

Even though they hadn't done anything special, the date with Julian had been magical. Other than her mother, she'd never felt as close to anyone, not even Parker.

She could see herself spending her life with Julian, and it would be a good one.

Except, she couldn't help the feeling that it was all too good to be true. Life had taught her that shit happened often and for no good reason, and when everything seemed to be going her way, she should brace for a disaster to ruin it.

Ella still remembered how elated she'd felt when Parker was born. Being a big sister had been a wish come true, and for one wonderful year their family was as happy as could be.

But then her father was killed, and nothing was the same again. From the height of happiness, their family had descended into the pits of despair.

It had taken years for the pain of his loss to recede. The wound had crusted over, but the part of her heart that had died with her father remained numb.

Then things started to look up when Romeo showed up in her life. She'd thought she was falling in love, but that had been another disaster in the making.

Every time Ella had allowed herself to be happy, the universe decided that she didn't deserve it.

What was it going to throw at her now?

Gorchenco's goons sniffing out her trail?

Would Logan turn out to be a Doomer and storm the village because she somehow revealed its location even though she didn't know where it was?

What if he ended up hurting Julian?

A shiver running down her spine, Ella curled up on her side and tucked her hands under the pillow. She needed to fall asleep and dream of him.

Hours passed as she tried to deep breathe herself to sleep, and when that didn't help, to count sheep. Eventually, though, exhaustion did the trick. Once again, Ella found herself walking along the shoreline, but Logan wasn't there.

Should she try and call him? Would it work?

"Logan, where are you?"

The good thing about dreamland was that there were no

other people on the beach unless she willed them to be there. Maybe she should try to do the same with Logan?

Closing her eyes, Ella willed him to appear at her side.

When a couple of minutes passed and nothing happened, she was ready to call it quits, but then the air in front of her shimmered, and Logan stepped out through what looked like an arched doorway. It blinked out of existence as soon as he was entirely on Ella's side.

"You called?" He arched a brow.

"Yes, I did. I want to talk to you."

Suspicion clouded his dark eyes. "About?"

"Gorchenco."

Hopefully, Logan would buy the excuse. She knew he would get suspicious if she claimed to just want his company.

"What do you want to know?"

"Is he okay? I worry about him."

As much as she wished it was just an excuse, it wasn't. Gorchenco was too smart to buy her staged death. Something must've happened for him to concede defeat so quickly. It wasn't like him to give up so soon.

"You must have a sixth sense, Ella. Gorchenco had a heart attack."

When she gasped, he lifted his hand to quickly qualify. "He's not dead. He's recuperating on his Russian estate."

"How do you know that?"

"Did you forget? I do business with him."

"Right. He supplies you with weapons."

"Indeed. No one can get the stuff he does. He must have excellent connections in the Russian military. Maybe even to Putin."

"Perhaps they are related. Did you notice how much alike they look?"

He chuckled. "I don't think they are, but maybe. Who knows? They might be distant cousins."

If only she had a way to verify Gorchenco really had had a heart attack, she would know whether Logan was a separate entity from her or not.

"I don't know if I believe you. He seemed very healthy to me. He didn't overeat, or over drink, and he didn't smoke." Except for the one time he'd lit up a joint for her.

Logan shrugged. "You don't have to take my word for it. Who knows? Maybe your guilty conscience is making it up."

"Right. As if I would feel guilty for escaping from the guy who bought me and wanted to keep me against my will."

Logan shrugged again.

Tomorrow, she could look for information about Gorchenco on the internet. Perhaps his supposed heart attack would be mentioned somewhere. But if it was, it would probably be in Russian. Unfortunately, she hadn't learned it and would have to find someone who could read it.

Except, that would take time, and the need to know the truth couldn't wait that long.

"I need to ask you something."

"I figured you didn't call for me to talk about your husband."

"He is not my anything," she bristled. "That wedding was a sham. But that's neither here nor there. I need to know whether you're really a figment of my imagination or are you real?"

"Why? Do you want me, Ella?" He smirked. "Do you crave what only I can give you?"

"And what's that?"

He cupped the back of her head and leaned, so his lips hovered a fraction of an inch away from hers. "Passion, Ella," he murmured. "Like you've never experienced before."

For reasons she refused to examine, he was affecting her, and she hated it. Why was he making her feel things she wanted to feel for Julian and no other?

Pushing on his chest, she took a step back and was surprised that he didn't try to stop her.

"Tell me the truth, Logan. Are you real? Or am I making you up?"

He caressed her cheek with the tips of two fingers, much in the same way Julian had done, but Logan's touch felt more erotic in nature than loving.

"If I tell you, my sweet Ella, you have to promise not to tell anyone."

Seeing no other choice, she nodded.

"I need to hear you say it."

"I promise not to tell anyone about you."

He smiled with too much satisfaction over her small concession. "Very good. Just so you know, your promise is binding."

"What does it mean?"

"It means that you really can't tell anyone."

"Well, I promised."

Not that she had any intention of keeping the promise if he admitted to being a Doomer. Except, she couldn't ask him if he was without giving herself away.

"I'm real. I'm a telepath like you, and that's why I find you so fascinating. I've never met a woman who could do what I can."

"If you were a telepath like me, you could've contacted me while I'm awake and not only in my dreams. Although that would've been one hell of an achievement since I have very strong protective walls up. Even my mother can't communicate with me unless I allow it."

"There is no fooling you, is there?" He sighed as if resigned to revealing his big secret, but it looked fake. "I don't know anyone else who can do what I can, and the name I invented for my ability is dream-walker."

"So, you can enter my mind while I dream but not while I'm awake?"

"It's more complicated than that. The best way I can explain it is that when you dream you create another dimension, a non-physical one, and we can meet there if I happen to be dreaming at the same time."

"Can you do it with anyone?"

He shook his head. "Only with people whom I've met in person, and only those who have at least some telepathic ability. I think the telepathy is the conduit for the dream encounters."

For a change, he sounded sincere, and Ella believed him.

"So other than me, who else have you shared dreams with?"

"Very few people." He caressed her cheek again. "I told you, my sweet Ella. You're a rare treasure, and I intend to find you. And when I do, you're not going to escape me as easily as you did the Russian. I'm going to keep you forever."

50

VIVIAN

*a*s the door to Ella's room opened, Vivian reminded herself to stay calm and say nothing about the pink spikes on her daughter's head.

It had been quite a shock to see her return from her date with Julian looking nothing like her sweet little girl. Between the horrendous eye makeup that had been smeared all over her face and the dark shading under her cheekbones, she'd looked like a character from the zombie apocalypse.

But the smile on Ella's face and the dreamy look in her eyes had been worth every splash of paint Amanda had applied to her face and hair.

Evidently, the date had gone very well. Vivian couldn't wait to hear the details.

"Good morning." Ella shuffled into the kitchen in her bunny slippers.

Her eyes seemed blurry, and at first glance, the dark circles under them looked like smeared makeup that she hadn't done a good job washing off last night. On closer inspection, however, that wasn't the case.

"Good morning. Did you have trouble sleeping again?"

"Uh-hum." Ella lifted the coffee carafe and poured herself a cup.

"Good dreams or bad ones?"

"A little bit of both."

When Ella didn't elaborate, Vivian decided to drop the subject and move to the one she was more curious about.

"How did it go with Julian?"

A smile brightened Ella's tired face. "Great. I dragged the poor guy all over the mall, and he didn't complain even once."

"That's your proof that he's a keeper. I was right."

Ella rolled her eyes. "As if it was needed. Julian is every mother's dream son-in-law. The question I keep asking myself is what the heck does he see in me?"

She took another sip of coffee. "If it was about my pretty face then the makeover should've turned him off." She chuckled. "You should have seen his expression when he opened the door to let me in. He looked horrified."

"You went to his house?"

Ella shrugged. "I returned the clothes I borrowed from him and used it as an excuse to ask him out."

Ella had asked Julian out? Not the other way around?

If it weren't early in the morning, Vivian would have opened a bottle of champagne to celebrate. There was no doubt Ella was getting better.

"I'm so happy that you initiated it."

Cradling the cup in her hands, Ella leaned forward. "It was a test. I wanted to see his response. If he was willing to be seen with me in public when I looked like a cross between a fairy and a zombie, it would prove that he liked me for me and not just for my pretty face."

"Given the way you were soaring on a cloud last night, I assume that he passed your test with flying colors."

Ella raked her fingers through her short hair that thankfully wasn't spiky anymore. With the glue washed out, there was nothing to hold it up. It was kind of cute, making Ella look like a pink-haired pixie.

"He exceeded my expectations. First of all, he admitted to hating the new look, which was really brave of him. And he was so much fun to be with. I wasn't stressed, and I wasn't anxious. I was as comfortable as if that was our hundredth date and not the first."

Vivian wasn't sure that was a good thing.

There should have been at least some sexual tension between them. A new couple that hadn't been intimate yet shouldn't feel so comfortable with each other on their first date or even the fifth or the seventh.

"Good morning, Mom, Tinker Bell," Parker said as he entered the kitchen. "Is there anything to eat?"

"For you." Ella rubbed her fingers over his head. "Fairy dust should do."

"I'll make French toast for everyone." Vivian got up.

He blew at the imaginary dust. "I shall destroy your magic with my telekinetic power."

Ella ruffled his hair. "Any luck discovering what your special talent is?"

He grimaced. "It's not telekinesis, that's for sure. And it's not telepathy."

"Did you try remote viewing?"

"I don't know how."

"Simple. You close your eyes and imagine some place you've never been to, and then look for it on the Internet to see if you were right."

His eyes brightened. "I'm going to do it right now."

Vivian waved her spatula. "Can it wait until after breakfast?"

"Sure. What else can I try?" he asked Ella.

"Precognition, but I guess that's trickier. You can try to guess the lottery numbers and then check if you were close."

That got Parker even more excited. "Why didn't you tell me about it before? I could've asked Mom to buy me a ticket when we went shopping yesterday."

Ella chuckled. "Don't you want to test it first before spending your allowance money on it?"

"I was only going to spend one dollar." Parker pouted.

Letting out a big yawn, Ella got up and stretched. "I need to get dressed."

"Any plans for today?" Vivian asked.

"I thought about hanging out with Carol. She's such a fascinating woman."

"Has she invited you?"

Ella waved a hand. "She said I can come over whenever I want. But I'll text her and ask if today is good for her."

"Don't forget that later today we are going to Dalhu's art exhibition. You need to come home and change clothes." Vivian glanced at the pink hair. "Maybe wear a wig too. We still have the short black one Amanda gave you."

"It's fine, Mom. I just need to put the gel on to spike it."

"Please don't. Maybe I can blow dry it for you, slick it back and away from your face?"

"Can we talk about it when I come back?"

Which in Ella speak meant forget it.

Vivian sighed. "Did you at least buy something nice to wear yesterday?"

"I got everyday stuff. I'll borrow something from you."

With Vivian's closet getting frequent new updates courtesy of Magnus, Ella had plenty to choose from.

"Okay. Just be back on time. The exhibition is at six-thirty, and I want us to have dinner before we go. You need to be here no later than five."

"I'll be back long before that."

51

ELLA

*A*s Ella walked down the pathway leading to Carol's house, she was still asking herself the same question that had been bothering her since she'd woken up that morning.

How could she find out whether Logan was a Doomer without asking him point blank if he was? Which she couldn't do because she was pretending not to know anything about immortals.

Besides, after he'd threatened to find her and keep her, it was better if she didn't engage with him at all. The chances of Logan ever finding her were slim, so she wasn't scared, but it creeped her out.

Next time he showed up in her dream, she was going to ignore him and pretend he wasn't there. And she was certainly never voluntarily inviting him again.

Eventually, he would get tired of that and leave her alone.

But then she would have to find some other way to determine if he was a Doomer. Regrettably, it seemed like she had no choice but to dream share with him at least one more time.

Because if he was, she needed to tell Kian or Turner. Not

that either of them could do anything about it, but maybe she should go away from the village for a while and hide somewhere until Logan stopped popping up in her dreams.

She should describe him to Dalhu and Robert, the two ex-Doomers who'd left the Brotherhood and joined the clan. Carol had access to one of them, and maybe she could arrange a meeting with the other.

During the makeover, Ella had planned to ask Amanda about a meeting with Dalhu, but even though the goddess's daughter was nice and friendly, she was also as intimidating as her brother. Maybe even more so because she couldn't be manipulated like a man.

Even without realizing it, men were more inclined to listen to a pretty, young girl, as well as help her. Ella had no doubt that if a guy came to Kian with the same ambitious plan as she had, Kian would've thrown him out much less politely than he had her. The end result was the same, but at least she'd gotten to say what she'd come for.

When the path she was walking on intersected with another, Ella checked the village's map on her phone and continued straight.

If she'd followed the directions Carol had given her, she would've gotten lost for sure. Luckily, Magnus had overheard them talking and gave Ella a map, but only after she'd refused his offer to walk her there. It was time she got familiar with her new home.

"There you are." Carol waved at her from the doorway. "I was afraid you got lost."

"I almost did. It's good that Magnus gave me a map."

"There is a map?" Carol threw the door open. "I didn't know that."

Inside, a guy Ella didn't know was sitting on the couch and watching a football game.

"This is Ben, my roommate."

"Hi." The guy waved his hand without turning his eyes away from the television.

"Ben, pause that stupid game for a moment and come say a proper hello to Ella."

"That's okay. Let him watch. Parker and Magnus are also glued to the screen. I don't know what it is with guys and football. I think it's boring."

"Sacrilege," Ben gasped dramatically and offered his hand. "I love the hair."

"Thank you." She fluffed it with one hand while shaking his with the other.

"You're welcome. Well, nice meeting you and all that, but I'm going back to my game."

"Sure. And nice to meet you too."

Threading her arm through Ella's, Carol led her outside to the back yard. "What happened to the spikes?"

"Too much hassle." She sat on the double chaise lounge next to Carol. "I'll spike it when I go out."

"It looks good like this too. It's soft." Carol smoothed her hand over Ella's short hair. "You look cute."

"My brother calls me Tinker Bell."

Carol shrugged. "That's cute too. He could have come up with something much nastier."

"That's true."

Leaning sideways, Carol lifted a ginger ale soda can from the side table and handed it to Ella. "I was in the mood for a beer, but given your tender age, I decided against it."

"Isn't it too early for that? It's only eleven in the morning."

Carol smirked. "I don't care for conventions. I do pretty much as I please."

Yeah, she did, and that was why Carol was Ella's new role model. Eva was a bit too extreme to emulate. Or a lot.

"I wanted to ask you for a favor. Can you get your ex-boyfriend to talk to me? Or is it against the rules because he's Sharon's now? Do I have to ask her?"

Carol narrowed her eyes at her. "Why do you want to talk to Robert?"

"I want to ask him questions about the island. Kian challenged me to come up with a better plan, but I can't do that without having more information about it."

"You went to Kian with your crazy idea?" Carol shook her head. "You have guts, girl, I'll give you that. But he was just teasing. Kian doesn't expect you to come up with a plan."

"I know that. But I want to prove to him that I can."

That had been her original plan, but now she needed information for a different purpose.

"I see." Carol leaned back on the lounger and crossed her arms over her chest. "I can probably answer any questions you might have. I've already talked with both Dalhu and Robert extensively, picking their brains about the security measures, possible access points, and anything else I could think of."

Crap. What should she ask?

Perhaps she should just go for it and have Carol think what she would.

"How can you tell if a guy is an immortal if he's not showing fangs or glowing eyes?"

Logan had both in some of her dreams, but she could've given them to him. Dream Logan hadn't looked exactly like the real one, with his appearance changing according to how she was feeling about him that night.

Carol tapped her nose. "I can smell the difference between a human and an immortal."

Great, not so useful in dreams. Besides, until she transitioned, Ella wouldn't be able to smell the difference anyway.

"Do Doomers smell different than clan males?"

"No."

"So how do you know if an immortal guy is a Doomer?"

"Easy. I know all of my relatives. I might not remember everyone's name, but I know their faces. If I meet an immortal guy that I don't know, then he must be a Doomer."

"What if he is neither?"

Carol shook her head. "There are no other immortals. It's either them or us. But what does any of this have to do with the island? Everyone there is either a Doomer or a human."

There was another possibility Ella hadn't considered before. What if Logan was a clansman? Maybe he belonged to the Scottish branch?

She shouldn't assume that they were all decent people just because their ideology and leadership were good.

In the same way that there could be decent Doomers, there could be rotten clansmen.

"It's all new to me." Ella waved a dismissive hand. "I was just curious. But now I feel like I should learn the face of every male clansman, so if I ever meet a Doomer, I would know what he is. Do you have something like a yearbook or a directory?"

"No, but with all the newcomers, that's a good idea. We should have one and post it on the clan's virtual board. Although if you're worried about randomly encountering a Doomer, don't. The chances of that are very slim."

"I'm not worried." Hopefully, Carol couldn't smell the lie. "I just wanted to know if there was a way to differentiate between the good guys and the bad."

Carol chuckled. "Their attitudes. Doomers still think women are good only for breeding. They also think that humans are too dumb to govern themselves and should be enslaved."

Hmm, that was a clue. Maybe she could get Logan engaged in an ideological debate and see where he stood on those. Not that it would be proof positive. Entire human societies still believed that women were inferior. On the other hand, very few thought that slavery was a good idea, except for the traffickers, of course, but that was mostly about women as well.

Regrettably, it seemed like she had to arrange for another dream meeting with Logan and find out what his position on male slavery was.

It wasn't much, but it was better than nothing.

"Anything else you wish to know about Doomers?"

"Yeah. I want to know as much as possible about the island and what's going on there. How are the visitors screened, and how is it possible to hide its location so well, and who's in charge…"

Over the next hour or so, Carol provided her with so much information that Ella was afraid she'd forget half of it if she didn't write it all down.

"I think that's enough for today. Next time I'll bring a notepad."

"You could've recorded me on your phone."

"Shit, I should've thought of that. I'll go home and write down what you've told me. But next time I'm going to record it. If that's okay with you."

"Sure. Just make sure to keep your phone away from your little brother. Some of the things I've told you are not for his young ears."

Just thinking about it Ella felt herself blush. Carol was very open about her sexual promiscuity, and very blunt in her descriptions too.

It was cool that she'd confided in Ella so openly, not treating her like the young, inexperienced human she was. If Ella ever needed advice on sex, she now knew who to turn to.

"Maybe I should write it down and lock the notepad somewhere he can't get into. He's a nosy little guy, and way too good with technology. He probably knows my lock code."

"Not so little anymore." Carol winked. "I give him a year or two before he starts chasing immortal females around the village. Not that they'll be running away all that fast. An immortal male who is not a cousin is a rare find."

"Ugh, gross. I can't think of my little brother as some gigolo."

Carol stifled a snort, turning it into a cough. "Of course not. Now tell me, are you coming to Dalhu's art exhibition this evening?"

"Yes. My mother is a fan of his work."

"What are you going to wear?"

"I don't know yet. I'll borrow something from my mom. I don't have any fancy stuff. Why are you asking?"

"I ordered this really sexy dress online, and it's a bit snug on my butt. We are about the same height, and I thought you'd look great in it." She pushed to her feet. "Let's go to my room. I want you to try it on."

"I thought we were done with the makeover." Ella followed her inside.

Carol patted her arm. "This is a different kind of makeover." She winked. "I'm going to make you look so sexy, Julian is going to salivate."

"Oh. I don't know if that's a good idea."

"Trust me. It is."

52

AMANDA

*A*manda followed Dalhu as he walked from one room to another, regarding his work critically, the muscles of his shoulders getting tighter instead of looser.

There was a reason she hadn't allowed him anywhere near the office building while her team of helpers had worked on transforming the place into an art gallery.

Dalhu had agreed to do the exhibition grudgingly and only because she'd convinced him that selling his art and donating half of the proceeds to the clan's humanitarian effort would erase the last doubts some of the clan members still harbored about him.

Showing him the completed project ensured that he couldn't change his mind at the last moment and cancel the entire thing.

"What's the matter? You don't look happy."

Stopping in front of a landscape, he rubbed his jaw. "It's not good enough, Amanda. I should have waited until I'd gotten it right."

She wrapped her arm around his middle. "You are a perfectionist. If I wait until you deem your work worthy of display, no one will get to see it, and it would be a shame. People love your landscapes, there is so much feeling in them."

He turned to look at her with an arched brow. "What are you talking about? Those are depictions of nature. They have no feelings."

Leaning her head against his shoulder, Amanda sighed. "It's the feeling they evoke, which is probably how they make you feel, and it shows in your work."

Her guy was so incredibly talented and yet so unaware of his own process, perhaps because he'd never taken classes and had never been taught how to reach down into his soul and transfer what he found to his art.

He did that on pure instinct.

"I think you are either imagining things or trying to boost my confidence." He turned her toward him and kissed her lips. "You're amazing, do you know that?"

"Of course, I do."

Dalhu chuckled. "Thank you for organizing this. I've never been to an art gallery, but I'm sure you topped them all. Everything looks beautiful."

"You're welcome, my love." She kissed him back. "I had a lot of help, which just shows how many people love your work."

"Not necessarily. You're one hell of a bossy lady, and people are afraid to say no to you."

She slapped his bicep. "Not true."

"Oh, yeah? I bet most of the Guardians you've roped into moving furniture out of the offices have never even seen my work."

"Yes, they did because they helped hang it on the walls. You should have heard them oohing and aahing."

A soft growl started deep in his throat. "I'm sure it wasn't over the landscapes. Did you let them hang the nudes I did of you?"

"I did no such thing. You asked me not to." Which was a shame. Amanda wasn't bashful about her body, and those were some of Dalhu's best works. "They are still at home, hidden under the bed."

She shook her head. "You should at least let me hang them in the bedroom. No one goes in there but us and Onidu, but he doesn't count."

"You've invited people in there before."

"Only ladies."

"Not true. Kian was there, and so was Anandur."

Amanda waved a dismissive hand. "First of all, they are my relatives. And secondly, it was a one-time thing because Wonder fainted after seeing Annani's portrait and we had to take her somewhere private. Speaking of that portrait, you haven't seen what I've done with it yet. Come on."

She took Dalhu's hand and pulled him behind her to the next room. "What do you think?"

As befitting the work and its subject, Annani's portrait was the only painting in the room. Amanda had had several chairs brought in for people to sit down and ponder its many layers of meaning. A casual look just wouldn't do. It was a piece of art worth spending time admiring.

53

ELLA

*a*fter styling her short hair as best she could, Ella pulled on the little black dress Carol had loaned her.

It was short and tight, but the round neckline wasn't too deep, and it didn't show much cleavage, which made it passable for the occasion.

Ella liked it.

It was sexy, young, and nothing like the wardrobe the Russian had commissioned for her.

No bad memories there.

The problem was that she didn't have shoes to match. The black monster boots could go with it if she wanted to look edgy, but that would mean spiking her hair and applying tons of makeup, which she wasn't in the mood for.

After all, Dalhu's art exhibition was in the village, so she didn't need to disguise her appearance.

Well, that was what she told herself. The truth was that she wanted to look nice for Julian, and he didn't like the Goth getup.

Talking with Carol had been educational on many levels.

Apparently, sex with an immortal male was an entirely

different experience. Carol had compared it to eating at a Michelin four-star restaurant, qualifying that statement by emphasizing that currently the most stars a restaurant could get were three. In contrast, she'd said, sex with a human was like eating a stale, gas-station sandwich.

Yuk.

Carol's detailed descriptions of the differences had started a low burn. And when Ella had gotten home and allowed herself to imagine Julian doing some of those things to her, that burn intensified tenfold.

Could he be so dominant in the bedroom?

According to Carol, all immortal males were dominant. It was how they were designed. It was the rare exception to find one without a dominant streak, which had been the case with Robert, and one of the main reasons things hadn't worked out between him and Carol.

Ella was starting to suspect that Carol actually wanted to go to the Doomers' island because of all the great sex she'd be expected to have with immortal males.

Strange female.

But whatever, to each her own.

Ella couldn't fathom having a lover she didn't have feelings for, let alone several a night.

Yuck, and yuck again.

There was just one guy she could envision being with, and that was Julian.

Liar.

She could almost hear Logan whisper the word in her ear. Maybe in addition to being a dream-walker he was also a warlock?

Had he put a spell on her the one time they'd actually met in person, and was he now tempting her in her dreams?

Last night, when he'd told her that he intended to find her

and keep her for himself, Ella had experienced two conflicting emotions.

One had been fear, the other arousal.

It was very disconcerting.

Her attraction to Logan didn't make any sense. So yeah, he was handsome and mysterious, and Ella had no doubt that he was dominant as hell in bed, but he was also scary, and most likely human, which meant that he couldn't be all that great.

Ella shook her head. As if that was even a consideration. Maybe for Carol, but not for her.

Sex wasn't nearly as important to her as having a good, loving relationship, and in that respect, Logan wasn't in the same league as Julian.

Heck, he wasn't even in the same galaxy.

She should remember that every time thoughts of Logan drifted through her head. Even magic couldn't help him become a decent man.

Releasing a relieved breath, Ella applied a little eyeliner, some lip-gloss, and then brushed her hair one last time before leaving her bedroom.

"Mom, do you have a pair of black pumps I can borrow?"

"I do. But they have very tall heels. I don't know if you'll be able to walk in them."

Ella grimaced. "I had practice."

"I'll go get them." Vivian looked her up and down. "You look lovely. Where did you get the dress?"

"Carol loaned it to me."

"It looks great on you. With the heels, you're going to look like a fashion model."

"Yeah, a very short and padded one."

Ella wasn't fat, but the models she'd seen in magazines looked like they hadn't eaten anything other than lettuce in months.

Her mother waved a dismissive hand and headed to her room. A moment later she returned with a pair of gorgeous pumps.

"Here you go, sweetie. Try them on."

They weren't the same make as the ones Pavel had gotten her, but they looked just as pricey.

"Oh, wow, Mom. Fancy, fancy. You've never worn shoes like these before."

Her mother nodded. "They are not practical, and they cost way too much for collecting dust in my closet, but Magnus insisted I had to have them. You know how he is with clothes."

"He sure is stylish." Ella braced a hand on the kitchen counter as she slipped her feet into the shoes. "Suddenly I feel so tall."

As the front door opened, Scarlet bounded in first, with Parker and Magnus walking in behind her. Luckily, she skidded to a stop as Ella lifted her hand instead of jumping on her.

Parker whistled. "Nice dress." He looked down at her feet. "And shoes. You look like a runway model."

Vivian waved a hand. "Told you. But do you ever listen to your mother?"

"Do the walk," Parker said. "The one with a hand on your hip and swaying from side to side like models do."

"I don't want to." She would feel silly strutting like that in the middle of her kitchen, especially with Magnus watching.

"Why not? In the old house, you used to do it all the time." Parker moved a chair to make a clear path for her. "Just do it!"

Bossy dweeb.

Ella still didn't want to do it, but surprisingly, she found herself putting her hand on her hip and doing the runway walk like she used to.

Parker whistled.

Vivian clapped her hands.

Magnus smiled.

Ella felt strange.

She hadn't wanted to do that, and yet here she was, putting on a show for her family because Parker had told her to do it.

Unless she felt like it, Ella wasn't in the habit of obeying her little brother's commands.

Something wasn't right about this scenario.

JULIAN

*H*alfway to the village square, Julian bumped into Jackson and Tessa who were heading the same way.

"Hi, Julian," Tessa said. "Where is Ella? Isn't she going to the exhibition?"

"She's going with her family."

Jackson shook his head. "It's a missed opportunity, my man. You should've asked to accompany her."

Smiling, Tessa patted Julian's arm. "It's not too late yet. Go get her."

Raking his fingers through his hair, he hesitated for about a second. "Yeah, you're right. I should." He turned around. "Thanks for the advice."

"Any time," Jackson called after him.

This dating thing was turning out to be much more complicated than it seemed at first glance. It wasn't the same as prowling for hookups and making booty calls. There were rules to follow of when and how and where, and the embarrassing truth was that Ella, an eighteen-year-old high school graduate, probably knew more about it than he did.

As Julian knocked on her front door, he hoped the last moment change of plans wasn't going to get him in trouble with her. He hadn't even texted her to let her know that he was coming.

Parker opened the door and grinned. "Hi, Julian. Are you going with us to see Dalhu's paintings?"

"If you don't mind me tagging along." He wanted to take Ella and go, but that would be rude.

"Of course, we don't. We would love for you to join us," Vivian said from behind Parker. "Don't just stand there. Come inside."

"Thank you."

Talk about awkward.

Standing by the entry door, he didn't know whether he should come in and shake hands, or just wait for everyone to be ready to leave.

"Ella!" Parker yelled. "Come out already. Julian is here!"

That solved the dilemma.

"She can't hear you, Parker," Vivian said. "I'll tell her."

Julian heard her bedroom door open, and then the clicking of heels as she walked down the short corridor. And yet, when she entered the living room, he hadn't been prepared for the punch to the gut impact her appearance delivered.

His jaw going slack, Julian gaped.

Even the Goth getup and pink hair hadn't been as startling.

When he'd first seen Ella in the ambulance, she'd worn a shell-shocked expression and an elegant cream-colored pantsuit, looking confused and just a little disheveled. Later, when she'd put on his clothes, she'd looked young and fragile.

Since then, he'd seen her mostly in jeans and T-shirts, looking like a typical teenager, and that included yesterday's disguise.

"You look amazing," he finally managed to say.

Her pink hair was slicked back and held away from her gorgeous face with a pin. Long earrings dangled from her ears, nearly reaching her bare shoulders, and the short black dress she had on was lovingly hugging every curve of her delectable body.

Then there were the shoes. They made her shapely legs seem to go on forever.

Damn, he might develop a shoe fetish because all he could think about was her wearing nothing but those damn heels as she wrapped her long legs around his waist.

"Thank you." She turned in a circle, letting him see her from all angles. "Do you like the dress?"

His Ella wasn't a shy girl, that was for sure. And she wasn't even trying to hide the satisfied smirk on her lush lips. The girl had seduction on her mind, and if he needed proof, the sweet scent of her nascent arousal confirmed it.

"I love it. But you should wear something over it." Like a long coat and a scarf. "It's getting cold outside."

"I've got just the thing," Vivian said. "I'll get it for you."

Ella smiled. "Thanks, Mom."

Julian could only imagine the looks she was going to get from all the single guys, which was nearly every male in the village. He had a feeling the bro code was not going to cut it tonight. The men were going to go after her like a pack of hungry hyenas and try to take her away from him.

He hadn't claimed Ella as his yet, and she hadn't claimed him either, which in their eyes would mean that she was up for grabs.

Except, luck seemed to be on his side.

If he hadn't bumped into Jackson and Tessa, Ella would have arrived at Dalhu's art exhibition with her family, and the situation would've been difficult to salvage.

Now everyone was going to see them arriving together, and Julian was going to do his damnedest to demonstrate that Ella belonged to him.

He should remember to thank Jackson and Tessa again for their excellent advice.

ELLA

"This is the goddess?" Ella arched a brow as she and Julian entered a room with only one large portrait hanging on the wall.

The girl in the painting looked younger than Ella, but as she looked closer, she realized how wrong her first impression had been.

The eyes staring at her from the picture were smiling as if the goddess was hiding a secret or planning some mischief, but they were also ancient and full of wisdom.

It was astounding how Dalhu had managed to capture both in one painting. Even without knowing much about art, it was apparent to Ella that the guy was extremely talented.

"Larger than life, and I mean it literally." Julian chuckled. "This canvas is probably taller than her. Annani is tiny. She's shorter than you." He glanced at Ella's high heels. "Even without the shoes."

"A big wonder in a small package." Ella giggled. "I guess you have two wonders. A small one and a big one."

"Funny that you should say that. Wonder is Annani's best

friend. They've known each other since they were both young girls."

"No way. Wonder looks my age. Well, so does Annani, even younger, but Annani has smart old eyes. Wonder doesn't."

"It's a long story. But Wonder was buried in the ground, surviving in stasis for thousands of years. She was awakened only recently. So, you are right about her being young. She hasn't really lived for all those years."

"What do you mean by stasis?"

"When deprived of air and nutrients, immortals go into stasis. They can survive like that for thousands of years. Maybe even more. Although Wonder's is the longest anyone has heard of."

"Fascinating." Ella took a few steps back and looked at the portrait again. "I can't wait to meet the goddess in person. Is there a chance she might visit anytime soon?"

"I don't know. Annani is impulsive. She doesn't plan ahead." He furrowed his brows. "Actually, that's not true. She has charted a course for the clan thousands of years in the making. I guess she acts impulsively only on a personal level."

"I totally believe it. Her eyes are ancient and smart but also full of humor and life."

Julian wrapped his arm around her shoulders. "Ready to move to the next room?"

"Sure. What's in there?"

"I don't know. Let's find out."

They stepped out into the corridor and entered a room across from the one they'd just left.

Ella glanced at the printed sign propped on a tripod. "Early works in charcoal."

Julian walked over to the wall. "I wonder who those dudes are. I don't recognize any of them."

"Maybe he drew pictures of his old buddies." Ella joined

him in front of the portrait he was looking at and threaded her arm through his. "Handsome, but foreboding. He doesn't look like a nice guy."

"That's because he isn't," Amanda said as she entered the room. "This is one of Navuh's sons." She pointed at a larger portrait of a stunning man with a severe expression and hair that was so dark it looked pure black. "And that's Navuh. The bane of our clan's existence."

"Funny, he doesn't look evil," Ella said. "And his son doesn't look much like him either."

"You think?" Amanda put a hand on her hip and looked at one portrait and then the other. "I think there is a familial resemblance."

"They are both dark and wear twin severe expressions, but they don't look much alike. The son probably looks more like his mother."

"Perhaps." Amanda moved to the next charcoal drawing that was hanging on the opposite wall. "What about this one?"

Since the tripod with the sign on it was in the way, obscuring both Amanda and the portrait she was pointing to, Ella couldn't offer her opinion without getting around it.

But as she cleared the contraption and the portrait came into view, her throat clogged up and her heart started racing.

Logan's eyes were mocking her from the picture, just as dark and intense as she'd remembered them. His lips were curled on one side in a smirk.

Pointing, she tried to say his name, but nothing came out.

"What's the matter?" Julian asked.

She kept pointing like an idiot and then wagging her finger at the picture, but she was still unable to speak his name.

"What are you pointing at, darling? Is there a scary spider on the wall?"

Ella shook her head. "No spider." Encouraged by finally

being able to speak, she tried to say Logan's name again, but her throat contracted once more, and a splitting headache assailed her out of nowhere. It was so bad that she whimpered and her hands flew to squeeze her temples.

"Let's get you out of here." Julian wrapped his arm around her waist and turned her around. "Maybe fresh air will help."

Outside, the headache eased enough for her to be able to draw in a breath.

"Better?" Julian asked.

"Yes, thank you."

"What happened in there?" Amanda asked.

Ella opened her mouth, but nothing came out. Afraid of the pain coming back, she shook her head.

Amanda regarded her with worried eyes. "Okay, let's try something else. When I ask you a question either nod for yes or shake your head for no. Can you do that?"

Ella nodded.

"Did something in that room scare you?"

She nodded.

"Was it the picture?"

She nodded again.

"Was it because the guy looked scary?"

Ella shook her head.

Amanda's frown deepened. "Was it because you recognized him?"

Ella nodded.

"Did you see his picture somewhere?"

Ella shook her head.

Her expression incredulous, Amanda asked her next question. "Did you meet him in person?"

Ella nodded.

"Damn." Julian's arm tightened around her middle. "Was it in the auction house?"

She shook her head.

"After?"

She nodded.

"With Gorchenco?"

She nodded again.

"We should go talk to Dalhu," Amanda said. "And Kian."

KIAN

*K*ian watched Amanda enter the room and saunter toward him and Syssi while smiling at the people admiring her mate's work. But he knew his sister well, and there was worry in her eyes.

When she reached him, she put a hand on his shoulder and whispered, "Something is wrong with Ella. You should come with me."

Syssi leaned closer to Amanda. "Is she sick? Should I go find Bridget?"

Despite her worry, Amanda chuckled. "Julian is glued to her side. I think one doctor will do. I don't want to talk here. I took them to your office."

Kian didn't like having people there while he was away, but with most of the offices converted to an art gallery for one day, Amanda didn't have much choice.

"Did you call her parents? I mean Vivian and Magnus."

It hadn't been done officially yet, but everyone in the village already thought of Magnus as Ella's and Parker's father.

"Parker is with them. I don't think he should see Ella like that."

Now Kian got really worried. "Let's go." He took the stairs two at a time, rushing into his office ahead of his wife and sister.

As he saw Ella sitting at the conference table, he let out a relieved breath. She looked pale and scared, but other than that she seemed fine.

Julian looked worse.

Amanda and Syssi entered right behind him, and a moment later Dalhu came in holding one of his charcoals.

"That's what started it." Amanda waved her hand at the portrait. "Ella pointed at it and tried to tell us something, but couldn't. It was like a blockage of some sort was preventing her from speaking. I asked her several yes and no questions, and basically, we ascertained that during her time with Gorchenco, she met one of Navuh's sons."

"His name is Lokan," Dalhu said. "And Ella is most likely under compulsion not to talk about him. He has the ability to compel humans. One of the other brothers can compel immortals as well."

Kian looked at Ella. "Is that so? Did this man compel you not to talk about him?"

She lifted her hands in the air as if to say that she didn't know.

"Is this the guy you told me about? The one who talked with Gorchenco about the island?

She nodded, but then grimaced and pressed the heels of her palms to her temples.

Dalhu put the portrait on the floor, bracing it against the wall. "She'll get a headache every time she tries to override the compulsion. You should keep your questions to a bare minimum."

"Understood."

As Dalhu pulled out a chair for Amanda, Kian pulled one out for Syssi and another for himself.

"Okay. So, what we know so far is this," he said as he sat down. "Gorchenco has dealings with the Doomers, supplying them with weapons. Ella also told me that he visits the island. He took her with him when he met with Lokan, and during that meeting, Lokan must have put her under compulsion not to talk about him. The question is why?"

"While we ponder that, I'll get us drinks." Amanda got up and walked over to the buffet.

"Who wants what?" She opened the fridge. "We have coke, sprite, water, and beer."

"I'll take a beer," Julian said.

Ella cleared her throat. "Water for me."

It seemed she could talk as long as it wasn't about Lokan.

"I'll take water too," Syssi said. "Is there any Perrier?"

Pulling out the bottles and cans, Amanda brought them to the table and handed them out.

"I assumed you'd like a beer." She handed Kian a Snake's Venom.

"Is there a way to break compulsion?" Syssi asked.

Kian shook his head. "Not that I know of. Only the one who put it on can remove it."

"Crap," Ella said. "So, I'm trapped."

Syssi crossed her arms over her chest. "Maybe Annani can do that. She compelled my parents to keep us a secret. Perhaps if she can compel people, she might be able to also remove a compulsion even though she wasn't the one to do it."

"Perhaps." Kian nodded. "But I doubt she'll hop over to help us out unless it's an emergency."

"It might be," Ella murmured and then grimaced.

"Don't force it," Julian said. "It might be dangerous to you. If you get a terrible headache every time you try to talk about him, you might suffer neurological damage."

Ella nodded and lifted the water bottle to her lips, drinking half of it in one go.

"That's good. Drink up." Julian massaged her shoulders.

"What about Merlin?" Syssi asked. "He has a potion for everything. Maybe he has one for that too?"

"I doubt it, but it won't hurt to ask." Kian pulled out his phone.

ELLA

"I can cook up something, a kind of a tongue relaxer," Merlin said. "But I've never tried to use that to release someone from compulsion."

At this point, Ella was willing to try anything. It was so incredibly frustrating not being able to speak up and say what she wanted. Not that there was much more she could add to what everyone in Kian's office already knew.

Except maybe for the unimportant detail of Lokan using Logan as his fake name, which was very unimaginative on his part.

She was sure to tell him that the next time he invaded her dreams, along with a few other choice words.

Except, she couldn't do that because it would give her away. Logan aka Lokan didn't know where she was and with whom. Otherwise, he would've said something to that effect, or asked her questions about the people she was with.

And it wasn't because he was so cautious.

In his wildest dreams, Logan couldn't have anticipated her finding out who he was, so there was no reason for him to be overly careful about what he asked her or what he told her.

She was pretty sure that he was only interested in her because of her telepathic ability and her pretty face.

Still, it seemed that Dalhu didn't know about Lokan's dream-walking ability, and perhaps that was information that could be potentially helpful.

"How long is it going to take you to prepare the potion?" Kian asked.

"I need to get the ingredients first. I can have it ready by late morning tomorrow." He gave her a pitying look. "Come to my house at around ten."

"Okay," Ella said in a small voice.

Merlin was cool, and she liked him, but the idea of drinking some concoction he made was a bit scary. Sometimes, she wasn't sure how sane the guy was.

"I'll come with you," Julian said.

That was a relief. At least she would have a real doctor with her in case something went wrong. "Thanks, I appreciate it."

"Well." Kian tapped his fingers on the table. "There isn't much more we can do today. I suggest you go home and get some rest, Ella. Try not to think too much about this and give your brain time to recuperate."

"I will."

"I'll take you." Julian rose to his feet and gave her a hand up.

"Thanks." She turned to Kian. "Sorry for giving everyone a scare."

"Take care of yourself, darling." Amanda gave her a peck on the cheek.

As they headed outside, Ella wondered if she should find her mother and tell her what had happened or wait with it until they got home.

The problem was that in order to tell her mom, she would have to fight the compulsion again, and according to Julian, it was dangerous to her brain.

"Julian." She looked up at his worried face. "Can I ask you a favor?"

"Anything."

"Can you tell my mom and Magnus what happened? I don't want to talk about it because of what you said it can do to my head."

"Sure, no problem."

"Thanks." She leaned into him.

"You're cold." He tightened his arm around her.

The shawl she'd borrowed from her mom wasn't doing much to block the night's chill. Or maybe she was cold because of the exhaustion that followed the excruciating headache attacks when she'd fought the compulsion.

She was cold all over, her feet hurt from the shoes, and her home was another fifteen-minute hike through the village.

What had been supposed to be a fabulous day had turned into a miserable one.

The story of my life.

When another uncontrollable shiver shook her body, Julian swung her into his arms and held her tightly against his chest. "Better?"

"Yes. Thank you." She was too tired to object, and he was too warm and solid to resist. "The moment I get too heavy for you, put me down. I should be fine in a minute or two."

Dipping his head, he planted a kiss on her forehead. "Silly girl. You'll never get too heavy for me. Even if you gain a hundred pounds."

"God forbid." She put her hand over his mouth. "Don't speak such blasphemy."

Julian chuckled. "Now I know that you're okay. You didn't lose your sense of humor."

"You think I'm joking? You really don't know anything about girls, do you?"

His confused expression was just adorable. Teasing Julian was so much fun.

"Apparently, I don't."

She cupped his cheek. "Never ever mention weight to a girl. It's a touchy subject."

"Noted. What else?"

"That's it. I'm not going to teach you how to charm other girls. That wouldn't be in my best interest."

"You don't have to worry about that. There is only one girl I'm interested in, and if you're wondering who she is, it's the one I'm holding in my arms right now. I just regret having to take you home. I would much rather bring you to mine and never let you leave."

She would like that too, and not only because she was scared of Logan invading her dreams again. Tonight, she didn't want to sleep alone.

Would her mom mind?

Ella wasn't a little girl anymore. She was an adult, and if she wanted to spend the night at Julian's, she could.

"Take me to your house. I'll let my mom know that I'm staying with you."

He stopped walking. "Are you sure it's okay with her?"

"I'm an adult, Julian. And my mom adores you. So yes, I'm sure."

"What about telling her and Magnus about what happened earlier?"

She cupped his cheek. "Tomorrow, my dear, is another day."

The end...for now...

COMING UP NEXT
THE CHILDREN OF THE GODS BOOK 27
DARK DREAM'S UNRAVELING

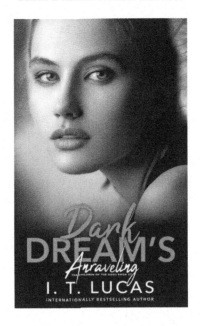

FOR EXCLUSIVE PEEKS AT UPCOMING RELEASES
JOIN MY *VIP CLUB* AND GAIN ACCESS TO THE VIP PORTAL AT

ITLUCAS.COM

CLICK HERE TO JOIN
(OR GO TO: http://eepurl.com/blMTpD)

(If you're already a subscriber and forgot the password to the VIP portal, you can find it at the bottom of each of my emails. . You can also email me at isabell@itlucas.com

---

Dear reader,

Thank you for joining me on the continuing adventures of the *Children of the Gods*.

As an independent author, I rely on your support to spread the word. So if you enjoyed the story, please share your experience, and if it isn't too much trouble, I would greatly appreciate a brief review on Amazon.

Love & happy reading,
Isabell

Don't miss out on
THE CHILDREN OF THE GODS ORIGINS SERIES
1: Goddess's Choice
2: Goddess's Hope

THE CHILDREN OF THE GODS SERIES

THE CHILDREN OF THE GODS ORIGINS

1: GODDESS'S CHOICE

When gods and immortals still ruled the ancient world, one young goddess risked everything for love.

2: GODDESS'S HOPE

Hungry for power and infatuated with the beautiful Areana, Navuh plots his father's demise. After all, by getting rid of the insane god he would be doing the world a favor. Except, when gods and immortals conspire against each other, humanity pays the price.

But things are not what they seem, and prophecies should not to be trusted...

THE CHILDREN OF THE GODS

1: DARK STRANGER THE DREAM

Syssi's paranormal foresight lands her a job at Dr. Amanda Dokani's neuroscience lab, but it fails to predict the thrilling yet terrifying turn her life will take. Syssi has no clue that her boss is an immortal who'll drag her into a secret, millennia-old battle over humanity's future. Nor does she realize that the professor's imposing brother is the mysterious stranger who's been starring in her dreams.

Since the dawn of human civilization, two warring factions of immortals—the descendants of the gods of old—have been secretly shaping its destiny. Leading the clandestine battle from his luxurious Los Angeles high-rise, Kian is surrounded by his clan, yet alone. Descending from a single goddess, clan members are forbidden to each other. And as the only other immortals are their hated enemies, Kian and his kin have been long resigned to a lonely existence of fleeting trysts with human partners. That is, until his sister makes a game-changing discovery—a mortal seeress who she believes is a dormant carrier of their genes. Ever the realist, Kian is skeptical and refuses Amanda's plea to attempt Syssi's activation. But when his enemies learn of the Dormant's existence, he's forced to rush her to the safety of his keep. Inexorably drawn to Syssi, Kian wrestles with his conscience as he is tempted to explore her budding interest in the darker shades of sensuality.

2: DARK STRANGER REVEALED

While sheltered in the clan's stronghold, Syssi is unaware that Kian and Amanda are not human, and neither are the supposedly religious fanatics that are after her. She feels a powerful connection to Kian, and as he introduces her to a world of pleasure she never dared imagine, his dominant sexuality is a revelation. Considering that she's completely out of her element, Syssi feels comfortable and safe letting go with him. That is, until she begins to suspect that all is not as it seems. Piecing the puzzle together, she draws a scary, yet wrong conclusion...

3: DARK STRANGER IMMORTAL

When Kian confesses his true nature, Syssi is not as much shocked by the revelation as she is wounded by what she perceives as his callous plans for her.

If she doesn't turn, he'll be forced to erase her memories and let her go. His family's safety demands secrecy – no one in the mortal world is allowed to know that immortals exist.

Resigned to the cruel reality that even if she stays on to never again leave the keep, she'll get old while Kian won't, Syssi is determined to enjoy what little time she has with him, one day at a time.

Can Kian let go of the mortal woman he loves? Will Syssi turn? And if she does, will she survive the dangerous transition?

4: DARK ENEMY TAKEN

Dalhu can't believe his luck when he stumbles upon the beautiful immortal professor. Presented with a once in a lifetime opportunity to grab an immortal female for himself, he kidnaps her and runs. If he ever gets caught, either by her people or his, his life is forfeit. But for a chance of a loving mate and a family of his own, Dalhu is prepared to do everything in his power to win Amanda's heart, and that includes leaving the Doom brotherhood and his old life behind.

Amanda soon discovers that there is more to the handsome Doomer than his dark past and a hulking, sexy body. But succumbing to her enemy's seduction, or worse, developing feelings for a ruthless killer is out of the question. No man is worth life on the run, not even the one and only immortal male she could claim as her own…

Her clan and her research must come first…

5: DARK ENEMY CAPTIVE

When the rescue team returns with Amanda and the chained Dalhu to the keep, Amanda is not as thrilled to be back as she thought she'd be. Between Kian's contempt for her and Dalhu's imprisonment, Amanda's budding relationship with Dalhu seems doomed. Things start to look up when Annani offers her help, and together with Syssi they resolve to find a way for Amanda to be with Dalhu. But will she still want him when she realizes that he is responsible for her nephew's murder? Could she? Will she take the easy way out and choose Andrew instead?

6: DARK ENEMY REDEEMED

Amanda suspects that something fishy is going on onboard the Anna. But when her investigation of the peculiar all-female Russian crew fails to uncover anything other than more speculation, she decides it's time to stop playing detective and face her real problem—a man she shouldn't want but can't live without.

6.5: MY DARK AMAZON

When Michael and Kri fight off a gang of humans, Michael gets stabbed. The injury to his immortal body recovers fast, but the one to his ego takes longer, putting a strain on his relationship with Kri.

7: DARK WARRIOR MINE

When Andrew is forced to retire from active duty, he believes that all he has to look forward to is a boring desk job. His glory days in special ops are over. But as it turns out, his thrill ride has just begun. Andrew discovers not only that immortals exist and have been manipulating global affairs since antiquity, but that he and his sister are rare possessors of the immortal genes.

Problem is, Andrew might be too old to attempt the activation process. His sister, who is fourteen years his junior, barely made it through the transition, so the odds of him coming out of it alive, let alone immortal, are slim.

But fate may force his hand.

Helping a friend find his long-lost daughter, Andrew finds a woman who's worth taking the risk for. Nathalie might be a Dormant, but the only way to find out for sure requires fangs and venom.

8: DARK WARRIOR'S PROMISE

Andrew and Nathalie's love flourishes, but the secrets they keep from each other taint their relationship with doubts and suspicions. In the meantime, Sebastian and his men are getting bolder, and the storm that's brewing will shift the balance of power in the millennia-old conflict between Annani's clan and its enemies.

9: DARK WARRIOR'S DESTINY

The new ghost in Nathalie's head remembers who he was in life, providing Andrew and her with indisputable proof that he is real and not a figment of her imagination.

Convinced that she is a Dormant, Andrew decides to go forward with his transition immediately after the rescue mission at the Doomers' HQ.

Fearing for his life, Nathalie pleads with him to reconsider. She'd rather spend the rest of her mortal days with Andrew than risk what they have for the fickle promise of immortality.

While the clan gets ready for battle, Carol gets help from an unlikely ally. Sebastian's second-in-command can no longer ignore the torment she suffers at the hands of his commander and offers to help her, but only if she agrees to his terms.

10: DARK WARRIOR'S LEGACY

Andrew's acclimation to his post-transition body isn't easy. His senses are sharper, he's bigger, stronger, and hungrier. Nathalie fears that the changes in the man she loves are more than physical. Measuring up to this new version of him is going to be a challenge.

Carol and Robert are disillusioned with each other. They are not destined mates, and love is not on the horizon. When Robert's three months are up, he might be left with nothing to show for his sacrifice.

Lana contacts Anandur with disturbing news; the yacht and its human cargo are in Mexico. Kian must find a way to apprehend Alex and rescue the women on board without causing an international incident.

11: Dark Guardian Found

What would you do if you stopped aging?

Eva runs. The ex-DEA agent doesn't know what caused her strange mutation, only that if discovered, she'll be dissected like a lab rat. What Eva doesn't know, though, is that she's a descendant of the gods, and that she is not alone. The man who rocked her world in one life-changing encounter over thirty years ago is an immortal as well.

To keep his people's existence secret, Bhathian was forced to turn his back on the only woman who ever captured his heart, but he's never forgotten and never stopped looking for her.

12: Dark Guardian Craved

Cautious after a lifetime of disappointments, Eva is mistrustful of Bhathian's professed feelings of love. She accepts him as a lover and a confidant but not as a life partner.

Jackson suspects that Tessa is his true love mate, but unless she overcomes her fears, he might never find out.

Carol gets an offer she can't refuse—a chance to prove that there is more to her than meets the eye. Robert believes she's about to commit a deadly mistake, but when he tries to dissuade her, she tells him to leave.

13: Dark Guardian's Mate

Prepare for the heart-warming culmination of Eva and Bhathian's story!

14: Dark Angel's Obsession

The cold and stoic warrior is an enigma even to those closest to him. His secrets are about to unravel...

15: Dark Angel's Seduction

Brundar is fighting a losing battle. Calypso is slowly chipping away his icy armor from the outside, while his need for her is melting it from the inside.

He can't allow it to happen. Calypso is a human with none of the Dormant indicators. There is no way he can keep her for more than a few weeks.

16: Dark Angel's Surrender

Get ready for the heart pounding conclusion to Brundar and Calypso's story.

Callie still couldn't wrap her head around it, nor could she summon even a smidgen of sorrow or regret. After all, she had some memories with him that weren't horrible. She should've felt something. But there was nothing, not even shock. Not even horror at what had transpired over the last couple of hours.

Maybe it was a typical response for survivors--feeling euphoric for the simple reason that they were alive. Especially when that survival was nothing short of miraculous.

Brundar's cold hand closed around hers, reminding her that they weren't out of the woods yet. Her injuries were superficial, and the most she had to worry about was some scarring. But, despite his and Anandur's reassurances, Brundar might never walk again.

If he ended up crippled because of her, she would never forgive herself for getting him involved in her crap.

"Are you okay, sweetling? Are you in pain?" Brundar asked.

Her injuries were nothing compared to his, and yet he was concerned about her. God, she loved this man. The thing was, if she told him that, he would run off, or crawl away as was the case.

Hey, maybe this was the perfect opportunity to spring it on him.

17: Dark Operative: A Shadow of Death

As a brilliant strategist and the only human entrusted with the secret of immortals' existence, Turner is both an asset and a liability to the clan. His request to attempt transition into immortality as an alternative to cancer treatments cannot be denied without risking the clan's exposure. On the other hand, approving it means risking his premature death. In both scenarios, the clan will lose a valuable ally.

When the decision is left to the clan's physician, Turner makes plans to manipulate her by taking advantage of her interest in him.

Will Bridget fall for the cold, calculated operative? Or will Turner fall into his own trap?

18: Dark Operative: A Glimmer of Hope

As Turner and Bridget's relationship deepens, living together seems like the right move, but to make it work both need to make concessions.

Bridget is realistic and keeps her expectations low. Turner could never be the truelove mate she yearns for, but he is as good as she's going to get. Other than his emotional limitations, he's perfect in every way.

Turner's hard shell is starting to show cracks. He wants immortality, he wants to be part of the clan, and he wants Bridget, but he doesn't want to cause her pain.

His options are either abandon his quest for immortality and give Bridget his few remaining decades, or abandon Bridget by going for the transition and most likely dying. His rational mind dictates that he chooses the former, but his gut pulls him toward the latter. Which one is he going to trust?

19: Dark Operative: The Dawn of Love

Get ready for the exciting finale of Bridget and Turner's story!

20: Dark Survivor Awakened

This was a strange new world she had awakened to.

Her memory loss must have been catastrophic because almost nothing was familiar. The language was foreign to her, with only a few words bearing some similarity to the language she thought in. Still, a full moon cycle had passed since her awakening, and little by little she was gaining basic understanding of it--only a few words and phrases, but she was learning more each day.

A week or so ago, a little girl on the street had tugged on her mother's sleeve and pointed at her. "Look, Mama, Wonder Woman!"

The mother smiled apologetically, saying something in the language these people spoke, then scurried away with the child looking behind her shoulder and grinning.

When it happened again with another child on the same day, it was settled.

Wonder Woman must have been the name of someone important in this strange world she had awoken to, and since both times it had been said with a smile it must have been a good one.

Wonder had a nice ring to it.

She just wished she knew what it meant.

21: DARK SURVIVOR ECHOES OF LOVE

Wonder's journey continues in *Dark Survivor Echoes of Love*.

22: DARK SURVIVOR REUNITED

The exciting finale of Wonder and Anandur's story.

23: DARK WIDOW'S SECRET

Vivian and her daughter share a powerful telepathic connection, so when Ella can't be reached by conventional or psychic means, her mother fears the worst.

Help arrives from an unexpected source when Vivian gets a call from the young doctor she met at a psychic convention. Turns out Julian belongs to a private organization specializing in retrieving missing girls.

As Julian's clan mobilizes its considerable resources to rescue the daughter, Magnus is charged with keeping the gorgeous young mother safe.

Worry for Ella and the secrets Vivian and Magnus keep from each other should be enough to prevent the sparks of attraction from kindling a blaze of desire. Except, these pesky sparks have a mind of their own.

24: Dark Widow's Curse

A simple rescue operation turns into mission impossible when the Russian mafia gets involved. Bad things are supposed to come in threes, but in Vivian's case, it seems like there is no limit to bad luck. Her family and everyone who gets close to her is affected by her curse.

Will Magnus and his people prove her wrong?

25: Dark Widow's Blessing

The thrilling finale of the Dark Widow trilogy!

26: Dark Dream's Temptation

Julian has known Ella is the one for him from the moment he saw her picture, but when he finally frees her from captivity, she seems indifferent to him. Could he have been mistaken?

Ella's rescue should've ended that chapter in her life, but it seems like the road back to normalcy has just begun and it's full of obstacles. Between the pitying looks she gets and her mother's attempts to get her into therapy, Ella feels like she's typecast as a victim, when nothing could be further from the truth. She's a tough survivor, and she's going to prove it.

Strangely, the only one who seems to understand is Logan, who keeps popping up in her dreams. But then, he's a figment of her imagination —or is he?

27: Dark Dream's Unraveling

While trying to figure out a way around Logan's silencing compulsion, Ella concocts an ambitious plan. What if instead of trying to keep him out of her dreams, she could pretend to like him and lure him into a trap?

Catching Navuh's son would be a major boon for the clan, as well as for Ella. She will have her revenge, turning the tables on another scumbag out to get her.

28: Dark Dream's Trap

The trap is set, but who is the hunter and who is the prey? Find out in this heart-pounding conclusion to the *Dark Dream* trilogy.

29: DARK PRINCE'S ENIGMA

As the son of the most dangerous male on the planet, Lokan lives by three rules:

Don't trust a soul.

Don't show emotions.

And don't get attached.

Will one extraordinary woman make him break all three?

30: DARK PRINCE'S DILEMMA

Will Kian decide that the benefits of trusting Lokan outweigh the risks?

Will Lokan betray his father and brothers for the greater good of his people?

Are Carol and Lokan true-love mates, or is one of them playing the other?

So many questions, the path ahead is anything but clear.

31: DARK PRINCE'S AGENDA

While Turner and Kian work out the details of Areana's rescue plan, Carol and Lokan's tumultuous relationship hits another snag. Is it a sign of things to come?

32 : DARK QUEEN'S QUEST

A former beauty queen, a retired undercover agent, and a successful model, Mey is not the typical damsel in distress. But when her sister drops off the radar and then someone starts following her around, she panics.

Following a vague clue that Kalugal might be in New York, Kian sends a team headed by Yamanu to search for him.

As Mey and Yamanu's paths cross, he offers her his help and protection, but will that be all?

33: DARK QUEEN'S KNIGHT

As the only member of his clan with a godlike power over human minds, Yamanu has been shielding his people for centuries, but that power comes at a steep price. When Mey enters his life, he's faced with the most difficult choice.

The safety of his clan or a future with his fated mate.

34: DARK QUEEN'S ARMY

As Mey anxiously waits for her transition to begin and for Yamanu to test whether his godlike powers are gone, the clan sets out to solve two mysteries:

Where is Jin, and is she there voluntarily?

Where is Kalugal, and what is he up to?

35: DARK SPY CONSCRIPTED

Jin possesses a unique paranormal ability. Just by touching someone, she can insert a mental hook into their psyche and tie a string of her consciousness to it, creating a tether. That doesn't make her a spy, though, not unless her talent is discovered by those seeking to exploit it.

36: DARK SPY'S MISSION

Jin's first spying mission is supposed to be easy. Walk into the club, touch Kalugal to tether her consciousness to him, and walk out.

Except, they should have known better.

37: DARK SPY'S RESOLUTION

The best-laid plans often go awry...

38: DARK OVERLORD NEW HORIZON

Jacki has two talents that set her apart from the rest of the human race.

She has unpredictable glimpses of other people's futures, and she is immune to mind manipulation.

Unfortunately, both talents are pretty useless for finding a job other than the one she had in the government's paranormal division.

It seemed like a sweet deal, until she found out that the director planned on producing super babies by compelling the recruits into pairing up. When an opportunity to escape the program presented itself, she took it, only to find out that humans are not at the top of the food chain.

Immortals are real, and at the very top of the hierarchy is Kalugal, the most powerful, arrogant, and sexiest male she has ever met.

With one look, he sets her blood on fire, but Jacki is not a fool. A man like him will never think of her as anything more than a tasty snack, while she will never settle for anything less than his heart.

39: Dark Overlord's Wife

Jacki is still clinging to her all-or-nothing policy, but Kalugal is chipping away at her resistance. Perhaps it's time to ease up on her convictions. A little less than all is still much better than nothing, and a couple of decades with a demigod is probably worth more than a lifetime with a mere mortal.

———

For a **FREE** Audiobook, Preview chapters, And other goodies offered only to my **VIPs**,

JOIN THE VIP CLUB AT ITLUCAS.COM

———

TRY THE SERIES ON

AUDIBLE

2 FREE audiobooks with your new Audible subscription!

THE PERFECT MATCH SERIES

PERFECT MATCH 1: VAMPIRE'S CONSORT

When Gabriel's company is ready to start beta testing, he invites his old crush to inspect its medical safety protocol.

Curious about the revolutionary technology of the *Perfect Match Virtual Fantasy-Fulfillment studios*, Brenna agrees.

Neither expects to end up partnering for its first fully immersive test run.

PERFECT MATCH 2: KING'S CHOSEN

When Lisa's nutty friends get her a gift certificate to *Perfect Match Virtual Fantasy Studios*, she has no intentions of using it. But since the only way to get a refund is if no partner can be found for her, she makes sure to request a fantasy so girly and over the top that no sane guy will pick it up.

Except, someone does.

Warning: This fantasy contains a hot, domineering crown prince, sweet insta-love, steamy love scenes painted with light shades of gray, a wedding, and a HEA in both the virtual and real worlds.

Intended for mature audience.

PERFECT MATCH 3: CAPTAIN'S CONQUEST

Working as a Starbucks barista, Alicia fends off flirting all day long, but none of the guys are as charming and sexy as Gregg. His frequent visits are the highlight of her day, but since he's never asked her out, she assumes he's taken. Besides, between a day job and a budding music career, she has no time to start a new relationship.

That is until Gregg makes her an offer she can't refuse—a gift certificate to the virtual fantasy fulfillment service everyone is talking about. As a huge Star Trek fan, Alicia has a perfect match in mind—the captain of the Starship Enterprise.

FOR EXCLUSIVE PEEKS

Join The Children Of The Gods VIP Club
and gain access to the VIP portal at itlucas.com

CLICK HERE TO JOIN
(or go to: http://eepurl.com/blMTpD)

INCLUDED IN YOUR FREE MEMBERSHIP:

- **FREE** narration of Goddess's Choice—Book 1 in The Children of the Gods Origins series.
- Preview chapters.
- And other exclusive content offered only to my VIPs.

Made in the USA
Columbia, SC
12 October 2020